A Shadow's Touch

The Light Within The Shadows

Anne T. Thyssen

Copyright

Cover designed by GetCovers
ISBN: 978-87-94501-04-0

Important!

Warning!

This book contains kidnapping, torture, explicit sex scenes and is therefore rated 18+.

Prologue

The man was pushed against the wall as the Shadow Lord leaned closer, his dark powers swirling beneath his skin, craving a taste of life. The man's essence would fuel him, feed him, and make him stronger. Each life essence had a distinct taste. The more corrupt, the more sour, but acquiring the sweeter souls had become increasingly challenging. There was a time when the Shadow Lords ruled, effortlessly obtaining souls. Breeding cages existed solely to feed their corrupt bodies. However, this Lord was now reduced to hunting people in the dark in order to survive.

As he drained the man, the taste was akin to a sour apple, hearing him choke as if the Shadow Lord's hand were wrapped around his throat. It wasn't. The Shadow Lord effortlessly held him a few inches off the ground by the collar of his dirty jacket. The man wasn't entirely corrupt, but as the Shadow Lord absorbed his life essence, he glimpsed the man's cheating nature, not only in games but also in matters of the heart. Loyalty eluded him. The thrill of deception and betrayal was too enticing. While the man's life essence tasted sour, the Shadow Lord accepted it, as it still provided him with energy. However, the more challenging part was accepting another person's memories. Seeing the darkest aspects of people was never easy. Having lived for hundreds of years, the Shadow Lord had witnessed much.

He had once wielded great power, but now he was reduced to a mere shadow in the night, feared only by himself.

The man before him grew paler, dark veins spreading across his body. His eyes turned white, losing their sight. His hair greyed, and his body wrinkled. He stopped breathing, his heart ceasing to beat in his chest. The Shadow Lord let him fall to the ground in the dark alley, hearing the light thud as his body hit the cold stones. He smiled slightly, feeling better now. He adjusted his fine clothes, far superior to those of the common man. He could survive on that energy for a few weeks, but he knew he would have to hunt more souls soon. The cities were dangerous hunting grounds, but they were also where souls congregated. Souls were scarce in the countryside, although he preferred the solitude it offered.

As the Shadow Lord turned, he was startled by a small figure appearing at the end of the alley. His powers stirred with intrigue at the sight of the little dark figure observing him. Children's souls were often the purest. Unfortunately, due to their small size and immaturity, they didn't provide much power. The taste was delightful but not sustaining enough. Nevertheless, he considered taking the little one with him and allowing her to grow. He could do it as they did in the old days, patiently waiting for souls to mature. He approached, noticing the little figure becoming clearer as she emerged from the glow of a burning lamp near the alley. The girl was very young, a tiny little thing. She would provide nourishment if she were to grow stronger. He smiled as he stopped in front of her, and the girl looked up at him with enormous light blue eyes. He crouched down, captivated by her fearless gaze. Had she grown accustomed to the harsh realities of life? If so, no matter what he did for her, her soul would be tainted. He had encountered more corrupted children's souls than those of their elders, but he also knew that it was the elders who had led them astray. The girl observed him with curiosity, as though he were something she had never seen before. He likely wasn't. There were very few of them left, all hunted by the Halos, also known as the Lights, although that title was typically reserved for those in training. Halos were the hunters.

"Hello, little girl," he said, his voice carrying a slight echo as his powers swirled with newfound energy beneath his pale skin.

The girl blinked, remaining calm as ever.

"Are you lost?" he asked.

She continued to look at him, making him wonder if the girl was either deaf or mute.

"Do your parents know where you are?" The Shadow Lord asked to ensure that no one would come looking. He did not need the chaos a lost child would bring. The Halos were excellent trackers, and he had not survived this long, evading their light-bringing grasp, for nothing.

"Are you all on your own?" he continued.

Finally, the girl nodded, looking somewhat sad as her eyes wandered to the stony ground. The Shadow Lord smiled at the sight of her shrinking. One lost little soul among the darkness where he reigned. It felt too easy. A fresh, grown, and pure soul could last him years if taken good care of. It was why breeding cages were often used under his rule. If the Halos had never appeared, becoming his weakness, he could still be a ruler. He had once been one of the strongest lords out there. And look at him now... what hadn't he become? Stealing lost children in the night. It was pathetic and low, but everyone had to survive in their own way.

"How unfortunate," he whispered, his voice filled with a joy that couldn't be missed. "Shall we go somewhere warmer?"

The girl looked up at him, her eyes wide as she studied the dark figure in front of her. His eyes glowed with a red hue, while shadows masked most of his face. But as he asked the question, she remained silent.

"Come, it is too cold for you to be out here in such clothes and... without shoes?" The Shadow Lord had noticed that her little white dress was not at all suitable for the low temperatures of the night, and now he saw that she was barefoot as well.

Her feet were dirty, but her dress was not. The Shadow Lord examined her more closely, seeing her in a new light. Her appearance raised questions as he wondered where the little girl had come from. He looked around, listening for sounds, but there was nothing. It was a silent night, and he was hiding in the lower part of a larger city. Here, he could hunt in peace, as no one would find the sight of strange dead bodies alarming. So what was a little girl like her doing there? It wouldn't change what he was about to do, but now he had questions.

"Aren't you cold?"

She nodded, confirming she wasn't deaf. The Shadow Lord smiled.

"Then let's go somewhere more comfortable," he said.

His hand began reaching out, his long dark nails resembling claws. The girl noticed how they grew, like a horrifying nightmare inching closer to her. In fear, she took a step back. The Shadow Lord noticed, hissing slightly as a warning for her not to run.

"You aren't going anywhere," he informed her, moving faster to ensure the little girl wouldn't escape.

She noticed his speed, fear spreading within her and triggering a hidden power. The Shadow Lord was unprepared for the sudden burst of light emanating from the little girl as she screamed, releasing a flow of energy. Her whole body became radiant, her blue eyes transforming into shiny orbs. He recoiled, the light burning him like fire. He hissed and yelled in pain while the girl continued to scream, the light more powerful than he had witnessed in hundreds of years. He had kept himself hidden, evading the Halos. The Shadow Lord stumbled back, nearly tripping, as the girl turned into the brightest little sun. He retreated as far as he could, desperately seeking a few surviving shadows to merge with and escape. But her light illuminated the entire alley, obliterating everything in its brightness. It began consuming him from within, making him feel as if he were melting. He tripped and fell to the ground, his impending demise near as all darkness was eradicated from his being.

The girl shone her light upon him, continuing until she grew tired and felt utterly exhausted. When the light vanished, there was no one left in the alley. She blinked rapidly, stumbled back a little, her body trembling. Then she walked away, barely comprehending what lay beneath the surface of her being.

Chapter 1

A loud screeching sound echoed in the dark tunnel as the tip of a dagger ran across it. The sound served its purpose of instilling fear in the victim hanging farther away, their wrists locked in iron chains as they hung naked from a high ceiling. The room was small and circular with a large iron grate, allowing the mid-day sun to pour in and cold rain to stream down from above, but the Shadow Lord had only arrived at night. While he could endure the sun's rays, nothing fuelled him like the night. It gave him power that resonated with his energy. He crept closer, ensuring the shadows concealed him, while the sound of his dagger still reverberated through the tunnel leading to the circular room. An evil smile played on his lips as the priest prayed for his life. Nothing would save him, not even the information the Shadow Lord sought. The Priest of Light already bled, as the Lord had visited him many times in the night, but his commitment to protecting the ancient scrolls fuelled the priest just as pain fuelled the Lord.

The sound ceased as the knife reached the end of the tunnel. The priest lifted his head slightly, blood dripping from his split lips and small cuts tracing paths down his naked body. Yet, he could not see where the Lord was hiding. The Lord emerged from the darkness like a predator, slicing the priest's chest. Shock and pain mingled in a wave that spread through his body, making him wish for death. However, Erars had no intention of killing the priest until he had obtained what he desired. He began circling the priest, the dagger's tip cutting slightly but not drawing blood. The priest squirmed and prayed to the almighty Goddess of Light, but Erars had lived long enough to know that no one saves you in your dying days. How many people had he not witnessed begging for life and receiving death instead? The mercy granted to those who prayed for it was a lie. There was no one who came to save you when you needed it.

"How do I find it?" Erars asked, delving a little deeper.

"In her light, we find the truth. In her light, we find our peace..."

"In her light, you find your purpose, blah, blah, blah..." Erars taunted, finding the words of praise directed towards the Goddess irritating to his ears. Learning about her was not why he was there. He wanted answers about something darker.

He moved to the front of the priest. One of his eyes was closed due to swelling around the eyebrow. Erars smiled, relishing the sight of the priest's tormented body. The priest bore swirling symbols all over his body, another demonstration of his dedication to the Goddess of Light.

"Where can I find it?" he repeated.

The priest shook his head, mumbling faster, causing Erars to roll his eyes.

"She isn't listening. Not down here, not with me," Erars spoke, tauntingly walking around, never letting the priest know when he would strike.

"She is always with us," the priest defended.

"No, she is not. She allows her light to shine down on us in the day, but now it's dark, and who rules in the darkness?" Erars asked.

"She is with us."

"In spirit?" he chuckled.

"Always."

"Your devotion has always baffled me. Even as I tear you apart limb by limb, you still pray and hope for salvation. But we all know where you will end up. Swallowed by my darkness, never witnessing that eternal light."

"We go where we need to go," he whispered.

As an elder, having lived many years, Erars was surprised the priest had survived this long compared to the younger priests he had hurt as well.

"Poetic, but useless."

"They will hunt you," he threatened.

"Oh, the Halos? We have met before. I am still here."

"You cannot escape their light. They will come for you."

"I am trembling."

"Many of your kind have been eradicated already!" he shouted with the last bit of power he had before coughing, causing blood to drip from his mouth.

Erars watched the pitiful sight of the priest, raising an eyebrow.

"I know, and it has made the world mine," Erars said. "With the other lords gone, who do you think has taken charge?"

The priest stared at him with empty eyes, his life slowly fading away.

"I do," Erars answered for him, pointing the tip of the dagger at himself. "I should thank the Halos."

"They do not want thanks from your repulsive..." a fit of coughing interrupted the priest, preventing him from finishing his intended words. Erars could piece together the rest.

"Let me tell you a story," Erars said, beginning to pace in front of the priest. "Long ago, before these lands showed any evidence of human rule, when we Shadows ruled over the land, taking the souls we desired without fearing any consequences. We were not just scary bedtime stories for children but their real-life nightmares. During that time, a tiny and insignificant shadow was born. His mother, the woman chosen to carry darkness within her, was a stolen and rare artifact. She was indeed a princess. The father believed her status would bring power as well, but what she birthed did not live up to his expectations. The little Shadow Lord, like all unaccepted children, was cast out into the cold. His mother died in childbirth, as expected. One life must end to give rise to another."

"You're leeches! Even as babies!" the priest coughed.

"I do not deny it," he chuckled. "But the little one was supposed to die as well. To everyone's surprise, he did not. Slowly, he returned to the dark world, smarter, angrier, more wicked, and thirsting for revenge. However, there were many powerful Shadow Lords back then. Yet, one day, these women appeared, full of light and power, ready to fight back. It's interesting how rapidly it all occurred and where they came from..."

"They were a gift!" the priest said, smiling as he thought of the Halos as saviors.

"Were they?"

The priest lost his smile.

"Or were they the perfect way of revenge?" he asked.

The priest paled, looking scared, then shaking his head.

"Maybe that little shadow knew he did not have the power to remove the stronger Shadow Lords. Maybe he needed others to do the dirty work."

"They are a gift!" he defended.

"Or maybe just foot soldiers."

"But that would make no sense. The Halos have brought peace. Protection! They hunt your kind."

"Maybe I am the only one who knows their weakness?"

Erars was toying with the old priest. There was nothing that cut deeper than fear, and he enjoyed bringing it out in people.

"No..." the priest weakly said. "They are a gift."

"Always so devoted. I did find it amusing as people began praising them, praying to them, when they truly came from darkness."

The priest remained quiet and did not want to engage anymore.

"But now it is time the world becomes mine. All of Aneria will be mine."

"Never," the priest said.

"Where is it?" he repeated his earlier question.

He moved closer, and the priest turned his head slightly.

"*Where?*" Erars spoke in a dark, echoing voice.

"You already have the scrolls. Find it yourself."

"But the veil is not easy to locate. I can decipher your scrolls, but they do not give me the exact location. I know it is entrusted only to those who have proven their worth, to priests who bear these marks..." Erars began tracing one of the marks representing a higher status, cutting into the dark red tattoos and creating new and unerasable scars. The priest whimpered, trying his hardest not to allow the pain to overtake him. "You are one of them. They prove it."

"I know nothing..."

"You know everything. Where is the veil?!" he snarled.

"Where you will never find it!" he snapped back.

"Where is it?!" he dug deeper.

"No..."

"Shall I really take it? Do you want me to consume your life energy to get my answer?" he growled.

The priest laughed, knowing it wasn't that simple.

"You can't break it. The seal protects our secrets."

Erars knew of the seals. The priest had created them for those carrying secrets so important they should never fall into the wrong hands. That was why Erars had not drained him yet. The memories were locked away and inaccessible. Erars went to the tattoo over his heart, seeing the symbol that allowed the locking away of the information he needed. He had tried many times to crack it and had succeeded once, but almost died in the process. It took too much power, and he was unsure if he should risk it, fearing this priest did not know the location. Other information was sometimes locked away as well, and the last time he had tried to break the seal, the high risk had not been worth the reward. He traced it with the tip of his dagger, unsure how to proceed next. Should he take the chance, possibly die, or should he see if he could break the priest yet?

"Where would such a valuable veil hide? One that divides our worlds?" Erars asked, locking eyes with the priest. "Somewhere hidden. Somewhere not obvious, but still not so unclear that if someone came across it, they would never know."

The priest remained silent, and Erars watched him for a little longer.

"You know," he stated.

"Even if I did, you can't just open it. You would need—"

"A Halo?"

"It will never work. The sacrifice must be a willing one," the priest said. "They will never do that."

"What if they were young? Could they be manipulated?" he asked.

"They protect the Lights. Your shadows will never touch them."

"Hmm, I do not believe that is true," Erars said before he reached out, placing his hand on the symbol. His dark nails grew longer as he dug them into the priest's chest, making him yelp in pain. "Without sacrifices, you gain nothing."

Erars knew what would happen once he began erasing the symbol. He might die, but to learn how to destroy the veil between this world and the Shadow World below, he needed to take the risk. So he began letting his darkness flow, but he couldn't do it too quickly. If the priest died before the symbol was erased, the information would be lost. He had to be careful, erasing the symbol little by little until it began disappearing from the skin. The priest gasped, writhed, and his heart raced in his chest, but slowly it happened. Sweat dripped from both of them, and Erars came closer to his answers. His own black heart pumped like crazy. The world turned blurry, and his legs began to shake. *A little more*, he thought. He just had to stay strong long enough. A simple image appeared in his head, but it was enough. He released the priest, whose head slumped forward, his body going still. Erars stumbled back, hitting the brick wall, laughing as he was once again able to break the symbol, but leaving the room was becoming impossible. The world tilted to the side, and he began passing out, falling flat to the ground.

Chapter 2

"Is that really all you've got, Nat?" Owin asked, tauntingly swirling the white staff in his hand while looking at Natava. She groaned in annoyance and rubbed her lower back where he had struck her. She narrowed her eyes, feeling her anger rise as he looked so smug. Just once, she wanted to show him that she wasn't that easy to overpower. Just once, she wanted to be the one to look smug. "You're letting your emotions rule you."

"I thought you taught me that they were good fuel."

"Good fuel, but also blinding," he corrected. "You're letting them blind you."

"Or maybe you're just that annoying."

Owin sighed, pressing one end of the staff to the ground and leaning his head against it as he observed Natava in front of him.

"You have a bad temper."

"Oh, was that a compliment? Well, thank you, Sir Owin," she replied sarcastically, pressing a hand to her heart and exaggerating her response. "You sure know how to flatter a lady."

"More like a princess," he laughed.

Natava groaned, swinging her stick around just to have something to do with her hands. "We don't know that."

"We do know," he said. "You're the future queen."

"I am the future of nothing. I am just a Light training to be a Halo."

"Sure, Your Highness."

Natava sighed, looking at him annoyed. "Don't."

"The announcement will happen soon. Everyone knows who will ascend. Why are you the only one not believing it?" he asked.

"Maybe because I am not a princess. I am just a simple Light."

"Simple? Your powers showed themselves when you were five, even before that. Only you can completely destroy our world with your powers."

"And somehow that is a clever move to put me in power?" she teasingly asked.

"You, on the throne, will scare anyone."

"I am that frightening?" she chuckled.

"No, but maybe with your future fiancé—"

"Fiancé?!" she snapped, looking at Owin, who realised that information had not yet been delivered to the princess.

"Oh, um..."

"Owin, what have you heard?" she asked.

"Nothing."

"Liar! I thought a knight couldn't lie."

"I am not lying. I must have heard wrong," he said.

"No, you know something. Was it your father? Did the Commander tell you?"

Owin's father had been involved in protecting the young Lights and Halos in the capital where they lived. There weren't many Halos left, and it was important to protect those who remained. It wasn't just the Shadow Lords that posed a threat to Aneria. Many creatures hid in the darkness, as did humans with evil intentions. There had been attempts to break into the marble castle before. That's why each Light had an assigned guard. Owin had become Natava's guard at a young age. They had grown up together. His father was tasked with protecting the leading Halo, the Queen of Aneria, and Natava's mentor.

"He said nothing."

"So you overheard it?" Natava asked. "Owin!"

"Well, you aren't just the queen, you're the future mother of one."

"Then why hasn't Massana given birth to anyone?"

"Because she was the chosen queen, not born into it," Owin said. "You were always meant for the throne."

"No," Natava refused. "I am not someone's queen or mother. I am me."

"You?"

"Me!"

Owin smiled a little, and Natava couldn't help but smile back.

"And who is this mighty Nat?" he asked.

"She is... fast!" Natava lunged at Owin, but he anticipated her move and backed away, laughing. "Clever!"

She made another attempt, but he dodged her and struck her back with the staff, causing her to groan.

"Clever, you say?"

Natava rubbed her back and swung the staff, meeting his. "And.. . strong!" she managed to say between gritted teeth.

Owin pushed her back, causing her to stumble, and while she was off balance, he swiftly slipped the staff between her legs, making her trip and fall flat on the elevated white platform. She groaned in pain and dropped the staff.

"Ouch..." she hissed.

"I think you might need to reconsider who this Natava is," he chuckled as he stood in front of her, leaning against the staff again.

Natava sat up, resting her arms on her knees, and sighed. "Well, if I can't even take you down, then how am I supposed to be a good queen?"

"You're not meant to seek out danger as a queen."

"I want to be a Halo. Not a queen!"

"But you're meant for the throne," he countered.

"Meant for the throne? Just a mother?"

"A mother to us all."

"That sounds so disgusting!" she snapped.

"I know, that's why I said it," he laughed, reminding Natava of the time one of her teachers had said the same thing, which had made both Owin, who as her guard had to be in the room, and Natava cringe.

For a long time, Natava had known what people really expected of her, and she had fought against it. But to no avail. She knew a pretty crown would be placed upon her head. While she was allowed to train with Owin, she knew she would never officially receive the title of Halo. She was destined to be Queen of Aneria and bring forth the next powerful line of Lights. Was that truly all she was good for? Natava wondered. To be a protective mother to them all? How was that her destiny?

"Really, Owin, is this my future?" she asked, feeling scared. She had come of age long ago, and ever since then, she could feel the weight of responsibilities tightening around her throat. Fortunately, Massana hadn't deemed her ready to be queen yet. She was almost 27 now, but Natava knew the time was approaching. Massana had been dropping hints about it. The future she had never wished for was looming. Massana had been her mother's best friend and had been chosen to lead after Natava's mother was killed. Everyone believed that Natava had died as well. Mysteriously, she had survived on her own as a small infant and child.

Owin came closer, sitting down beside her, and noticed that she avoided looking at him, not wanting to see the answer on his face. He understood. He hadn't had much choice in determining the direction of his life either. Owin was destined to become a knight, and when the time came to settle down, his father would undoubtedly have an opinion about it as well. But at least Owin could speak up against his father. He wasn't that important. He didn't have an entire kingdom depending on his choices. Not all kingdoms were allies to Natava. Some across the Long Sea or deeper down in Aneria desired power from her, wanting to take it. Once the Shadow Lords had been a collective fear uniting everyone, but as the Halos gradually gained control, things changed. People could become power-hungry again. They could fight for their own desires.

"Maybe," Owin said.

"Maybe?" Natava asked, turning to him.

He shrugged. "I don't see a way out, but you rarely do what people want."

That made Natava smile a little, and a small chuckle escaped her lips.

"So, I am that awful," she teased.

"Yes, I'll be glad when you're too busy with politics to have any time to train with me."

They both laughed a little, but neither wanted these training sessions to end. Natava sighed, resting her head on Owin's shoulder, and gazed at the imposing walls of the marble castle not far away.

"Have I ever told you how much I hate the sight of it?" she asked.

He chuckled. "Many times."

"I hate the sight of it," she repeated.

"Maybe one day you will learn to love it."

"My prison?"

"It's not a prison," Owin scolded, moving away and looking at Natava.

While he understood her struggles, she was also their future. Natava was nothing like any Light or Halo he had ever encountered. She had done something no one should have been able to do. At the age of five, she had already killed her first Shadow Lord. Her light had been visible all the way to the capital, miles away. That's how they had found her—the princess who had disappeared. Natava hadn't known what she had done, but when she recounted the events, everyone understood that the princess truly possessed the power her mother believed she did. The former queen had spoken of the future Natava would bring—a bright and peaceful one. But Natava was the one resisting it. How could they achieve such a future if she fought against it?

"What is it then? It has imposing walls that won't open for me, guards around me, and people constantly pointing out everything I do wrong. Is that not a prison?"

"You're supposed to lead us to greatness," Owin reminded her.

"But is greatness what we truly need? Massana rules just fine. Why am I needed?"

"Not all Shadow Lords are gone. Not all fighting has stopped. Many conspire against the Halos."

"Yeah, they are idiots who think the danger is gone."

"Exactly. They are, and now they want to become kings or queens. Now they want power. Natava, you are needed," he stated firmly. "You are needed here."

Natava heard what he was saying, but it didn't alleviate the burden she had felt on her shoulders since she was a young child. She had known this was her fate ever since she had appeared in her mother's womb. But why couldn't it be her choice? Why couldn't someone else be chosen? Who said she was the one to bring them a bright future? Maybe she would cause everything to crumble. No one could say for certain, yet people looked at her as if she were the Goddess of Light herself, descending to this earth to save them all. Natava thought it was ridiculous, but there was no escape for her. There was only one path already laid out before her.

Chapter 3

Natava and Owin sat outside, basking in the warm sun that heated their bodies, already warmed from their training. It was becoming uncomfortably hot, but neither wanted to move. Their conversation continued to flow in their minds as they enjoyed the comfortable silence. Natava leaned on Owin again, and they shared a smile.

After a while, someone came to find them. Owin sighed as he saw his father approaching them at a brisk pace.

"Here comes the Commander," he teased.

"I bet the queen has summoned me," Natava chuckled.

They exchanged a glance and smiled. Standing up, they waited for the Commander to approach them. He was the highest-ranking knight in Aneria. He stopped a short distance away, his eyes filled with suspicion as he glanced between them—a look that neither of them understood.

"Princess," he said calmly, but his voice carried a slight air of authority, "the queen has summoned you."

Natava tried to stifle her laughter as she looked at Owin, then nodded to the Commander and descended the stairs of the small platform. She walked past Owin's older version of her best friend, heading towards the entrance of the large square. Owin stayed behind for a moment longer, noticing the warning in his father's eyes. He began following Natava, but his father grabbed his arm to stop him.

"The princess is destined for much more than a knight can offer," his father warned in a low voice.

Owin said nothing, meeting his father's eyes for a brief moment before walking away. The warning had become a familiar refrain, but nothing escaped the notice of the older knight. He could see what his son desired, even if the princess had not yet recognised the look in his eyes. Owin caught up with Natava inside, knowing exactly where Massana would be. Whenever she summoned Natava for something important, she could be found in the large meeting room, pacing and examining the numerous tasks that needed attention.

Natava pushed open the white and golden doors, finding Massana pacing with a smile on her lips, but the strain was evident in the slight furrow of her brow. She held a piece of paper in her hands, scanning its contents. Hearing the door open, Natava stopped a short distance away.

"Ah, there you are, Natava. Training?" Massana asked.

It was clear that Massana had noticed Natava's skin-tight white training clothes.

"No, I was hunting gnomes," Natava replied. "One of them bit me when I tried to steal its treasures, but now I know where its cave is, and tomorrow I will go and steal them."

Massana raised an eyebrow, observing Natava with a weary expression in her eyes.

"He was feistier than I thought," Natava continued.

"I'm sure," Massana said wearily.

Natava smiled at her own dry humor, while Massana took a seat at the long, dark green meeting table. She extended her hand towards one of the seats closest to her, but Natava took the seat at the other end, making a show of pulling out the chair, causing it to screech and echo in the large meeting room. She sat down and smiled at Massana.

"Do you want us to yell at each other?"

"What?!" Natava yelled, placing a finger behind her ear. "I can't hear you."

"Natava!" Massana scolded.

Natava laughed, rising from her seat and walking closer before sitting down in the chair beside Massana.

"Goodness, you're a grown woman, and you still enjoy your games," Massana sighed.

"They're fun," Natava countered.

"They are not fitting for a future queen who must take her role more seriously."

"Yes, seriously," Natava mumbled, tapping her finger against the table in front of her.

"You are going to assume a very important role. You will decide how our world will be shaped," Massana reminded her. "This is not a game. You are the future queen."

"Queen..."

"Yes, queen. You were meant for this role."

"Me?" Natava asked.

"Yes, you."

"How? How have I proven myself?" she asked. "You and my mother fought your first wars before reaching your thirties. You were the most unstoppable Halos out there. You led your own patrols and killed more Shadow Lords than most."

"It was a different time," Massana reminded her. "I have not been in the field for many years. The Shadow Lords are mostly gone now."

"Some are still here."

"Very few, and we will eliminate the remaining ones. The world will no longer be shrouded in their darkness, but that doesn't mean people don't harbor darkness in their hearts. Darkness that we also need to eradicate."

"Is bringing light all we can do?" she asked.

"Is there anything else?"

"What if I don't want to be queen?" Natava asked.

"Then I am sure you have lost your mind."

"That's not funny."

"Isn't it the kind of joke you enjoy?" Massana asked.

Natava looked away, needing a moment to prevent her temper from rising dangerously. It was better to talk to Massana without screaming at the top of her lungs. Such conversations always ended in her defeat. After counting down silently, she refocused on Massana. Massana grabbed Natava's hand and squeezed it.

"You're going to rule for hundreds of years. This is what you're meant for," Massana said.

"And having children?" Natava retorted.

"There are worse fates."

"Why not wait with that? Better yet, why do I have to have children at all?" she asked.

"You need an heir."

"My mother was 322 before she had her first and only child."

"And maybe if she had had one earlier, there would have been more princesses to choose from," Massana said.

"Oh, now we're options to choose from. Why didn't you have any children? You're the queen now," Natava said.

"I am just a stand-in. I don't belong on the throne," Massana replied.

"But you're doing a much better job than me. I'm not good with children, and I don't want to be queen," Natava protested.

"We all have burdens to bear," Massana said. "I never expected to be queen either, but I embraced the role and did what I thought was best."

"So, what if I believe it's best for me to rule on my own?"

"You can take some time, but I would advise—"

"To get married?" Natava interjected.

"The sooner, the better. Our world has changed with the disappearance of the Shadow Lords. Now we fight in a different world, where alliances are formed through marriages."

"And who is this chosen one?" Natava asked.

"Chosen one?" Massana questioned.

"Don't act like you don't have someone in mind for me. Owin spilled the beans," Natava said.

"Owin..." Massana mumbled.

"Was he at the meeting?"

"Yes, but he could never keep anything a secret from you," Massana sighed.

"Why was my guard invited and not me? Am I not the one getting married?"

"I wanted to discuss whether the choice was suitable, but he wasn't actively part of the meeting. Only an observer."

"Who?" Natava asked, her voice filled with impatience.

"Someone good and respectable, and—"

"Who?" Natava interrupted.

"The Prince of Meladova."

"Meladova?!" Natava exclaimed. "They consider us beneath them. Aren't they our greatest threat? Weren't you planning to destroy them if they ever crossed the Long Sea and attacked us?"

"I did..."

"Why am I now marrying their future king?"

"Because it's how we ensure peace."

"There was a time when you would have chosen the sword," Natava retorted.

"I told you, our world has changed. Now it's about politics and humans who want to eliminate us to seize power for themselves. They have forgotten why we were crowned in the first place. Why this part of Aneria is our sanctuary. They have forgotten what we did for them because the Shadow Lords no longer pose a threat. People easily forget."

"But we don't," Natava snapped.

"But we are taught differently. Our world revolves around protecting humans not only from the Shadow Lords but also from the shadow creatures they create, the orcs of the Underworld, the Burned, and all the damned souls out there. We remember because we are forced to. Our lives, and the lives of many others, depend on it. But the humans live their lives focused on their jobs, families, and the love they find. We protect, and they barely notice it as long as they remain safe."

"Maybe we should bring them into the field then," Natava mused, smiling a little. But she noticed a weary look on Massana's face.

"We don't deliver punishments," Massana replied.

"Just lessons?" Natava questioned.

"No."

"How unfair."

"The world is unfair. You shouldn't have lost your mother at such a young age, but you did. How you survived is still a mystery to us, but considering your powers, it shouldn't be much of a surprise," Massana said, causing Natava to sigh and look away.

She barely remembered what had happened after becoming lost. Her mother had fled under a powerful attack, carrying her infant daughter, to protect her from a Shadow Lord whom Massana later hunted down. They searched for the queen but never found her or her daughter. Natava had only faint memories. Warmth. Coldness. And a creature reaching out to her. But what had she been doing there? Where had she lived? She was just a small infant when her mother had taken her away, her guards brutally and swiftly killed, and her father struck down. Massana had told Natava of the brutal and swift attack that had torn her parents away from her, but no one could say what Natava had done during those five years she was on her own. Only when she lit up the entire Aneria did they find the lost princess and bring her back, but memories and explanations were scarce. There was no trace to be found. Natava wasn't starved when they found her, so she could only believe that someone had taken care of her. But why couldn't she remember?

"They're not that special," Natava mumbled.

"We both know that's a lie."

"Then why not let me fight?" Natava asked, crossing her arms and focusing on Massana. "Why am I the one locked behind high walls when I could be useful out there?"

"Because losing you would be a devastating loss. You have great power, but you shouldn't seek death."

"So if I have a daughter, an heir, can I go into the field?"

Massana drew back in surprise at the suggestion and blinked rapidly as she looked at Natava in front of her, but the young Light remained serious.

"Natava..."

"Answer the question. If I give birth to this heir, can I fight?" she asked.

"NO!"

"Why not? I have given you everything you wanted, so I should be free to choose," Natava argued.

"That child needs to grow up."

"I was raised by you. You can train her," Natava said.

"Natava..."

"My suggestions are perfectly reasonable! You get what you want, and I get what I want!"

"But why are you so determined to seek out danger?! Many Lights never have a choice. They are meant to become Halos."

"Yes, so let me join them!"

"You have a different life. One without so much bloodshed. Natava, you have no idea what war does to you. You don't know the horrors that your mother and I endured. How our love..."

"Our?" Natava questioned, causing Massana to turn slightly pale as an old secret almost slipped.

"Yes, we stood by each other's side. We cared deeply for each other, but that didn't mean we could take away the pain or the nightmares that followed," Massana explained, feeling her heart pounding in her chest.

Natava accepted the explanation. No one knew of the true love that Massana and Hela truly carried for each other. A love they couldn't openly express because Hela was destined for something greater. Massana understood the importance, never allowing her heart to stop beating for Hela, but their love became a deeper secret than anyone else wanted. Massana remained by Hela's side, but only as a friend. Natava sighed and ran a hand over her long, blond ponytail. Massana saw so much of Hela in her, her heart breaking at the sight, but she was proud of Natava and how far she had come. However, Natava carried so much anger. A temper that seemed uncontrollable at times, and it worried Massana. Where did that anger come from? Why did Natava seem so unpredictable? Was it her powers giving her a stronger connection to the wild emotions, or had something else affected her that no one knew about? The princess remained a deep mystery, but Massana knew that no one was more suited to be queen than her. Natava possessed a power like no other. She belonged on their throne.

Chapter 4

Natava felt like she was talking to a wall. Whatever she threw at it was sent right back to her, and she grew tired of the endless discussion that seemed to lead her nowhere. It often felt like she was speaking to walls. People had this idea of her, seeing her as someone who brought them into a bright world. She was seen as a symbol, not as a person, simply because she had displayed immense power and killed a Shadow Lord at the age of five. Usually, their powers didn't manifest until around the age of 12, when they began their slow development into adulthood. But Natava had shown extraordinary power and killed the Shadow Lord. She couldn't recall him clearly, but his voice still lingered in her mind. Natava remembered his hand, the long black nails, reaching out for her. She recalled the fear as his claw drew nearer, and that's when she had unleashed a surge of pure power. Her mother was known to be a formidable fighter, one of the strongest Halos out there, and her powers had been remarkable. But they paled in comparison to Natava's. Why her? Why was she chosen for this greatness? Could she trade places? Could someone else carry the next heir? Or could she choose? Why not choose? she asked herself. Why did she have to bear this burden?

"I want to be a Halo," Natava stated.

"I know your wishes, but sometimes fate takes us in different directions."

"Is this court my fate?"

"It's your destiny," Massana said.

"All I hear are excuses to prevent me from fighting. I will give you the heir, so give me a sword!" Natava argued.

"Natava, we have discussed this. Let it rest. Accept the way things are."

"No!"

"No?"

"No! I won't. I will marry the prince, I will have that heir, but I will not stop fighting. I want to fight. I want to remind everyone of what we are still doing for them. I will bring peace, not with a pen, but with a sword," Natava declared firmly.

"We cannot risk losing you."

"Who says you will?" Natava asked.

"I never thought I would lose your mother," Massana whispered, causing Natava to look down and feel a twinge of guilt. "We all lost something great that day."

"Yeah..."

"But that doesn't mean we didn't gain something as well," Massana said, looking at Natava with a motherly gaze. Massana also wished for a different path for Natava, but she had to consider the greater good. She wished she could have been more affectionate, wished she could have allowed Natava to pursue her own desires. She wished she could have given the young Light more freedom, but sometimes choices were not within our grasp. Massana had learned that lesson early in her life.

"I guess that's me, huh?" Natava joked, attempting to lighten the mood.

"Yes, very much so."

They shared a small smile, but Massana soon sighed and sank back into her seat.

"If I could let you choose, I would," she admitted.

Natava was taken aback by the extended hand Massana suddenly offered and raised a suspicious eyebrow.

"Yeah?"

"I do wish it was that simple, but it never is for people like you."

"People with great powers?" Natava questioned.

"People with greatness within them."

Natava looked a bit puzzled, and Massana stood, beckoning her to follow. Natava trailed behind, knowing where they were headed. Massana often took her on these walks where they would discuss her future, her powers, and what it meant to be queen. Natava had long ago tuned out during these walks, as they strolled through the castle and its garden, greeting the people they encountered, be they servants, Lights, or Halos. It was important for a queen to always show respect, but Natava's mind was miles away as Massana continued to talk. Natava plucked a rose from one of the bushes, twirling it before catching up to Massana.

The interesting part was that Natava was as oblivious to Massana's words as Massana was to Natava's disappearing and reappearing at her side. Massana continued her talk filled with what she deemed as wisdom, while Natava found other things that captured her interest. Soon, Natava noticed both Owin and his father walking not far behind them. She turned, walking backwards, making a funny face at Owin in an attempt to disrupt the serious role he had to adopt as her knight when they weren't alone. Owin pressed his lips together, trying not to laugh, as his father walked right beside him. Natava bit off the top of the rose, spitting it out, which almost caused Owin to crack, but it wasn't enough. Natava sneaked up behind Massana, who had begun talking about the greatness of being queen and the importance of listening to the people as a leader, taking each problem seriously. Natava pretended like she was going to jump at Massana, looking over her shoulder and seeing Owin shake his head with a smile on his lips. His father looked displeased but said nothing. It wasn't his job to speak up against the princess's eccentric behavior. He was simply there to watch over Massana.

Natava knew she was on the verge of making Owin crack, so she quickly came up with an idea. She took another path through the garden, and Owin had no choice but to follow, walking behind his father and hurrying after Natava, who chuckled as she maneuvered through the tall bushes with Owin chasing her. Soon, she heard his laughter as he relaxed now that it was just the two of them. She moved around a statue, waiting for him to appear, and when he did, she peeked out from beside it. He smiled, and she took off before returning to Massana, who continued her long speech. Natava waited until she was close enough, then she jumped out from her hiding spot, scaring Massana, who let out a little scream and placed her hand over her heart. Massana turned and saw an empty spot beside her. This was not a new prank, but Massana had hoped Natava had outgrown her childish behavior. Once again, she was disappointed to see that she hadn't.

"Did you hear a word I said?" she asked.

Natava shrugged. "Not really, but I've heard it a million times."

Owin appeared beside her, and they exchanged smiles before Natava turned to Massana. Massana shifted her eyes between them, leaving Natava perplexed. Massana's eyes carried a peculiar look, and Natava wondered what she was thinking.

"Were you running around with Owin?" she asked.

"Yes. He is my guard. He is supposed to follow me, is he not?" Natava asked.

"Yes..." Yet it sounded almost like a question in Natava's ears.

"I have heard the speech, Massana. Greatness, be a good queen, make smart decisions, and so on, and so on."

"Yes, but did you hear about the ball?"

"Ball?"

"Your coronation ball," Massana reminded her, crossing her arms.

"My what?"

"Natava, you are going to be queen. We just talked about it," she said.

"Can't the council choose someone else?"

"The decision lies with me," Massana told her.

"Fine. Can you choose someone else?"

"We just had a long talk!" Massana scolded.

"Yes, and while I had to listen to you, you didn't listen to me," Natava retorted.

"I am listening, but I also know what this kingdom needs, and that is you, Natava."

Natava didn't agree, placing her hands on her hips, looking very unsatisfied.

"The announcement will happen in three days, and in five, we celebrate," Massana told her.

"Wait... three?"

"Yes, three," Massana said.

"So soon?!"

"Soon? You have, according to our laws, been ready to take over since you turned 18," she reminded Natava.

"Yes, but we all knew I wasn't ready. I am still not ready!" Natava argued.

"You are."

"I just jumped out behind a bush to scare you. Is that a queen?"

"I know you will rise to the responsibilities of your role once you are crowned," Massana said, sounding like she trusted her completely.

While it was a compliment to have Massana's full trust, Natava was unsure where it came from. She had done whatever she could to seem unfit to rule, and she knew there were many who still thought she needed more time, especially since Massana was doing such an excellent job of ruling. But Massana saw more in Natava than most. Hela had not been prepared to be queen either, and neither had Massana. But they all became the queens they needed to be once they finally sat on the throne, and therefore Massana had no doubt Natava would become the queen she needed to be.

"Why do you have so much trust in me?" Natava asked.

Massana laughed, thinking it was a funny question, then began walking again, signaling for her to follow her. Natava did, interested in their talk now.

"Well?" Natava asked.

"Of course, I trust you."

"But I act like a child!"

"I am glad you see it yourself," Massana said. "But you will learn. Sometimes we must experience in order to learn."

"So throw me into the water without being able to swim?"

"But I have given you all the tools you need to learn to swim. You will manage," Massana told her, surprising her as she again showed Natava her complete trust.

It took Natava aback. She was sure Massana was going to wait at least a few weeks, if not months, before the announcement, constantly postponing it a little because she was unsure if Natava was ready. But it didn't seem like that was Massana's intention at all. She was prepared to put a crown on Natava's head, and Natava was unsure how to feel about it. She had no interest in the crown, but having Massana's complete trust was very flattering, considering Natava had done a lot to show she was unfit to be a ruler.

"You truly think I am ready for this?" Natava asked.

Massana stopped and turned to her, placing a hand on her shoulder. They were about the same height, and Massana only had to reach out a little before touching her. The older woman with bright green eyes smiled at her and then nodded.

"I truly think you are," she answered, shocking Natava.

She had thought Massana only felt the need to make her queen because she spoke so often of it, like she wanted her crowned to make an example, but not because she truly trusted Natava not to make a mess of everything she had built and worked for.

"How soon must I marry?" Natava questioned.

"You still have some time. You don't have to marry immediately, but the negotiations have begun."

"Without me?"

"They have only begun, but after the coronation, you will be part of the meetings," Massana assured her.

"Great, then I can reject everything."

"Natava," Massana scolded.

"What?"

"We should always aim for peace. It's a—"

"Queen's job," Natava interrupted.

"Yes, so aim for peace," Massana told her and then continued to walk, expecting Natava to follow. But Natava had a hard enough time accepting she was going to be queen, now she also had to think about marriage and heirs.

Natava took a different path, and Massana noticed how she hurried away but allowed her the time alone Natava needed while she continued the walk on her own.

Chapter 5

Erars watched the little paper fly towards him as he commanded his shadows to manipulate it. He had already read it several times, yet he couldn't help but keep going back to it. A perfect plan was forming in his mind as he admired the beautifully crafted announcement that had been spread across Aneria. Riders had been dispatched to ensure that everyone could read the wonderful news. A young queen had been chosen, destined to ascend the throne as their new ruler. Rumors circulated about the next queen, with some believing she possessed unparalleled power, while others dismissed her as a weakling unfit for rule. Erars did not concern himself with the identity of the next monarch. His focus was solely on his own ambitions of becoming the most powerful Shadow Lord. However, the upcoming festivities in the capital piqued his interest. He required a Light to sacrifice themselves in order to create a rift between this world and the realm of Shadows, enabling him to remove all the Halos and claim their power for himself. As the priest had mentioned, it necessitated a *willing* sacrifice. Thus, he would not target one of the trained Halos who possessed enough experience to avoid being deceived. No, he needed a young Light who would boldly enter the lion's den without hesitation. Erars planned to sow chaos during the coronation ball, seize a Light, and manipulate her into believing that sacrificing herself was a great service to the world. Only then would he ascend to the pinnacle of power.

The tale Erars had shared with the priest was not entirely false. He had been born as a disappointment and cast aside to fend for himself. The genesis of the Halos was more intricate, though. While he hadn't directly created them, he had set something in motion. It had unfolded differently from his initial expectations, but that did not mean he couldn't turn the circumstances to his advantage. Erars playfully spun the letter, relishing its exquisite design and knowing that the forthcoming ball would be unlike anything witnessed before. Only a select few had received invitations: nobles, individuals of stature, allies, and, of course, all the Lights and Halos would be present. Meanwhile, the common people would revel in street celebrations. Erars had obtained his invitation by eliminating a lord, claiming it as his own ticket to find a Light to abduct.

"It's going to be an intriguing night, sweet Lights," he chuckled.

His eyes traced the paper, observing the two distinct signatures at the bottom. They differed from each other—one curving with elegance and patience, while the other displayed harsh edges and impatience. These signatures belonged to the current queen and the future queen. *How intriguing*, he thought, scrutinizing their contrasting styles. If one of them was destined to be the future queen, how could she sign her name in such a manner? The impatience conveyed in the signature almost resembled that of a man's writing. It exuded anger and frustration. What could be the reason behind it? Erars's thoughts wandered as he examined the signatures. Something told him that the new queen would be an interesting person, but unfortunately for her, her reign would be short-lived. He would ensure it. Once he had breached the veil between the two worlds, it would require another sacrifice to seal it. However, the veil resided at the heart of where the Shadows emerged, making it an impossible task to approach. In Erars's mind, his plan seemed flawless as it would shock all the Halos, obliterate them, and plunge the world into chaos. No one would possess the courage to offer themselves as a sacrifice. He knew that without the Halos, the world would regress to its chaotic ways. The Halos brought peace, and their absence would return the world to how it used to be.

"Enjoy your night," he whispered, his dark voice resonating within the study where he sat. "It shall be the final one filled with joy."

Natava loathed the dress. She detested the party, and she despised the ridiculous little golden crown they had placed in her hair, weaving braids tightly to prevent her from removing it without pain. Frustrated, she groaned and paced in her chambers, searching for an escape. Was her window really that high? She walked over, opened it, and peered down. Yes, it was too high. She would break her neck if she attempted to climb down. What about using a rope? she wondered, searching for some rope but ending up looking at the sheets instead. She smiled and began tying them together. Her coronation had already felt suffocating enough. She hadn't even spoken to many people that day, merely riding around Aneria, greeting the citizens. Massana had ridden beside her, smiling and appearing joyful. Even now, Natava could barely muster a smile, knowing everyone would see through it if she joined the party. They would notice the strain in her smile, the tension in her body, and realise she loathed every moment.

Just as Natava finished tying the last knot, someone knocked on her door. She looked around, uncertain whether to answer. If she were quick, she might make it down to the ground. But as she contemplated her plan, she realised that escaping wouldn't be so simple. People were still streaming inside, lords and ladies arriving to celebrate her. Guards and Halos that were not participating in the festivities, patrolled everywhere. She knew she could easily be discovered. Perhaps if she waited a little longer, she would have a better chance.

"Nat?" Owin called.

She breathed a sigh of relief upon hearing her friend's voice. It was just Owin, she thought. She walked over to the door, the white-golden dress flowing around her, adding to her frustration. She rarely wore such dresses. They were impractical for fighting, and she was unaccustomed to the way they felt against her skin. Natava opened the door, her annoyance evident on her face. Owin struggled to suppress a smile at the sight, but his eyes slowly travelled down her body, taking in every inch of her. She wore a long, form-fitting dress with her blond hair braided and heavy makeup. Golden spirals adorned the area outside her eyes, and dark lines traced their edges. She raised an eyebrow, daring him to say anything. Owin knew Natava felt out of place, but he found her incredibly beautiful.

"You look stunning, my Queen," he complimented.

"I look like a stranger. Get me out of this!" she complained, tugging at her dress and causing him to chuckle.

"It's just for one night."

"No, it's every night and day after that. I'll never see the training grounds again. Can I even go riding?"

"With an escort."

"Yes, I'm sure knights and Halos will be following me everywhere. I'll be like a blazing beacon in the night, with so many people trailing behind," she complained.

"It's not the end of the world."

"No? Maybe if I begged for it, things would be different," she teased, turning around and walking back inside.

It was a clear invitation for Owin to follow, and he closed the door behind him, noticing the sheets all tangled and tied together.

“Don’t tell me you plan to escape through the window,” he said.

“Why not?” Natava turned to him. “Is it a terrible plan?”

“It’s a very bad plan.”

“Why?”

“You’ve tried it before. How easily were you caught?” he asked, reminding Natava of the many times she had attempted to evade her duties.

“I was younger. Less clever.”

“Are you that much smarter now?” he teased, earning an annoyed look from her. “Not in the mood for jokes?”

"I'm not in the mood for anything except getting out of here! Save me!" she pleaded, clasping her hands together and begging him.

"I can't help you, and you know that."

"Yes, yes, it's your sworn duty to protect me, even if it goes against my own wishes."

"You're needed here, as the next queen. Massana is no longer queen. You are. We need you to take charge."

"I hate how everyone keeps saying that," she snapped.

"But you can't change who you are."

"What if I could?"

"Then we wouldn't be having this conversation," he teased, offering her a small smile.

Owin always had a way of making her feel a little better, and she smiled back as they locked eyes.

"You're probably right about that."

"Listen, your life may have changed from now on. Yes, you'll act more as a queen than a Light, but that doesn't mean you can't still enjoy the same things. There may be new responsibilities, but it doesn't mean you have to let go of the small pleasures, right?" he asked.

Natava's smile grew, enjoying Owin's words of reassurance, and she nodded.

"No, I hope not."

"So, shall we survive this night?" he asked.

"I might need some wine."

"Then we'll get you some wine."

"And if anyone asks me to dance, I'll kick them," she warned.

"I would advise against that. Remember, you need allies."

Natava sighed, not entirely agreeing with how she had to act, but she summoned a bit of bravery and straightened her posture.

"Okay, I can do this," she whispered to herself, seeing her friend smile at her and nod.

She walked past him and opened the door, and they proceeded down a long hallway, followed by a flight of marble stairs, until they reached the floor below. Once there, they encountered the invited guests. They nodded their heads, greeting Natava and wishing her a long reign. She had never been scrutinised as much as she was now, and she wasn't sure how to feel about it. She had never desired to become the next queen, but here she was, and now everyone looked at her as if she had already saved them from all the cruelties that existed in the world.

Natava entered the grand ballroom, where soft music played and people danced, ate, and conversed. Massana had already found a group of people to engage with, but when she spotted Natava, she beckoned her closer. Natava took a deep breath, preparing herself for what was to come. She walked over to the group, and Massana began introducing her to the people. Throughout the night, she gradually learned more about her allies than any textbook could have taught her. While she had studied their histories and family trees, it was an entirely different experience to get to know them in person.

However, the atmosphere in the room grew a little tense as a powerful family arrived—the royal family of Meladova. Natava's face paled, and her stomach churned into knots. Massana quickly approached them, greeting them and conversing with them as if they had been long-time friends, as though they hadn't engaged in threats just a short while ago. Natava thought the plan of arranging her marriage to the prince was terrible. She retreated further into the shadows, hoping to find an escape. As she neared the room's walls, she collided with Owin's chest. She turned her head, feeling relieved when she recognised her friend there.

"What are you doing?" he questioned.

"Slipping away."

"What?"

"I tried, but now that my lovely betrothed is here, I'm out."

"Natava, you can't leave," he said firmly.

"No? I think I can."

Natava attempted to slip away, but Owin grabbed her wrist, pulling her back. He then led her to a more secluded area, where they could talk without interruption.

"This is your night. Many people have come to see you."

"Well, now they've seen me," Natava retorted.

"You've barely spoken to a quarter of the people here. You're supposed to be here all night. Massana has prepared this for you."

"I didn't ask her to!"

"You didn't have to. This night is your chance. Your actions tonight will influence how people perceive you in the future. You must make a good impression tonight or risk losing support. No one wants a queen who doesn't appreciate her position," he reminded her, invoking a slight sense of guilt for wanting to slip away from the party. But could she truly endure more of this?

Chapter 6

A simple mask, a change of clothes, and a little help from his shadows allowed Erars to blend in perfectly with the crowd streaming into the marble castle, ready to celebrate their new queen and get to know her. Erars had to admit he found the new queen somewhat intriguing. After observing the way that she had written her name, he sensed a darker side within her. He believed there was a hint of darkness merged with her light, but he needed a closer look. Erars had to see the queen in person to truly know. He smiled faintly, grabbing a cup of wine as it passed by on a servant's tray. The grand party was filled with people from all over Aneria, oblivious to the threat lurking among them. Erars found amusement in their ignorance as he made his way further into the ballroom, surveying the surroundings. He was searching for a very young Light to abduct, unsure if they would be directly involved in the festivities or kept separate from everything else. It wouldn't surprise him if they kept the precious young ones somewhere else to honor their queen. Regardless, he would find them, even if it took all night. This was his opportunity, and he wouldn't let it slip away.

His eyes swept across the room, scanning a small group of Lights laughing and flirting with young lords. All Lights were born as women, and their guards had taken vows to never touch them, only to protect them. Could anyone blame the Lights for desiring to experience the touch of a man? However, these were older Lights, more challenging to manipulate. No, he needed younger ones, those who wouldn't grasp how he twisted their minds into believing they were sacrificing themselves for the greater good—or rather, his greater good. He moved through the room, feeling his powers swirl beneath his skin as he encountered various souls. Some were difficult to look away from, their purity and sweetness drawing him in, but he remained focused on his plan, searching for a suitable Light. He found a secluded corner, concealing himself in the shadows, observing from a distance all that transpired. The party resembled any other thrown by those of lesser stature. Nothing like the extravagant parties the Shadow Lords once hosted. *Ah, those were the days*, he thought, although he had never been a welcome guest. He had fought his way to the top, but to the Shadow Lords, status and family mattered. In many ways, the same held true for these people, but he had struggled to earn the respect of the higher Shadow Lords, and he never gained it. Yet, where were they now? All dead, while he thrived, slowly making his way to where he desired to be. It had taken many years, but he could already taste the impending victory.

Suddenly, his eyes caught sight of a small group of young Lights, children, running through the crowd, chasing one another. So, there were some here, he thought, observing as the group vanished among the larger bodies. He quickly finished his wine, ready to pursue one of them and isolate them from the rest, when a commotion occurred farther away. He shifted his eyes, attempting to see through the crowd to discern what had happened, but all he could make out was a woman storming out of the ballroom, her flowing dress catching his attention. It mattered little to him, and he resumed tracking the group of young Lights running away. He saw them hurrying down a hallway as he distanced himself from the ballroom. However, older Halos intercepted them, blocking their path and delivering a lecture. Internally growling, he acknowledged that he would need to exercise more patience before he could seize one of them.

Owin looked at Natava, silently pleading with her not to run off when the night had only just begun. She understood the weight of his expression and what he desired and needed from her. His importance to her made his plea even more significant. She stood there for a moment, carefully considering her options. While she knew she couldn't evade her engagement indefinitely, she preferred not to engage with the prince just yet. She would rather escape for the night. However, Owin continued to look at her with his small, pleading expression.

"I hate it when you look at me like that," she mumbled.

He smiled, aware of the effect his "puppy eyes" had on her. He easily got under her skin, but they both cherished the connection they shared. However, he understood that their relationship could never progress beyond friendship. Natava tapped a finger against her arms, crossing them over her chest as she searched for an escape from the ball. Unfortunately, it seemed there was no way out. She had to face her responsibilities.

"Fine, I will stay," she said. "But just for a quick chat."

"Don't forget, you're needed all night," he reminded her.

"I am in need of more wine."

She walked away and grabbed a cup, hearing Owin chuckle, which brought a smile to her lips. Before she could take more than a sip, Massana found her and called out to her. Natava inwardly cursed, slowly turning on her heel before making her way over to where the royal family of Meladova stood. Massana began introducing them, and Natava offered a weak smile to the King and Queen of Meladova before the prince was presented to her. She could understand why people found him handsome. Rumors definitely spoke of his charm. However, as their hands met and his lips lightly brushed against her hand, she felt a shiver run through her, making her feel uneasy. Sometimes it was easy to see a wolf in sheep's clothing, and she believed she stood before one now. Could he be trusted not to later attempt to seize all power? Well, at least then she wouldn't have to worry about ruling, she thought. But Massana believed in her. She had expressed full trust in Natava, unwilling to simply hand everything over to a stranger—a family that had recently threatened to kill Massana and seize her possessions if she didn't comply with their demands. In Natava's mind, none of them could be trusted. However, Massana believed in the potential of this alliance. She believed a powerful union could mend everything. Natava had a different view, but she kept her thoughts to herself. Massana and the King and Queen of Meladova gradually moved away, providing the two of them with more space. Natava wished they hadn't. The last thing she desired was to be alone with the prince.

"Lovely evening, isn't it?" he began.

"Yes... lovely," she mumbled, sipping her wine.

"A lot of people have turned up tonight," he remarked, glancing around the room at all the guests, and she did the same.

"It's a significant night."

"It will be even more magnificent when the two of us rule together," he stated.

"Most likely..."

"Then there will be something truly worth celebrating."

"Truly worth celebrating?" she questioned.

The prince, with his dark smirk and deep blue eyes that concealed sinister intentions, turned to her, causing goosebumps to rise on her skin.

"Well, considering your wild behavior, you aren't really suited to rule."

"Excuse me?" she said, unsure if she had heard correctly. Who openly insulted someone like that?

"You must be aware of what people think of you. You're not fit to rule. It's a good thing you will have a king now—one who truly understands the responsibilities of leadership."

Natava's entire body tensed with anger as something dark swirled within her. She heard the slight sound of a sword being grasped and partially drawn from its scabbard. Owin stood behind her, looking just as furious. She knew he wanted to strike down the prince for openly insulting her. She appreciated his unwavering loyalty, but she couldn't allow Owin to commit murder, as it would serve none of them and would lead to his own death. Striking down a prince due to a few insulting words wasn't the solution. Natava didn't need Owin to defend her honor. She could do that herself.

"You're right," she said, causing the prince's smile to widen.

"Of course I am."

"I am nothing but a foolish princess who has now been crowned queen. How will I know what to do?" she pretended.

"That's why I am here. That's why my family agreed to this. If we wanted to, we could have easily taken over your land," he boasted.

"Of course, such a powerful family could have easily overpowered us. A simple princess like myself needs a man in her life to truly become the queen she is destined to be," Natava continued.

"Exactly."

"I am just so delighted you're here," Natava continued, watching his smile darken.

"Really?"

"Yes."

She moved closer to him, and he leaned towards her, towering above her.

"Perhaps you should show your appreciation privately," he suggested. "Why wait for the wedding?"

Natava felt a wave of nausea, but instead, she took another small sip of wine, appearing even more willing than she truly was. It was all an act. She leaned closer, surprising the prince with her enthusiasm. However, it was merely a façade. She leaned close enough to capture his full attention, then she tipped the almost full cup and poured the wine over his dark royal clothes. He gasped, pulling back and colliding with another woman.

The guests turned their heads as they heard the commotion, their attention drawn to Natava and the prince, who shot her a murderous look.

"I don't need a king to rule. This damn engagement is over!" she declared, throwing the cup away and hearing it clang against the marble floor.

She stormed past the prince and the guests, who quickly made way for her, and she hurried back to her room. Owin had done an excellent job of convincing her to stay. She had been willing to stay because he asked her to, but now she had changed her mind. Natava refused to be made a fool of by the man Massana thought she should marry. She would never marry such a person. She would never allow someone like him to make her feel small. Natava stormed into her room, the double doors clashing against the walls behind them. She ripped the little crown from her head, groaning as it got stuck in her hair. She kept pulling, trying to untangle it, and finally freed it before throwing it across the room.

"Don't worry, I'll explain everything to Massana," Owin assured her.

"I don't give a shit!" Natava yelled. "I never wanted him in the first place. Let her think what she wants to think. If she believes I should be with that man, then I don't think I owe her an explanation!"

Natava didn't mean to be so rude to the woman who had cared for her and loved her like her own daughter, but she was too angry at the prince's words. His remarks swirled in her head, boiling her blood. She had never encountered someone so rude and arrogant, someone who believed they were a gift to the earth or any woman they married. He certainly wasn't a gift to Natava, and now she wanted to leave.

"Natava..."

"I want to be alone. Please leave," she said, trying to keep her voice as calm as possible. She didn't want Owin to think she was angry with him. After all, he had been ready to confront the prince.

"Are you sure?" he asked.

"Just... wait outside. I want to leave," she told him.

He nodded slightly, made a small turn as if to leave, and Natava thought that was it. But then he spun around and approached her. He surprised her as he reached for her, placing his hands on her neck and pulling her in for a powerful and heart-racing kiss. She whimpered, taken aback by the gesture, but leaned into the sweet touch. He had never done that before. Through the kiss, Owin expressed his feelings for her. Slowly, he backed away, his dark eyes filled with tenderness as he looked at her. He smiled, and she smiled back.

"How long have you wanted to do that?" she whispered.

"For a very long time."

She smiled at him, and she wanted to ask him to kiss her again, but no further words were exchanged. Owin backed away, walking out of the room and closing the doors behind him. Natava let out a shaky breath, not expecting that, but it had certainly turned her night around, making her feel better.

Chapter 7

It took some maneuvering and bending in ways she didn't think were possible, but she succeeded in getting the dress off. Now, she was wearing white pants, a shirt, and a jacket adorned with the symbols of the Halos. Even though she wasn't officially one of them, she could still wear the clothes as a representation. The symbols were swirling circles that didn't connect but went higher, creating a small loop. She tied her boots, ready for a ride or whatever activity they decided to do for the night to take her mind off the horrible ending of the ball. Natava got up from her bed and walked out to where Owin stood. He turned to her, still wearing his blue and white uniform that stood out among the white and golden uniforms worn by the Halos. He smiled at her, and she smiled back. She stepped closer, prepared to repeat what had happened in her room, when she heard a familiar voice calling out her name.

"Natava!" Massana yelled, coming down the hallway with a group of older Halos and Owin's father by her side.

"Massana," Natava mumbled before turning to face the older woman, who stopped in front of her, looking furious.

"Do you have any idea what you have just done?" she asked.

"I have an idea."

"The royal family of Meladova has left!"

"Good, I wanted them to," Natava said, unapologetic about what she had done to the prince, spilling her wine all over his fine clothes.

"How could you do such a thing? Now we may end up in a war unless I can calm things down!"

"Good, let's fight."

"Natava!" Massana scolded.

"That prince was an asshole! You didn't hear the way he spoke to me. They can't be trusted, and I refuse to marry such a person. He is awful! I won't sacrifice myself like that and end up miserable with a bastard like him," Natava yelled, surprising Massana with the power behind her voice as she leaned closer, getting almost in her face.

"Natava, this could result in innocent lives being lost if we don't try to rectify the damage," Massana reminded her.

"He is not worth it. They are not worth it," Natava said.

"How can you be sure?"

"I overheard everything," Owin interjected. "I heard what he said, and he doesn't have the best interests of our home and the people here at heart. He cannot be trusted."

"This is not up to you, son," his father cut in.

Owin sighed, feeling tired of his father dismissing him. Owin didn't believe Natava should be with someone like the prince. The prince had treated her horribly and would only become worse after they got married. He had seen men like that before—showing small signs of being horrible people and then revealing their true darkness after marriage, leaving their partners trapped. He didn't want that for his friend. She would never be treated poorly by a husband. He would die before allowing that to happen. Massana and Natava seemed locked in a staring contest, but Massana seemed unsure of what to think after hearing Owin speak as well. Slowly, her eyes darted to him, and he was prepared to defend Natava if necessary.

Massana opened her mouth to ask more, but then something shifted in the air. At first, no one was sure if they had heard anything or why they suddenly felt so cold. But then the screams began erupting outside. They all rushed to the big windows on their left, witnessing the city connected to the marble castle on fire and people screaming in fear for their lives.

"Shadows!" someone yelled, and they all saw figures moving around in the square.

Instantly, the screams filled the castle. They reacted quickly, turning on their heels and running towards the stairs. However, Massana stopped before descending the staircase and turned to Natava.

"What?" she asked, bewildered.

"Stay here," Massana ordered.

"Are you serious?"

"Yes. Owin," she commanded, and Owin gently grabbed Natava's arm.

Natava looked at him as if he were betraying her, but he agreed that Natava shouldn't run into danger. Natava pulled away from his grip, ignoring the given orders, and quickly slipped past Massana. She was too fast, and the hands gripping her as she stormed through the group slipped away as she sped onwards.

"Natava!" Massana yelled.

She didn't listen and instead ran back to the ballroom, which had once been filled with lights and candles but was now a dark wasteland with dead bodies strewn across the floor. Looking around, she felt the chilling temperatures and wondered how this had happened. A strange growl caught her attention from behind. She swiftly spun on her heel, discovering a shadow hound standing there with red eyes and a black body. Although it appeared translucent, she knew it could harm her. Natava surveyed her surroundings, seized a sword from a fallen knight, and prepared herself for the impending attack.

The hound pounced, leaping into the air and lunging at her. She swiftly struck it, causing it to whimper and collapse to the side. Its body seemed almost carved in half, but it slowly regenerated and turned to face her. Natava understood that swords were ineffective against shadow creatures. They could only disrupt their attacks but not destroy them. Light was necessary for that. Harnessing her inner powers, she felt them swirling within her and directed them to her hand. The hound growled, sensing the change, and emitted a faint howl. More hounds materialised from the dark corners, as if they had always been part of the wall. They merged together, forming a massive shadow wave, ready to engulf and crush her. Natava witnessed the sight, fear gripping her heart, but she remembered her training and remained resolute before she conjured a ball of light in her hand. As the wave approached, accompanied by howls and growls, she thrust her hand forward, allowing the light to grow stronger and stronger, holding the wave at bay. She heard agonised whimpering and cries of pain. The shadow creatures retreated, gradually merging with the dark corners of the room until they vanished. She knew they hadn't truly disappeared. They had simply retreated.

Hastily exiting the ballroom, Natava noticed that the screams had subsided slightly. Shadows roamed throughout the marble castle, attacking anyone they encountered. She hurried towards the source of the sounds, with shadows lunging out from the darkness, attempting to seize her and impede her progress. Using her light, she repelled them and deflected their attacks with her sword. Upon reaching the lowest floor, she discovered the doors barricaded, and guests pounded on them desperately, seeking escape as the shadow hounds closed in, hunting their defenceless prey. Where were the other Halos? In a desperate attempt to divert the hounds' attention, Natava emitted a piercing whistle. The hounds turned towards her, and she tapped into her inner power, allowing a brilliant stream of light to radiate from her being. The hounds whimpered once again and vanished.

The doors swung open, and the guests hurried outside, dispersing in all directions. Natava followed them, observing the ongoing battle in the square. She realised that the outside offered no safety either, and the guests soon grasped that fact, scattering in various directions. Uncertain of where to start, she heard a high-pitched scream and witnessed young Lights being pursued by shadow creatures, herding them towards a door leading outside the castle walls and towards the training grounds. Without hesitation, Natava pursued the shadows, and just as they forced the young Lights beyond the wall, she leaped towards them, slashing one of the shadows to create a path for herself. Standing before the shadows that began to merge, much like the hounds had done, she positioned herself protectively with the young Lights huddled behind her.

"When I say run, move back behind the walls," Natava commanded.

She didn't bother checking if they agreed. She expected them to comply. The shadow emitted a bestial sound, sending a shiver down Natava's spine. Using her light powers had drained her, as she wasn't accustomed to channeling such immense energy. Feeling a bit dizzy, she summoned her remaining strength, allowing the light to flow from her body as she yelled, "Run!" the young Lights sprinted past the writhing and screaming shadow, propelled by the power of the light. The longer it was exposed, the more the shadow diminished in size. Eventually, it dissipated into nothingness, and Natava let the light fade away, finding herself kneeling on one knee and leaning on her sword, planted firmly in the ground. She needed a moment to recover, but then she heard a slow, mocking applause. Natava raised her eyes, her vision still blurry, and saw a dark figure approaching. He was dressed like any other guest, and his calm demeanor perplexed her.

"Well, what do we have here?" he taunted.

Chapter 8

Erars was just as bewildered as the other guests when the chaos of screams and hunting broke out. The shadows recognised him for what he was and disregarded him, focusing their attention on others. He could freely move around without fear, but this unexpected turn of events disrupted his plans. He had been on the verge of capturing one of the young Lights, following a girl to a secluded hallway where she had become separated from the rest. However, when the chaos erupted, he lost sight of her and became more engrossed in the unfolding events. The sheer number of shadows that suddenly attacked the marble castle and its guests was astonishing. It made no sense how a single Shadow Lord could summon so many. Or perhaps it wasn't just one? Maybe the shadows had orchestrated the attack themselves, but they typically required a master to conjure a single thought.

As he encountered another shadow that paused, growling at him before realising that he emerged from the darkness as well, he examined it closely and realised that the shadow hounds emerged from the depths of darkness themselves. But how was that possible? Tearing the veil required a Light, yet Erars recognised the powers of these shadow creatures. Had someone already succeeded in breaking the veil? And if so, how? Erars knew he couldn't linger there. The chaos offered him an easy escape, and there was no reason to abduct a young Light if someone had already shattered the veil. But he possessed the scrolls! How had someone discovered their location? Why? Who else was plotting against the Halos besides him? He considered himself exceptionally audacious and doubted anyone else had the courage to undertake what he had planned. It annoyed him that someone had even attempted and seemingly succeeded.

Erars emerged outside, witnessing the ongoing battle, and strolled across the square as if taking a leisurely walk. The main entrance was blocked, so he sought another exit that would attract little attention. However, as he approached, a bright light erupted, even causing him discomfort from a distance. He heard a loud, beastly, agonised sound before observing three young Lights running past him and returning towards the castle. Now, he was truly intrigued. Erars followed the path from which the young Lights had come and discovered something intriguing on the ground. There sat a young woman, leaning on her sword, panting and sweating as she recovered from an exertion of her powers. Shadow creatures from the Shadow World were far more resilient than ordinary shadows from their realm. They were forged from darkness, requiring significant energy to defeat. Erars found himself inexplicably drawn to the young woman before him. He was almost impressed and began to slowly clap, taunting her with the sound. She slowly lifted her head, but upon hearing his voice, she fell silent. As she looked at him, he sensed his powers surging forward, as if hands yearned to touch and reach out to her. He discovered an unprecedented purity within her soul, an allure he had never encountered before. It astonished him as he looked down at her, her eyes slightly closed, seemingly unable to focus on him. He crouched down a little, smiling.

"You're a very interesting one, aren't you?" he asked.

"Who are you?" she darkly asked.

Still disguised as an ordinary guest, Erars removed his mask, casting it aside, before allowing his true form to emerge. His blond hair turned dark, his skin grew paler, and his eyes transformed into a dark red. His nails turned black and pointed, while his clothes remained unchanged. The young woman's eyes widened with fear as she looked at him. This only drew him closer. Fear was akin to sustenance for him, and he almost felt compelled to touch her—not to drain her, at least not initially, but to feel and memorise her. *Very interesting,* he thought.

"You did this!" she accused, gripping her sword tightly and slashing through the air as he backed away.

Erars emitted a hissing sound, standing upright again. He glanced at his arm, where the tip of her sword had grazed him, observing black blood streaming from the wound. It quickly closed up, but he felt annoyed that she had managed to surprise him. Slowly, she rose to her feet, and he patiently waited for her to regain her balance.

"Why now?!" she demanded, clutching the sword tighter.

Clearly, she had expended too much power. Was she not yet a Halo? Had she not received the necessary training to utilise minimal energy, reserving her true outburst for when it was needed? She appeared old enough to have attained Halo status, yet she seemed to lack the strength to summon another powerful surge of light. Or perhaps she sought answers. Erars wondered the same. Who had shattered the veil? He needed to find this other Shadow Lord whose plan seemed remarkably similar to his own.

"How did you do this?!" she yelled, demanding an answer.

"I must admit, I'm somewhat surprised myself," he chuckled.

She did not find any humor in his words and stepped closer, displaying remarkable bravery. Erars was surprised by how she could appear so angry yet possess such purity within her. Halos were not known for being the purest souls to be found. The burdens they carried and the actions they took to protect themselves and those around them often took a toll. However, this one seemed to have remained untainted.

"Why did you do this?" she asked.

"I have done nothing, Light," he taunted.

"You want the crown?" she accused.

"That would be nice," he laughed, causing Natava to narrow her eyes, feeling repulsed by the sight before her.

"You will never have it."

"Won't I?" he asked.

"Who are you?"

"Just another nightmare," he answered.

Natava tightened her grip on the sword, and Erars noticed, his eyes briefly flickering down before refocusing on her.

"Going to kill me with that? You must know it takes more," he taunted.

Natava didn't care. She lunged at Erars, slashing through the air, but he swiftly moved back. Annoyance began to well up within him. He hadn't come here to fight. Yet as she came at him again, he used his powers to push her back, sending shadows in her direction. She groaned as she landed on the ground. Erars contemplated draining her for her powers when he sensed a shift in the air. He turned his head and witnessed a dark wave advancing towards him. While the shadows recognised him for what he was, this wave possessed a distinct command and purpose, and it showed no signs of halting. Erars leaped to the side, landing not far from Natava, and they both watched as the wave crashed against the walls, causing them to crack and collide.

"No!" Natava yelled.

She sprang forward, witnessing the wave attempting to tear down the entire wall. Natava had to stop it. She had to eradicate the shadows before they completely ravaged the castle. Natava delved deeper than ever before, tapping into an immense well of power that left her feeling dizzy, yet she remained standing. Focusing on the shadow wave, she allowed her powers to surge out of her, illuminating her entire body so brightly that she became unseeable. The wave began whimpering and emitting a peculiar sound of agony. Erars, too, felt the searing intensity of her light, shielding his face with his arms as her radiance inflicted burns upon him.

The shadow let out louder screams, unable to endure it any longer, and disintegrated, vanishing into the night. Erars emitted pained sounds as well and knew he had to flee before she annihilated him with her light. Soon, however, her radiance faded, and he observed as the woman collapsed to the ground, this time losing consciousness. Remaining on the ground for a moment, Erars observed the fallen body in the distance. He had never witnessed anything quite like it before. While he found her purity intriguing, the level of power she had exhibited was on a different scale.

Erars slowly rose, dusting off his clothes, and noticed the eerie silence that had settled. He knew it was time to make his escape—no one would even realise he had been there, except for the fallen Light on the ground. He approached, studying the young woman, an idea taking shape in his mind, one he probably shouldn't entertain. Uncertain if the veil had been shattered or if other Shadow Lords were involved, Erars considered the possibility that the Light before him might be of use. Though she had displayed incredible powers, among the shadows, she would grow weaker. Moreover, she had captured his attention in ways he hadn't deemed possible. After all, he had come tonight to abduct a Light. He just hadn't expected to be drawn to this particular one. Reaching for the young woman, he effortlessly lifted her into his arms and walked away, blending into the night, a smile playing upon his lips. This was going to be very interesting, he thought.

Chapter 9

Natava felt overwhelmingly dizzy. She had never before attempted to harness such an immense amount of power against such formidable creatures. She understood that certain shadow creatures posed greater challenges and required a more concentrated infusion of light to harm them. But the exertion had drained her to the point of unconsciousness. Was this normal? She had never engaged in combat, never faced an opponent who demanded her to fully utilise her powers, not since she was a child. The Shadow Lord she had encountered earlier had possessed power, but it paled in comparison to the creatures she had confronted tonight. Was it still nighttime? Her head throbbed, and her shoulders ached. Why was she in such agony?

Groaning, Natava opened her eyes slightly and found herself staring at a brick wall. As her vision gradually cleared, she quickly realised she was not in her home, not in her room. She had no idea where she was. She surveyed the circular room, only to discover that she was suspended above the ground by iron chains and metal cuffs around her wrists. Ah, that explained the pain in her shoulders, she thought. But why was she there? What was the last thing she could remember? She remembered the battle against the shadow creatures, believing they were the reason behind her current imprisonment. However, she had caused them to vanish. She had inflicted enough damage to force them to retreat. Had they returned? An image of a Shadow Lord emerging from the darkness flickered in her mind, and she realised that only one person could have taken her. But why? Soft footsteps reached her ears, and she peered down the small, dark tunnel in front of her. The sun's rays shone down on her, causing her to sweat and feel even more uncomfortable. She noticed red eyes emerging from the shadows. The tips of boots came into view, and she could just make out the figure of the Shadow Lord, observing her as she dangled from the ceiling.

"Who the fuck are you? Why did you take me?" Natava demanded.

It made no sense for him to abduct her, letting her live. Killing her would gain him more power.

"You're a very powerful one, aren't you?" he replied, his voice dark, sending shivers down her spine. But she refused to show any fear. She would not allow him to witness her weakness.

"Who are you?" she repeated calmly.

"Just another Shadow Lord," he answered.

"A weasel hiding in the dark," she snapped, causing him to chuckle.

"No, I am far more dangerous. But I am also patient."

"Patient? You destroyed the marble castle and killed so many people!" Natava snapped.

Erars smiled, but he knew he was not the one responsible for it all. He felt no remorse for the lost souls. Why should he care? But he wanted to discover who orchestrated the attack because they had disrupted his own plans.

"I thought you were a trained Halo," he remarked.

Natava looked at him, confused, uncertain why he was changing the subject.

"But you seemed uncoordinated. Untrained."

"Fuck you!" she retorted.

Erars chuckled. "And for a Light, you're quite rude."

"We aren't all sunshine and rainbows."

"No? You harbor a great deal of purity within you. I want to drain it," he calmly stated.

"Then why haven't you?" she asked.

"I am more intrigued by the possibility of using you," he disclosed.

"Using me? For what?"

"Believe it or not, I didn't plan the attack," he confessed, leaving Natava utterly bewildered.

"But you were there. Why else would you be present?"

"To steal a Light."

"What?" she exclaimed.

"I have grander plans for this world. I have waited many years, searching high and low for answers. Now, I have found them. I just require one more thing—a Light, preferably a young one."

"But I'm here," she pointed out.

"Yes, my plans were thwarted as others took matters into their own hands," Erars explained.

"I don't understand."

"Nor do I fully, but I will unravel the mystery. It seems that others also desire to shatter the veil."

"Shatter... You mean the barrier between this world and the Shadow World?" Natava gasped.

"Yes," he replied.

"No, you can't!"

"I fear that others already have."

"Impossible."

"No, it's actually quite possible. All it takes is one little Light, thinking she's doing us all a favor."

"I am not doing you a favor!" Natava snapped.

"Yes, manipulating you would indeed be quite a challenge."

"Then what do you want from me?!" Natava snarled.

"I want you to do what all you Halos have already done for me," he explained.

"For you?"

"I can't have other Shadow Lords attempting to take what is rightfully mine. And with the kinds of powers you possess, even with the shadow creatures likely guarding them, they won't be safe from you," he told her.

"Why don't you hunt them down yourself?"

"No, I prefer to have others do the boring and tiring work. That would be you," he explained.

"Never."

"I don't think you've encountered a Shadow Lord before or witnessed what we are capable of."

"But I have, and I killed one."

Erars grew even more intrigued and stepped slightly out of the shadows. Natava watched him, surprised that he would reveal himself. In the light, she could see him more clearly, triggering old memories of how she had slain the other Shadow Lord when she was just a child. It pained her to recollect because there were so many unanswered questions.

"Hmm, interesting that you're still so sweet if that is true," he said.

"I am not sweet! And once I break free from these chains, you're dead!"

"Here, you will gradually grow weaker," he explained. "This is my realm."

"Yet you appear when the sun is high in the sky."

"While it usually fuels you, your body will be drained. Without food and water, with the scorching heat beating down on you and the chains digging into your wrists, you will only grow more exhausted."

Natava despised how right he was. While the sun fuelled her, and the night fuelled the Shadow Lord, she couldn't deny the draining of her body's natural energy as she hung there above the ground, extended and in pain.

"I will not help you," she declared.

"We shall see. What is your name?" he asked, surprising himself with the question.

"Go to hell," she cursed.

He chuckled, shaking his head.

"I'm Erars. Don't forget it because you have no idea whose dark world you've just entered," he warned her.

"I will break free. Others will come for me!"

"So many perished that night. Why would anyone come looking?" he asked.

"There is no body!"

"But why should that matter?"

Natava narrowed her eyes, and Erars grew intrigued. Was she more significant than he had initially realised? She dressed like any other Halo, but why was she so convinced that people would come searching for her?

"Are you important?" he asked.

Natava kept her lips sealed, refusing to give anything away. She had been kept hidden and protected all her life. She had never been publicly recognised as a Halo, and she had only recently been crowned Queen. Natava wasn't surprised that the Shadow Lord didn't recognise her. After all, she had fought like any other Halo.

"You seem so certain," he pointed out.

"Maybe we simply understand the meaning of compassion."

"Yes, and that's precisely what will lead to your downfall."

"It's what keeps this world spinning."

"This world was perfect before all of you arrived. Well, almost. I needed all of you to remove some people for me," he revealed.

Natava felt confused by his words and looked at him, her head slightly tilted to the side.

"Why do you speak as if all of this is part of your plan?" she asked.

"I told you, I'm a patient person. I can wait for hundreds of years before finally claiming what is rightfully mine," he explained.

"And what is yours?"

"All of this. Everything you see around you, wherever you go. And once I've rid the world of the Halos, I will restore the glory of the Shadow Lords. We will once again dominate this world, with me as their true leader."

"Who the hell are you?" she whispered, struggling to comprehend Erars's words.

"Soon enough, you will learn of my power as well. You will see why submitting to me is the smarter choice. Choose the winning side. I might just spare your life, at least until I tire of you," he told her.

"You're a monster."

"I'm well aware."

He laughed as he walked away, saving the real fun for later. Natava tugged at her chains, attempting to swing her body, but she felt so exhausted, and she knew he was right. With time, she would have no strength left to fight him. Erars had meticulously planned this.

Chapter 10

It was dark in the middle of the night when Erars returned. Natava's head kept falling forward, so exhausted she was. But when she heard him creep closer, she quickly grew alert. Though she was starving and thirsty, she tried her hardest to appear composed and hide her exhaustion. Erars emerged like a thicker shadow in the darkness. He went to turn on a small candle on the wall, and she wondered why, as his vision was perfect in the darkness.

"Now you can see me," he taunted.

"Does the torture begin now?"

"Hmm, maybe," he teased.

He began circling her like a predator. She struggled to turn her head and keep an eye on him, but it was difficult to track his movements. Suddenly, he was gone. She looked around, thinking she had missed him, but no, he had disappeared, only to reappear right in front of her, shocking her and making her heart race. However, he did not touch her. He merely scared her and then drew away again. He chuckled softly, and she cursed him silently. Erars looked her up and down, sizing her up, which infuriated her even more, considering she was already in such a vulnerable position. She kicked out, but he easily grabbed her ankle, holding on tightly.

"Let go!" she demanded.

When she tried to pull back, he dug his nails through her clothes and into her skin.

"Shit!" she hissed.

"What is your name?" he began.

"Fuck you."

"Wrong answer," he told her, digging a little deeper, making her hiss in pain. But then he let go and disappeared from sight. She understood his tricks, never revealing where the next attack might come from.

"I will never serve you. What Light would?"

"The impressionable ones would," he spoke right outside her ear, making her gasp and turn her head, but he didn't stay there for long.

Suddenly, he appeared on her other side and reached out to grab her face, attempting to turn it. However, the moment his skin made contact with hers, he hissed and drew back, his skin sizzling as if he had been burned. Natava watched, surprised, as the Shadow Lord recoiled and clutched his wrist.

"Oh, that's power," he snarled, before turning to her, looking furious, his red eyes glowing even brighter. "In all my time, no one has been able to simply burn me without using their powers. Who are you, little Light?"

Natava smiled, amazed that she had been able to do that. She hadn't intentionally used her powers, and no Shadow Lord had ever touched her before.

"Apparently, someone not to be messed with," she chuckled.

Erars did not find her words amusing. How could the Light burn him like that? She hadn't even summoned her powers, and yet just touching her skin caused him pain. It shouldn't have been possible, and while it intrigued him, he also knew it made it harder for him to get close to her.

"So powerful," he mumbled as he began circling her again, running his hand down her back as he moved around her.

"Hey!" she protested, twisting around to avoid his touch.

He could touch her clothes, but he realised her skin posed a problem. Or perhaps she simply needed more time in the darkness with him. Maybe then he would be able to get closer. He stopped in front of her and began unbuttoning her jacket. Natava twisted, trying to kick him and summon whatever energy she had left to use her powers, but she was completely drained. Once he had her jacket open, he lifted her shirt slightly.

"Do not fucking touch me!" she warned.

Erars smiled before moving closer, this time more carefully. He used more of his powers to create a protective layer around his fingers. He wanted to see if he could minimise the damage she inflicted or even infect her slightly. They both hissed in pain when he barely grazed her skin, but it was more bearable this time. He pressed a little closer, utilising more of his powers, and it became easier. Dark veins started spreading from the spot he had touched, but they seemed to vanish instantly.

"You even seem immune to any infections from my shadows," he remarked, pulling away. "How can you be this powerful and yet so young? Who are you?"

Natava said nothing, glaring at him instead. Erars slowly began piecing things together. He wasn't certain, but there were rumors he had heard over many years.

"I had heard of a powerful Light, destined for great things and to rid this world of darkness. But she was also described as untrained, wild, and uncontrollable. No one knew if she was fit to be a ruler, yet her coronation took place." A dark smile crept onto his lips as he observed any shifts or signs on her face that he might be onto something.

Natava clenched her teeth so hard that her jaw hurt. Erars observed the myriad of emotions flickering behind her eyes, and he now understood who he had truly captured. *A very rare Light, indeed*, he thought.

"You're our new queen. Sorry, I forgot to bring a gift for the occasion," he chuckled.

"I am no queen."

"A queen who doesn't want to be a queen. You must be the only one I know with no interest in the crown," he pointed out.

"Or maybe you've simply surrounded yourself with the wrong people."

"No, I simply know what lies within people's black hearts. It isn't sunshine," he explained. "Even Shadow Lords can't stand each other."

"Then you must understand why I have no interest in your company," Natava retorted.

Erars chuckled, appreciating her sharp tongue. She was an amusing little Light, but she would be crushed among his shadows. Until he had her where he wanted her, she wouldn't be able to use her powers. The queen would soon realise that once you were ensnared in the world of shadows, there was no escape.

"I will leave you to your own delightful company, then."

"You're just going to leave me hanging here?" she asked.

"Oh, now you want me to stay? Do you prefer me over the darkness?" he asked, a sinister smile spreading across his lips. The flickering candle on the wall provided little light, causing the shadows on his face to dance and contort, intensifying his evil appearance.

"I'm simply curious why you haven't tortured me yet."

"There are many ways to torture and break people. I prefer barely lifting a finger," he explained.

"That makes no sense."

"Doesn't it?"

Erars continued to smile as he backed out of the small room where Natava hung. She shouted after him, disliking how he walked away like that. She feared he might emerge from the darkness, and when the flame suddenly went out, she was trapped in an eerie silence. Slowly, she began to realise how he could break her without even lifting a finger, as he had claimed. It sent a chill down her spine, and she expected that throughout the night he would appear, keeping her awake and perpetually on edge.

Chapter 11

A loud clap echoed in the circular room, and Natava jolted awake, scanning her surroundings to find Erars standing further away, a smile on his lips, partially concealed by the shadows once again. It was daytime, yet rain had begun to fall, and she couldn't help but notice how cold she felt. Goddess, would she be able to endure being trapped by him without breaking? Natava was already beginning to doubt it as she witnessed the true sinister nature of his tricks. She wondered what might have transpired if the Shadow Lord had gotten hold of her when she was just a child. Would he have subjected her to torture as well? She was only five years old, but she had no doubt that their wicked intentions knew no limits.

"Morning," he said.

"Is it?" she asked, surveying her surroundings.

"Almost over. Did you sleep well?"

"We both know I didn't."

"We do."

"Why don't you come out here and join me in the light?" she taunted.

"Well, if you insist. I am in the presence of a queen, after all," he teased, walking closer and stepping into the light.

She was taken aback by his willingness to do so, knowing that they typically preferred the cover of darkness. Erars began circling around her once again, his fingertips lightly grazing her clothes and hair. She tried to wiggle away from him, attempting to kick him once more, but her movements were too quick, causing her to jump momentarily before falling back down. The chains prevented her from going too far, delivering a powerful shock through her body.

"Argh!" she exclaimed as her shoulders were nearly wrenched from their sockets.

"Careful," he warned.

"Stop touching me!"

"No," he replied. "My powers are drawn to you."

"Oh, I am flattered."

He laughed, nodding slightly.

"You should be. You would attract any Shadow Lord from miles away."

"Is that supposed to be a compliment?" she snapped.

"We recognise when a soul is untainted. We sense when it emanates pure light," he explained. "It is indeed a compliment."

"Yet you desire to consume that soul!" she snarled.

"I wonder now, with your immense power, if I can even touch it. Shall we find out?"

"I'll pass."

"Oh, you don't want to indulge in a little experimentation?" he laughed, prompting an eye roll from her.

"As if I have a choice when it comes to your desires."

"Together, you and I could accomplish great things. The other Shadow Lords will always regard you as a threat. I see you as a tool."

"How delightful. But I'll pass once again. I already have a crown," she said.

"One you apparently despise. But if you're on my side, I will ensure that no one can harm you," he promised.

"And I'm supposed to believe that?"

"Once I have restored the world to its former state, you won't want to be on the losing side," he warned.

"No? I would be dead."

"Or confined to breeding cages," he stated.

Natava looked at him, filled with fear. She had learned about the world as it once was. All Lights received an education, and hers had been particularly extensive due to her involvement in politics and alliances with other kingdoms. She vividly remembered the gruesome tales of what women endured, solely for the purpose of the Shadow Lords having more children or feeding off them.

"They would burn," Natava sneered.

"Despite your power, you would gradually be crushed by the darkness, and they would have their way with you," he asserted.

"There are so few of your kind remaining. Even if you were to restore the world, what then? You would become the sire of all future Shadow Lords."

"You Halos believe you have utterly eradicated us, that only a handful remain," Erars said.

"But there are!"

"No, they lie in wait, hidden from sight. They struck during your coronation ball."

"And you truly expect me to believe that you had no involvement in the attack?" Natava asked.

"I didn't."

"You're a liar! Nothing that comes out of your mouth is the truth," she snapped, moving her face closer to his. "I will believe nothing you say."

"Fine, don't believe me. Maybe time will change your mind. You and I are going to spend a lot of time together."

"Lucky me," she growled.

"You are. Very few get to live in my presence for long, but somehow my powers have taken a liking to you."

"It's not a compliment!"

"It would be if you understood what it entails."

"More torture?"

"Power," he explained.

"Power?"

"If you accept it."

"No, I will pass."

"We will see, Your Highness. Time can be both an enemy and a friend."

Erars began walking away, and she called after him, cursing and vowing to make him pay for everything once she was free. Erars found her struggles amusing. He followed the tunnel back to his hidden palace, cloaked by shadows from the outside, rendering it impossible to find. Only he knew its location. The palace was built in the middle of nowhere, his father's old house that he had taken over after the old Shadow Lord died. Now Erars ruled there. He had spent the night and day deep in thought. There was more to why he had taken the Light. Something he had not realised. Initially, he thought his powers only wanted to devour, but while they hungered for the Light, destruction was not their sole purpose. She drew him in in a way he didn't think was possible. He thought he might be imagining the interest his powers had taken in the Light, but as he went to see her again this morning, he felt it swirling beneath his skin, a desire to touch. It was a new feeling for him. His powers had never wanted anything other than to devour. Now they wanted to explore.

Erars walked through the long hallways, the shadows moving around as they watched their master pass by. They took care of the place, keeping it clean and standing. It was many years old and had survived the elements. Sometimes lost souls found their way there, people lost in the cloak he had created. And when they did, he had his fun with them. He enjoyed drawing it out. As he had explained to the queen, there were many ways to break someone, and he relished finding all those hidden places to dive into and ruin them little by little.

However, he knew that capturing the queen was a significant gamble on his part. Normally, he would never risk so much, but there was a lot at stake here. He had feared that the veil had been torn by now, but he hadn't felt a shift in the balance of the world. As a Shadow Lord, he should have felt a complete change in energy as the shadow creatures took over all the light, but he hadn't. However, he couldn't deny the incredible power exhibited by those creatures from the coronation ball. They had to be from the depths, but how had they escaped? Perhaps a temporary tear? Or a failed attempt to unravel the veil?

The Halos had closed the veil long ago, weakening the Shadow Lords by depriving them of a significant source of power. This was another outcome Erars had not foreseen when he left clues for the Halos on how to become stronger and conquer the world as their own. They needed insider knowledge, and he subtly provided that. There was a time when their powers could barely cause any damage due to the freely roaming shadows and the darkness cast over the world by the Shadow Lords. They had thrived in that darkness while the rest trembled. But although they had successfully eliminated the powerful Shadow Lords who could have easily torn Erars apart if he had attempted something himself, there were many things he had not anticipated.

The closure of the veil was not something he had prepared for. He had not given them any clues about how to achieve that. It was something they had figured out on their own as they grew more powerful. He had only provided information on how to get close to the Shadow Lords and ensure their proper demise. But he had not taken into account the loss of access to the Shadow World. He would break the veil, and once he did, he would become even more powerful. First, he needed answers about who had infiltrated the queen's party and how they had managed to release those powerful shadow creatures from their cage.

Chapter 12

Owin paced around the tense room where a large round table stood in the centre. A giant map was spread out on it, with small figures representing the kingdoms. Owin could hardly relax, and no one else could either. The attack had left the walls around the marble castle almost completely destroyed, with only fragments remaining. So many lives had been lost—commoners, Halos, and knights alike. Even some princesses had perished, leading to anger from the kingdoms whose daughters had not been kept safe. Everyone held their breath, uncertain of what would happen next. Would war break out? And if it did, what would come next? Natava was missing. As the bodies were collected, it became clear that the queen was nowhere to be found. No one had slept since they discovered she was gone, and her whereabouts remained unknown. There were many theories and suggestions on where to search first, but no decision had been made.

"How did these creatures even find their way inside?" his father questioned.

They had reviewed the attack many times, but no one had the answer. The creatures had struck swiftly and forcefully, catching them off guard. Parts of the city had been set on fire, distracting the knights who patrolled the streets. The Halos were quickly overwhelmed by the shadow creatures before the knights were targeted. These knights were ordinary humans trained to serve the Halos. Though their lives were not as long, they were still skilled soldiers to have in their ranks.

"They are not from this realm," Massana said.

"This realm?" Owin questioned.

"I believe someone tore open a hole between the worlds."

Everyone stared at Massana. She had been silent since they arrived in the room. No one had slept. They had all spent the entire day pacing around, trying to clean up as much as they could. Then they discovered Natava was missing and gathered in this room.

"How is that possible?" his father asked.

"Through a sacrifice," Massana replied.

"A sacrifice?"

"A willing Light must give their life for it. Only then can the veil between our worlds be torn open."

"And when you say worlds?" Owin asked.

"Between this world and the Shadow World. It's where the Shadow Lords derive their true power. It's their place of origin."

"And now that it's torn open?" Owin asked.

"I'm not sure if it is. The energy would have shifted, but perhaps someone made a small crack."

"A crack?"

"Just enough to let a few through," Massana explained.

"Are any other Lights missing besides the queen?" his father asked.

"No, no one else is missing, but we lost many that night," Massana whispered.

"So, they took her for that purpose?" Owin asked. "To use her as a sacrifice."

"She must willingly offer herself," Massana reminded him. "If she does not, it won't work."

"But could it create a larger opening?" Owin asked. "Could it be enough to release so many shadow creatures that they could take over again?"

Massana remained silent, but her hesitation spoke volumes. Owin ran a hand through his hair, feeling a chilling fear. He had been taught about the horrors of the past when the Shadow Lords ruled. If they were to regain power, it would be catastrophic. Many would die as examples, while others would suffer for their sick pleasures. They would all be doomed.

"They could," he mumbled.

"I don't know."

"You hesitated!"

"Yes, because I don't know!" Massana yelled. "I can't say if a sacrifice will change anything. If offered willingly, it would tear open the veil, and our worlds would be connected again. That's what I know."

"How did you close it in the first place?"

Massana appeared devastated, and everyone looked at her with fear. They knew about the veil, but not the secrets behind it.

"Massana?" Owin pressed.

"A sacrifice," she whispered.

"You sacrificed one of your own?!"

"No! Well, yes, but it was a willing sacrifice."

"Willing, you say? Just as willing as Natava will be after enduring all that torture?"

"Owin, enough!" his father scolded.

"They sacrificed one of their own!" Owin exclaimed.

"We did it for the greater good, and it was voluntary. While a Light has to die to open it, another Light must enter the Shadow World and close it from the inside by surrendering themselves. It's a payment."

"Payment?!"

"Yes, a payment."

"And this Light did it willingly?" Owin questioned.

"She did."

Owin shook his head, unwilling to believe that this Light simply sacrificed herself like that. They existed in the light. He could only imagine the terror and pain the Light had experienced as they entered the Shadow World, to be devoured by darkness.

"Hela was ready to do it," Massana explained. "I was willing to take her place. But someone else ended up going in."

"Who?"

"Hela's mother."

"Hela's mother?" Owin asked.

"Yes."

"Natava's grandmother is trapped down there, or is she dead?" he asked, unsure of how it worked when they closed the veil.

"We don't know."

"So, if they tear the veil open, not only will a Light die, but another must enter?"

"Yes..."

"No, we cannot allow that!" Owin exclaimed. "How do we stop it?"

"We must first determine if the veil has been torn open, and if there is a crack, we will search for another way to mend it. I will consult the Priests in the Sun Tower to see if they have any knowledge of repairing a crack," Massana replied.

"I will go and see if the veil is torn. Where is it located?" Owin asked.

"You're not going," his father interjected.

"I am!"

"You're not!"

"I am going! And while I am out there, I will also search for clues about Natava's whereabouts," Owin declared before turning his attention to Massana. "Where is the veil?"

Massana sighed and pressed her finger into a dark spot on the map. The Hallows were known to be a dangerous and dark place, inhabited by unpleasant creatures, but Owin refused to be scared. He was determined to find out if the veil had been broken, and if it had, he would find a way to mend it without any more Lights being sacrificed.

"Very well. I will go prepare," he said. However, before Owin could turn away, his father grabbed his arm.

"You're not going," his father stated firmly.

"I thought we just agreed that I would," Owin snapped back.

"No, it's too dangerous," his father warned.

"Then I will not go alone. I will bring a group with me."

"We both know that as soon as you can, you'll go off on your own."

"I am an excellent tracker and much faster on my own."

"I will not allow my only son to walk straight into danger."

"Fine, then I won't," Owin retorted.

"Owin!"

"Let him go," Massana intervened, surprising them both. "Take some Halos and knights with you, but stay together as a group, Owin. Your father is right. These are dangerous times. We must be cautious and stick together."

Owin wasn't pleased with the arrangement. He was confident that he could move faster on his own. He even believed he could find Natava on his own. However, he knew he had to be smart. Something strange was happening, and the tension in the air was thick. He wouldn't be surprised if wars were about to break out among the kingdoms. And then what? Would the remaining Shadow Lords be able to take over? Would darkness once again shroud everything? It was crucial that if there was a crack between the worlds, they mend it as quickly as possible and ensure that Natava did not become a sacrifice.

"Go with him," Massana ordered the few Halos in the room.

They nodded, and the three of them left to gather more knights and Halos. Owin quickly dressed and packed for the journey ahead. But as he grabbed his bag and turned towards the door leading to the hallway, his father stood in his path.

"Father, not now. I am going. Massana agreed," Owin said.

"I heard what Massana said, but she's not your father," his father snapped.

"I am going."

"I know I cannot stop you, but I'm asking you not to go."

"Oh, so now it matters where I go?" Owin asked.

"It has always mattered to me. You think it didn't please me when I knew you would be around Natava? I knew she would never go into battle."

"Which is why you wanted me to be her knight?" Owin questioned.

"Yes, I wanted you to be by her side because I knew she would never seek out danger unless it came looking for her first."

"Good to know you have such trust in my abilities," Owin said, trying to slip past his father. However, his father continued to block his path.

"I have trust in my son, but I don't want to see him dead."

"I won't die. I will find out if there truly is a tear in the veil, and if there is, I will find a way to fix it. If I come across Natava, I will make sure to bring her back with me," Owin told him.

"No, don't."

"What?"

"Don't bring her back with you," his father warned.

"Why not? Don't we want our queen home?"

"Of course we do, but whoever took her, whoever attacked us, is powerful, and your group is small. Owin, you need more people if you're going to strike and win," his father explained.

"We will be fine."

"Don't be foolish or reckless," his father lectured.

Owin was tired of the lecture, and learning that his father had never trusted his ability to protect himself in battle hurt even more. He was tired of being seen as weak, and he refused to leave Natava behind if he discovered where she might be. She mattered to him not just because she was his queen, but also because she was his friend and someone he had deep feelings for. He had finally found the courage to kiss her, and then she was stolen from him. He would bring her back, no matter what, and not even his father could stand in his way. Owin pushed his father's arm aside and opened the door.

"I will bring her back," he declared as he left, aware of the impact his words had on his father, but Owin didn't care. He would save Natava. He would find her.

Chapter 13

The rain intensified, and although the respite from the scorching sun was welcome, Natava couldn't help but shiver from the coldness of the water. She seized the opportunity to let the droplets quench her thirst, but soon the incessant dripping into her eyes, mouth, and nose became suffocating. Hanging there, she felt her body on the brink of collapse, realising she couldn't endure this position for much longer. Time seemed elusive as disorientation began to cloud her senses. Natava couldn't believe she was already near her breaking point. Was she truly so weak? She glared at the dark tunnel, silently imploring Erars to return. Only he had the power to release her from this predicament. Despite her futile attempts to find an escape, there was nothing that could save her from being trapped, suspended from the ceiling.

"Damn it, don't do this to me," she whispered, shaking her head. Unable to bear it any longer, she called out for Erars, hoping he could hear her. The rain had been falling relentlessly throughout the day, casting a dark veil outside, but it was unclear whether the changing from day to night or the rain itself had caused the dimness.

"Erars!" she yelled, but coughed as water lodged in her lungs. "Erars!"

Nothing happened. Frustrated, she groaned and attempted to wriggle free from her confinement, but her efforts were in vain. Her energy was rapidly draining.

"Erars!" she tried once more, before slumping forward, tears welling in her eyes. Natava was surprised she could even shed tears in her tired state. She felt utterly drained, making it almost impossible for tears to flow, yet there they were, stinging her eyes as the warm drops mixed with the cold rain. Was this to be her end? She had barely tasted the fruits of life, and yet it seemed she was destined to perish in this moment. Natava closed her eyes, letting out a deep sigh, allowing the rain to further cool her body. The shivering intensified, her teeth chattering uncontrollably, until finally, she heard it—the sound of footsteps drawing near. By the edge of the tunnel, a drain was visible, preventing the water from flowing inside. Emerging from the shadows, Erars slowly came into view, observing the queen, who looked at him with fear and was uncontrollably trembling. Fear was his sustenance, his delight, and witnessing someone so defenceless evoked a strange sense of satisfaction within him. He smiled, prepared to taunt the queen, but she spoke before he could.

"Please, let me down," she pleaded softly.

This plea was something he had never encountered before. Others had begged for mercy, pleaded for their lives, offered anything to be left alone, but he had never cared. Now, the queen implored him to release her and end her suffering. He had already intended to free her, knowing her body couldn't withstand this suffocating state forever, but her plea tugged at his dark heart in an unfamiliar way. His powers seemed restless, no longer finding the same pleasure in witnessing the fear in her eyes. Erars retrieved a key from his dark pants and held it up. Natava could hardly believe he would set her free. She was convinced he was merely toying with her, teasing her with the sight of the key. Yet, he approached the lock securing the heavy chain and the iron hoop embedded in the stone wall. He unlocked it, slowly lowering her down. Relief washed over her as she could finally relax her strained arms. Though still bound by chains, she could now breathe more easily. Erars approached her, the sound of splashing water growing louder. He crouched beside her, then reached out, grasping her chin and turning her face to meet his eyes.

"It seems your power has all but drained away," he teased.

Natava glared at him but remained silent.

"And your words as well," he added.

"Go rot," she spat.

"Do you wish to return up there?" he asked.

Natava sighed, briefly looking down, before extending her chained hands. Now that she was devoid of strength, he could unlock her without fear. The moment she was free, however, she seized the opportunity to grab him, pulling him down and forcefully knocking her head against his, eliciting a groan. Pushing herself up from the ground, she fled. She followed the tunnel to its end, only to find herself in a strange, misty realm. Perplexed, she looked around, her confusion growing. Where was she? Shouldn't this tunnel have led her outside? Unable to comprehend the situation, she spun around, desperately searching for an exit. A dark figure emerged from the grey fog, laughter echoing in the surroundings.

"Do you truly believe it would be that easy?" Erars taunted.

"What is this?" she demanded.

"A little trick," he replied.

"Where are we?"

"But if I reveal that, you'll flee," he retorted.

"Of course," she acknowledged.

"Then I shan't divulge it."

Natava's legs trembled, and standing became an arduous task. She felt an overwhelming urge to collapse, but before doing so, she needed to understand the nature of this sorcery. She longed to escape this suffocating, misty world, much like she had yearned to be free from the circular chamber.

"What is this place?" she panted, leaning forward and resting her hands on her knees.

"My home," he disclosed, placing his hands in his pockets and regarding her with an air of superiority.

Natava dropped to her knees, utterly exhausted.

"Very well, I won't run," she conceded.

With a snap of his fingers, the peculiar grey world began to fade, leaving Natava bewildered. She surveyed her surroundings, struggling to make sense of it all. Soon, she found herself in a dim hallway, adorned with ancient statues and paintings. It resembled a grand estate, yet she had never laid eyes on it before. The dark blue walls and eerie silence created an unsettling atmosphere. The tunnel that led her here remained visible. The knowledge that her little torture chamber was not far away sent chills down her spine.

"And now?" she asked.

"Now, you have a moment to recover," Erars replied.

Erars observed Natava as she took deep breaths, gradually regaining some strength. It took a while, but then she rose, pressing a hand against her aching thigh before standing fully upright.

"And now?" she repeated.

Erars approached, causing her to retreat, but he simply passed her, glancing over his shoulder as if inviting her to follow. She obliged, and together they walked through the ancient house. Natava noticed the swirling dark energy and the shifting shadows in the corners, unsettling her further. Nothing about this place resonated with her. She was meant for a brighter world, yet here she was, trapped in Erars's dark realm. They entered a dim dining hall, a long table occupying the centre. Erars proceeded deeper into the room before turning to face her. Her eyes fell upon a plate of food at a distance. Had he anticipated her surrender, or was it for his own consumption? She had no intention of partaking in whatever he offered, nor would she become his servant. While she had requested to be released from her chains, she would never bow.

"What is the meaning of this?" she asked.

"Feeling hungry?" he asked.

"No."

"Don't lie. Let's not lie to each other, considering we will have to work together," he remarked.

"We will never work together," she asserted.

"Doesn't it feel better to stand on your own two feet rather than hang from the ceiling?" he taunted.

"I prefer the ceiling."

"Very well, let us return then."

Erars advanced towards her, and a sharp surge of fear raced through Natava's heart, causing it to quicken its pace.

"No! Wait..." Natava pleaded.

Erars smiled, halting just a short distance away from her. Natava's hand was raised as if signaling him to slow down.

"I'm listening," he said.

"I refuse to serve you. Just imprison me instead," she declared defiantly.

"So you can wither away?" he questioned.

"Why not?"

"You are destined for more, Your Highness," he taunted, employing her title mockingly.

"More? You want to exploit me."

"Indeed. I had hoped for an easier Light to manipulate, but you may suffice," he mused.

"Suffice for what exactly?" she asked.

"Many things. Firstly, to eliminate those who obstruct my plans, and secondly, to aid me in tearing this world apart."

"How do you expect to rule anything when it lies in ruins?" she challenged.

"You shall see."

"Enough with the enigmas. If you truly did not order the attack, you could take care of those interfering with your plans on your own."

"I did not," he admitted. "I was there to seize a young Light."

"And you confess it so proudly. Do you feel no remorse?"

"None whatsoever."

"Good to know," she muttered. "But you can handle them yourself."

"I fear there may be a group of them, and you were able to repel the shadows they unleashed upon us all. It would be better if you dealt with them," he suggested.

"Are you afraid?" she taunted.

Erars chuckled. "Never, but I am strategic. I know when to fight and when to avoid getting my hands dirty."

"I'm sure you have plenty of others to do your dirty work for you."

"I excel at manipulation."

"And once again, you say it with such pride. But what else can one expect from a Shadow Lord?" she snapped.

"Nothing but suffering," he declared, although he was uncertain how much pain he could inflict upon the Light standing before him. His powers seemed oddly drawn to her in ways he had never experienced before. He inched closer, watching her take a small step back, yet she held her ground, impressing him. Reaching out, his fingers almost grazed her skin as he slowly tasted her purity. She sucked in a breath, sounding as if she were choking, but then she acted swiftly, pushing his hand away and breaking the trance. "Powerful."

Erars sounded impressed, which perplexed Natava. She was certain he would attempt it again, but he did not. However, he did seize her, wrapping a hand around her throat. She expected him to teach her a lesson for fighting back, yet he maintained his grip without inflicting harm.

"And tasty," he whispered, leaning closer until only inches separated their faces.

A peculiar energy pulsed between them. Her heart raced with fear. She remembered how the first Shadow Lord she encountered had regarded her with hungry, crimson eyes. Erars's eyes held hunger too, but it seemed even more unbridled, as if something burned within them while he observed her. He cruelly smiled, then slowly released his grip, creating space between them.

"You should consider my offer. Stand at my side and reap the benefits," he suggested.

"A Shadow Lord and a Light working together?" she questioned.

"It may sound amusing to you, but I have collaborated with Lights for a long time. They simply never knew," he divulged.

"That makes no sense," Natava insisted.

"It does to me," he chuckled, walking farther away and pulling out a chair near the food. He gestured for her to sit, but she shook her head and began inching away.

"We agreed no running," he reminded her.

Natava couldn't help herself. She continued to retreat further and further. This Shadow Lord frightened her in ways she couldn't comprehend. She recalled the fear from her initial encounter with a Shadow Lord, but this was different. The way Erars looked at her and touched her unsettled her. It was as if he desired something more from her, something she couldn't fathom. He spoke of her aiding him, yet the intensity in his eyes conveyed unspoken demands. Natava knew she had to escape. She needed to break free from it all. She continued walking backwards.

"If you run, I will chase," he declared.

"Then come and catch me."

Natava swiftly spun on her heel, mustering her remaining strength to flee the dining hall. She was confident she could find her way outside if she kept running. There had to be a window or an exit for her to discover. Yet, as she sprinted down the lengthy hallway, it felt as though she were running endlessly. Natava eventually had to halt, looking back. Erars was nowhere to be seen, yet she realised she had distanced herself significantly from the dining hall. So why was she unable to reach the window at the opposite end? She resumed running, only to find the window moving farther away. Eventually, she had to pause once more, placing a hand against the wall, panting heavily. She couldn't understand it. How could her means of escape seem to elude her the faster she ran? A hand glided over her back, and she emitted a startled gasp, pressing herself against the wall as Erars materialised. He grinned maliciously while observing her.

"You're trapped," he declared, closing in on her, effectively cornering her.

"Now what?" she asked.

"Now you understand that there is no escape from me," he stated, lifting his hand slowly but refraining from touching her. He placed it against the wall beside her head, effectively trapping her.

"I will never serve you," Natava asserted.

"But slowly, you will crumble. I will become your entire world. The queen will kneel at my feet," he declared.

"No, she will burn you with her light."

Erars observed as her skin faintly glowed, surprised to see even a spark of power remaining within her. However, it quickly dwindled, and she was unable to rekindle it.

"Fuck," she muttered.

"I must admit, you impress me. By now, no Halo should be capable of conjuring even a small spark, yet there you are, your skin emitting a glow. I could sense a tinge of sting," he acknowledged.

"Why bother feeding me if it only strengthens my powers?" she questioned.

"There are numerous ways to make someone submit to you. Revealing a little warmth to the Light won't hurt. She will realise that being on my side is not so terrible."

"Do you truly believe I will ever join forces with you?" she snapped.

"Someone is making swift progress," he informed her. "Those shadow creatures you encountered are no ordinary beings."

Natava remained silent, aware that it had taken a considerable amount of her power to banish them once more. She had felt so drained afterwards that she had lost consciousness. She averted her eyes, uncertain of what to make of it all. Why had those creatures possessed such formidable strength?

"I'm certain you are aware of the existence of a world beneath ours," Erars continued.

"The orcs?" Natava guessed.

Erars chuckled. "No, and you knew that answer was incorrect. Try again."

"I am aware of the world lying beneath ours. I know what lurks there."

"Then you must understand the consequences if the veil were to rupture," he remarked.

"It would bring about our destruction."

"But the Shadow Lords would once again thrive."

"Is that what you need me for?" she asked. "I will not sacrifice myself for that."

"Why do you think I sought a young and impressionable Light?" he asked.

"To manipulate her into making the sacrifice."

"Yes, and I believe others are pursuing the same thing, if they haven't already obtained a suitable candidate. Why else would they attack your party?"

Natava began piecing together the puzzle herself. She knew she shouldn't entertain his words, but she couldn't resist. She felt compelled to explore further.

"To steal a Light. But if the veil is already torn, why steal one?"

"Perhaps it isn't fully torn. Perhaps someone, or many, managed to create a small hole, enough to allow the shadows to escape. Or maybe you were truly their target," Erars suggested, uncertain which of the possibilities held the truth. However, he could see that it piqued the queen's curiosity as he presented the various scenarios.

"What if it is indeed cracked?"

"Then it won't require much to tear it wide open," he stated.

"Could you do it on your own?"

What was she doing? Natava wondered. Why was she engaging in conversation with the Shadow Lord? Yet, she knew escape was futile, and if he was willing to provide answers, why not seek them?

"It cannot be torn fully open. I believe the hole that was made required the combined efforts of numerous Shadow Lords, and I would be surprised if none of them perished in the process," Erars explained.

"So, if all of you were to gather and completely rupture it?"

"That would be impossible. We would need as many Shadow Lords as there are people in this kingdom, and while we are not as few as you may think, we are not that numerous either," he divulged.

"There used to be more," she taunted.

Erars grinned slightly as she attempted to assert her power, but the Light was under his control. As he had mentioned, manipulation took many forms, and he could discern that Natava was becoming captivated by everything he revealed. She couldn't resist him, and sharing his thoughts only served to further sway her to his side.

"There used to be, but we now require a Light to sacrifice herself in order to rupture it completely."

"And am I that sacrifice?" she asked.

"If you join my side, you won't be," he assured her, extending his hand to stroke a finger down her cheek. He could feel his powers permeating through his touch, connecting with her on a deeper level. "You would belong to me entirely."

"Is that something desirable?" Natava questioned.

He chuckled softly. "Very desirable, because no one would harm you."

"I cannot thrive in a world shrouded in darkness."

"That's all right. I would wear the crown regardless. You would simply be liberated."

"Liberated?!" she laughed incredulously.

"Liberated, Your Majesty. Under my protection, you would have the freedom to go wherever you please, shielded from any harm."

"But you despise Halos. You detest the Lights. Why would you ever want one by your side?"

"I never truly hated them. They served their purpose to me," he confessed.

"Served their purpose?"

"I have been manipulating people long before your birth. This world belonged to me long before the Halos even assumed control."

"You're one of the ancient leaders?"

"No, but I am their downfall."

Natava grew increasingly bewildered by their conversation, and as she opened her mouth to ask more questions, she realised what was unfolding. He desired her curiosity because it drew her in. He wanted her to be intrigued, yearning for more from him, as it would gradually diminish her perception of him as an enemy. She was falling right into his trap. She pressed her lips together, crossed her arms, and erected an almost invisible shield around herself, which brought a smile to Erars's face upon noticing it.

"No more questions?" he asked. "Aren't you interested in discovering more?"

She remained silent, and he began to laugh, finding it amusing.

"Very well. Are you hungry?" he asked once again.

Erars incessantly repeated that infuriating question, and of course, she felt hunger gnawing at her. He knew that too, but he wanted her to admit it. He wanted her to acknowledge that she needed the sustenance he could provide. She was becoming increasingly aware of his tactics and how rapidly she was ensnared in his web.

"No," she replied firmly.

"Wrong answer," he declared.

"Does that mean I will return to my wretched torture chamber?" she asked.

"No, there are various ways to punish you."

"What ways?"

Natava regretted posing the question as soon as the words left her lips. He seized her arm, dragging her along with him, and she had scarcely any strength left to resist. Erars led her back to the dining room, commanded her to sit, and then pushed the iron plate farther away, to the opposite side. He took his place and picked up a fork, impaling the succulent meat and devouring it. While Shadow Lords could subsist solely on souls, he derived pleasure from an ordinary meal every now and then. It provided a sense of serenity to savor delicious food. Natava glared at him, witnessing her chance to satiate her hunger dissipate before her eyes. He speared another piece of meat, teasingly wiggling it in front of her eyes. The temptation to reach out and seize it nearly overwhelmed her, but she remained seated, arms tightly folded across her chest.

Chapter 14

Owin looked at the group gathered around the fire, noticing that a few were engaged in conversation. They had been travelling for several days, and the journey ahead promised to be long and arduous. It would be at least a week before they even reached the dense, ominous forest known as The Hallows. Owin absentmindedly poked at the fire with a stick, unsure of what to do with himself. When he was on horseback, constantly vigilant like the rest of the group, it was easier to distract his mind. But now, as he sat there waiting for time to pass, it became increasingly difficult to prevent his thoughts from wandering. He should be sleeping, but the idea of closing his eyes seemed impossible when Natava was out there. Who knew what was happening to her? What were they doing to her? Natava wasn't just any Light. She was the queen. Although she possessed considerable power, Owin knew it could be shattered in the darkness where the Shadow Lords resided. They would bring her to her knees, likely break her, and force her to spill her blood in order to tear open the veil. But would it still be voluntary if she was broken? What were the rules? Owin had heard about the veil, but he didn't know how to break it. Perhaps it was for the best that this knowledge was not widely known, but unfortunately, their enemies were already aware. Natava was gone, but luckily, no one else had suffered the same fate.

"Do you hear that?" whispered a knight beside Owin, clearly unable to sleep due to fear of lurking dangers.

The knight reached for his sword as Owin scanned the darkness surrounding them. Some knights and Halos patrolled the area while others slept. Owin strained his ears and distinguished the familiar sound of an animal rustling through the forest undergrowth.

"It's a rabbit," he reassured.

The other knight, young and inexperienced, clearly new to the title or perhaps new to missions altogether, relaxed slightly. Owin had accompanied his father on missions, although they were never full of dangers. Now he understood that his father had always shielded him from the hardships of the real world. Despite being trained as a knight, it was more of a title he carried rather than one he had truly earned. It frustrated him that his father didn't see him as someone capable of genuinely protecting others. He was merely meant to follow Natava around. He didn't mind that, as Natava herself desired to fight, but both of them were being kept in a safe bubble where nothing could harm them. Initially, he had thought it was only Natava being coddled, but he too was being sheltered. It caused him to roll his eyes slightly as the younger knight calmed down.

"Perhaps," the knight responded.

"What did you think it was? An orc?" Owin teased.

"At least a bear," the knight admitted.

"They don't typically venture this far. They prefer colder climates," Owin explained.

"I see..."

"No, there's a greater chance that an orc has emerged from beneath the ground," Owin teased, observing the wide-eyed reaction of the knight beside him.

While it was said that another world, the Shadow World, existed beneath theirs, it was a realm they couldn't truly reach. The Underworld consisted of tunnels and caves running beneath the surface, where orcs often took up residence, along with the mountain chains further north. Owin had only read about them and never encountered one, and he knew they would never venture out into their current location. Nonetheless, it amused him to frighten the young knight a little.

"Did you volunteer for this mission?" Owin asked.

"I was asked to join," the knight replied.

"By whom?"

"By the knight who trained me, Sir Gawain. He believed it would be a good first mission," the young knight explained.

"A dangerous one like this?"

"We are only scouting. We're checking if the veil has been removed," the knight defended.

"But many things can go wrong. The Hallows is a treacherous place, harboring many more evil creatures. Have you ever seen a snake as large as a house?"

"What?" the knight asked, taken aback.

"Or a spider? Or those two-headed salamanders known as Sarcas?"

"Sarcas are mere myths," the young knight protested.

"Are they?" Owin asked. "How many of us have ever ventured into the forest?"

He knew he was being a bit cruel now. Not even Owin himself had witnessed the horrors concealed within the darkness of the forest located in The Hallows. It was said that few emerged from it alive, so why wouldn't there be gigantic snakes, spiders, and Sarcases? Why wouldn't there be evil creatures lurking in the shadows, waiting to emerge and consume them? Owin could envision it happening. Numerous threats lurked in the darkness, making it easy to imagine the presence of evil creatures. However, the young knight appeared ready to soil his pants. Owin had succeeded in frightening him. It was a wicked form of entertainment, yet it temporarily diverted his mind from the potential dangers that Natava might be facing. Would she still be herself when they finally found her, or would she be a shattered soul? He feared the worst.

"Don't pay him any mind," the older knight interjected, joining them and settling on the ground in front of the fire.

Sir Gawain, the knight who had trained Owin, cast an annoyed glance at him. Although Sir Gawain had played a part in Owin's training, he was primarily training the other younger knights.

"It could be true," Owin defended himself.

"But dwelling on the worst-case scenario will only weaken our resolve. If we are shaken, how can we fight?" The older knight smiled, his white beard stretching with the gesture.

"Perhaps it's wise to be prepared," Owin suggested.

"Or perhaps you're merely trying to frighten the newcomers."

Sir Gawain glanced at the young knight beside Owin, who looked at him with a slightly accusatory expression.

"I went through the same ordeal," Owin stated.

Sir Gawain continued to smile. Owin was aware that he wasn't really being scolded but was simply having a bit of fun. The journey had put them all on edge, and the absence of their queen filled them with fear and anxiety.

"Have you been there before?" the young knight asked Sir Gawain.

"Once, but only briefly. It was another scouting mission. There were rumors of a dangerous spirit retreating to that area before reemerging in the dead of night, killing people in nearby towns," Sir Gawain recounted.

"And was it a spirit?" Owin asked, never having heard of spirits existing.

"We never found out. We couldn't locate her, and we didn't stay in the forest for long. None of us enjoyed being there. It exuded a dark energy. However, someone claimed to have spotted her. She was pale, as white as snow, with long dark hair and blind white eyes."

"And what about the attacks?" Owin asked.

"We discovered it wasn't a spirit after all, but a Dark Scorpion. They too prefer hunting at night, and one had developed a taste for human flesh. Once they acquire a taste, they keep returning."

"So, you eliminated the Dark Scorpion?" Owin asked.

"Yes, we stayed in one of the nearby towns, hoping it would come by, and eventually, it did. We took care of it, and the attacks ceased," Sir Gawain replied.

"But did you see the spirit?" the young knight pressed.

"One of my companions believed he did, but no one else caught a glimpse. It was peculiar, though. He started behaving strangely afterwards."

"What do you mean?" Owin asked, now interest in the story as well.

"We spent a few days in the forest, and he claimed to have seen her on the first day. After that, he became restless, pacing around constantly. He was jumpy, and when he tried to sleep, he would start sleepwalking. We almost lost him in the forest once. It was early morning when we found him, but the sun was already high in the sky. He seemed as confused as the rest of us, as if he didn't know what had happened."

"And what happened next? Did he become even stranger?" Owin asked.

"After we left the forest, he returned to normal. However, he did tell me that he still dreams of her and sometimes sleepwalks, finding himself heading back to the forest," Sir Gawain informed them, his voice lowering and taking on a haunting tone.

The two knights exchanged glances, then saw the older knight's smile, as if he were now playing a trick on both of them.

"Really?" Owin asked, chuckling.

"No, he never acted strangely. He believed he saw her, though, but nothing out of the ordinary occurred."

Both young knights breathed a sigh of relief, and the older knight chuckled, thoroughly amused by their reactions. But the two younger knights weren't upset. They were simply glad there was no evil spirit toying with their minds, slowly driving them insane.

"Of course, there may be something lurking in those forests. Few who enter come out alive."

"Perhaps that's why no one can truly reveal what lies hidden there," Owin remarked.

"Maybe, or maybe the forest itself drives you mad."

"Mad, you say?"

"Sometimes rumors hold such power that they can make you see things," Sir Gawain explained. "Sometimes they convince you of a truth that is entirely false."

"So, how do we protect ourselves from going mad?" the young knight asked.

"You can't," Sir Gawain said darkly, observing the fearful expression on the knight's face before bursting into laughter.

Owin rolled his eyes, while the other knight grew tired of their bad jokes. The younger knight stood up and left his spot to go sleep.

"Oh, a sensitive one," the older knight said.

Owin shook his head but couldn't help laughing. He was familiar with the jokes and tales the knights often used to tease one another. He had been tricked many times before.

"Your father was quite displeased with your decision to join this mission," Sir Gawain noted.

"You'd rather have me safely locked up in the castle too?" Owin asked.

"No, I think your father has always been overly cautious when it comes to you. But after losing your mother, you became the most precious person in his life."

Owin's eyes shifted from the flickering flames to the older knight sitting before him, who wore a gentle smile. Owin's mother had passed away from a fever when he was a young boy, and it had profoundly affected his father, making him more withdrawn and somber.

"Me?" Owin questioned.

"Indeed, you."

"He always finds something to lecture me about," Owin admitted.

"Perhaps because he worries so much. He doesn't want you to make a mistake that could cost you your life."

"I'm not so sure that's the reason," Owin sighed.

"Then what do you think it is?"

"I'm a disappointment."

"What father could ever think that of you?" the older knight asked. "You're an incredible fighter—smart and agile. Fear doesn't control you in difficult situations. I've seen you in battle before."

"I have fought other knights."

"No, you've fought other troublemakers, criminals," Sir Gawain corrected.

"I've never fought a Shadow Lord."

"Very few have. Even many Halos haven't faced them. They train numerous young Lights to become Halos, but they no longer engage in battles against Shadow Lords. Now they handle smaller matters, things that knights like us can easily handle. Times have changed," Sir Gawain explained.

"And yet it's not enough," Owin stated.

"What do you mean?"

"They've come out of hiding now and taken Nat... Our queen, I mean." Owin realised he shouldn't casually use his nickname for her. He needed to remember her status. She wasn't Nat anymore. She was their queen.

"We will retrieve her."

"But will we get her back as the person she is? Shadow Lords are known for their torturous methods. They revel in pain and fear. The things they used to do in the old days... they were horrific."

Owin had read stories about how humans, particularly women, were treated. It went beyond cruelty and evil. It couldn't be properly described with words. And the Lights didn't appear until many years later. It was said that they were a gift from the Goddess of Light, but no one truly knew their origin. No Halo had ever explained the details of their creation, and Owin wasn't sure if the younger Lights were trained in that aspect of history. Perhaps it was better that no one knew. Just like the information on how to break the veil, it was kept secret to prevent people from attempting it. Yet, the Shadow Lords had learned how, and now they were attempting to unleash the evil shadows.

"Yes, the things they did in the past were truly horrific, but our queen is no ordinary Light. She is no ordinary woman. She can protect herself," Sir Gawain said, surprising Owin with the depth of faith the older knight had in her.

Owin had always been by Natava's side. He had witnessed the power she possessed. He had seen her intelligence and incredible abilities. However, many others failed to perceive her in the same light. They only saw the childlike aspects of her, the carefree side, the unsuitable ruler. He knew she had wished it to be that way, hoping she would never have to bear the burdens of being a queen. However, Massana trusted Natava and believed in her, not the crown. But Natava thought Massana was fully capable of ruling until she decided to choose someone else more fitting.

"You seem surprised," Sir Gawain noted.

"I don't hear many people speak of her like that or show her the same level of trust."

"Do you not trust our queen?" he asked.

"I know our queen. I know the power she possesses, but few others see it. They don't see beyond her childlike demeanor. They don't see her as suitable to be our queen," Owin explained.

"Many of them are blind or believe they could do a better job, but we know how well-suited she is for the role. No one is more powerful than her."

"But what good will her powers do if she is trapped in darkness?"

Sir Gawain sighed, understanding how the darkness would affect her and how torture and starvation would weaken their queen. Yet, he still had faith that she could endure until they found her.

"They will use her as their sacrifice. They will hurt her and offer her as a gift to the Shadow World to tear open the veil," Owin continued, feeling a sharp fear in his heart as he had no idea what might be happening to his dear friend. He could already sense the pain of losing her. His mind conjured the most horrifying scenarios of her demise.

The older knight noticed Owin spiraling and called out to him, redirecting his focus.

"You believe in our queen, don't you?" he asked.

"Always," Owin promised.

"Then why do you doubt her strength so much?"

"I don't doubt her strength, but I worry for her and the pain she will have to endure."

"You've always cared deeply for her," the older knight said, his tone not condescending or accusatory. It sounded understanding. But Owin knew no one could accept his feelings for her. Not only would Natava outlive him by many years, but he was her knight, not her king. He could never rise to her level, so he had to accept their roles and positions. However, he longed for something more. He had already taken a small step. After that terrible prince had spoken to her, treating her as if she were a foolish woman, Owin couldn't resist. He had to show her someone who would truly appreciate her, and his emotions got the best of him. He allowed his feelings to take over, and he kissed her. How he yearned to kiss her again. He hoped he would get the chance. Once he had her back, he vowed that no one else would take her away. Owin would do everything in his power to keep her for as long as he lived. No one would ever lay a hand on her again. He would ensure it.

"We are good friends," Owin said, choosing not to reveal the depth of his feelings for their queen.

"Friends, yes," the older knight mumbled, seeing right through Owin but having no reason to pry for further information. It was clear how Owin felt about Natava. He only hoped she felt, or would feel, just as deeply.

Chapter 15

Natava stared up at the dark ceiling, unsure of what to do with herself. Her stomach felt like it had been tied into a knot. Erars knew how to play with her, keeping them in the same routine. He hadn't taken her to the circular room where she had been exposed to the powerful rain and sun. Instead, he had brought her to a dark room and told her she would stay there. Each day, he would try to entice her with food and charming talk, attempting to make her see the benefits of becoming his ally. But Natava refused every time. Sadly, that also meant no food. Food was only for those who agreed to Erars's plans, and she would not bow to him. She knew that the moment she did, it would doom them all.

Erars was smart, she had to admit. He knew how to manipulate her mind like no other. He quickly identified her weak spots and mercilessly targeted them. Each day, he became more intriguing to her. She never thought she would find anything interesting about a Shadow Lord. They were monsters, after all. But despite withholding food from her, she found herself captivated by him. She had never talked to a Shadow Lord before. She never thought she would. They always went straight for sucking out your soul, feeding off it. But Erars had not touched her in that way, except once to test if her powers still burned him. However, she felt drained now. There was no spark inside her, not even a small one.

Natava had tried to find escape routes, such as through the window. But when she had opened it, she had been met with a foggy world. It made her wonder if she was still in Aneria or if he had taken them somewhere else. Of course, Erars would not tell her. If there was one thing that the Shadow Lord enjoyed, it was his mysteries, and it annoyed her immensely. Therefore, she had resigned herself to staring up at the ceiling, tracing circles in the air with her hand as if she were painting. But she couldn't hold her hand up for long. She was too hungry. She needed food soon, or else... What then? Was she meant to die of starvation? Was that a better fate? She sat up, contemplating it. Massana believed she was destined for greatness, but what if this was her fate? To die from hunger in a dark and dusty room where no one resided. She almost smiled at the irony. Natava hadn't cared about greatness, but dying in this lonely room wasn't her wish either. It seemed she couldn't have everything she wanted. Either it was the crown she despised or being trapped with a Shadow Lord.

Natava shook her head, despising both options. She wanted more. She had to be smart and figure a way out. Maybe Erars wasn't the only one who could be manipulative. Perhaps she could find her own way out, but she had to give in a little. She remembered from her training that sometimes it was worth losing a small battle to win the war. Allowing one or two battles to be lost to gather strength, to learn about the opponent, and then strike when it mattered. Erars had high demands, though. He wanted Natava to take care of the Shadow Lords that seemed to hinder his plans. She knew that the Shadow Lords weren't very affectionate towards each other either. They preferred solitude. But Erars seemed to look at the other Shadow Lords with nothing but hatred. He didn't seem to like anyone else with the same kind of power as him. Why was that? Shadow Lords still worked together, despite their desire to live alone. Erars seemed determined to destroy the others so that no one would stand in his way. Maybe if she helped kill the other Shadow Lords, it would weaken Erars. She could get close to him. She could take him down when he least expected it and also be allowed to hunt the other Shadow Lords. Had she not wanted to be a Halo after all? Perhaps this was the solution.

A smile spread across her lips as a plan formed in her mind. When there was a soft knock on her door, Natava walked over calmly, ready to do what needed to be done. She would show the manipulative Shadow Lord who had the last laugh, and that would be her. Erars stood on the other side, dressed in dark blue clothes with black spirals adorning his jacket and pants. His red eyes glowed slightly, and the same evil smirk spread across his lips when he saw her. She narrowed her eyes, feeling her anger rise, but she knew she had to be patient and suppress her anger.

“Hungry?” he asked.

The same question again, she thought, before meeting his eyes with a straight back.

“Starving.”

“Shall we, then?” he asked, extending his hand.

She raised an eyebrow, walking right past him, which made him chuckle as he followed behind her.

“Have you reconsidered my offer?” he asked.

"Help you and earn my place at your side?"

"From now on, by my side is where you'll be."

"But I haven't agreed yet," she said.

"That doesn't matter. I wanted a Light, and I've found one," he said cheerfully. "Now you belong to me."

Natava glanced at Erars, bewildered by his words. She felt a strange sensation when he claimed her, as if he were marking his territory. She never imagined a Shadow Lord would assert ownership over a Light. They were supposed to be enemies, destined to hunt and eliminate each other.

"A queen belongs to herself," Natava spoke.

"But you don't want to be queen."

"We must all accept our roles as they are," Natava said, surprised by her own words. She sounded too much like Massana.

Erars and Natava descended the long, dark staircase before entering the dining room and taking their seats across from each other. A few flickering candles provided the only source of light. Not even sunlight penetrated the house, further weakening her.

"Now," Erars said, running a black and sharp fingernail along the edge of the iron plate in front of him, "have you reconsidered?"

“Do I accept your offer?” she replied.

“Exactly,” he said, smiling evilly.

Natava acted as if she were considering it, but she had already made up her mind. If working with Erars would get her out of there and allow her to kill the other Shadow Lords before they could cause any real damage, then so be it. Erars might solve a lot of her problems. He might even help her prove herself as a Halo. Natava reached out but couldn’t quite reach the plate. Erars understood what she wanted but did not move.

“Well?” he asked.

“I will help you,” she replied.

Erars’ smile darkened even more before he pushed the plate towards her, and she began stuffing her mouth right away. Erars lived alone, and yet he had all this food provided for him. It made Natava wonder.

“Where do you get all this food?” she asked.

“My shadows provide me with everything I need,” he explained.

“And where exactly are we?”

Erars poured them both some wine, only glancing at her as she asked the question.

“If I am going to help you, shouldn’t I know where we are?”

"You will know soon. We won't stay for long."

"Why?" she asked.

"Because I think we should get to work fast, don't you?" he asked.

"Can I get a chance to recharge?" she countered.

Erars pushed the wine towards her, and she took a sip, noticing how sweet it was instead of sour. It felt almost refreshing. She ate quickly, finishing the food before downing the rest of the wine, then turned her attention to Erars.

"When do you want to leave?" she asked.

"Tomorrow."

"You've kept me hungry for days and tortured me for two. As I've already asked, can I get a chance to recharge?"

"No."

"Then how can I be of help to you?" she snapped.

"Because you won't be fighting immediately. You and I are going to check the veil first."

"The veil?"

"Yes, we are going to see how far the other Shadow Lords have progressed in breaking it, and if we can disrupt their plans a little," he explained.

"Why not send your shadows out to do that dirty work?"

"I fear the other Shadow Lords would prevent them from getting far or even bend them to their will. No, we have to go," he said. "Besides, I want to see it with my own eyes."

"What if it's broken? Or partially broken?"

"Then we better work fast," he told her.

"Fast?"

"Maybe the other Shadow Lords have already found a Light to manipulate and use for their own gain. They might have abducted one the night they attacked. And if they haven't, I can promise you they will try again."

"They won't get in so easily again."

"With the help of those powerful shadow creatures, they will get a Light," Eras assured her, making her feel a little worried by the seriousness in his tone.

"Massana and the rest of the Halos will take care of them as they did last time."

"No, you took care of them," Erars countered.

"What?"

Natava drew back a little, unsure of what he meant. Erars smiled, surprised that the Light didn't see the significance of her actions. It seemed to him that Natava didn't realise just how powerful she was.

"That last wave you stopped, if you hadn't intervened, the attack would have completely devastated everything and killed anything in its path. It would have taken a Light without anyone trying to stop them. Natava, you're the one who prevented them from committing mass murder," he explained.

"They had already broken inside."

"Yes, but that last wave was the true attack. The one that would have caused irreparable damage," he said. "Don't underestimate your powers. I won't."

The way he said it worried her and made her feel a little taller. Massana had always spoken about the power she was born with, but over time, Natava had mostly ignored it, associating it with a responsibility she didn't want. Now Erars spoke about her like she was a hero to the other Lights, and that made her feel good. However, she reminded herself that Erars was their enemy, and she should only harbor hatred towards him.

"I am not underestimating anything. I am a queen," she said, making Erars laugh as she amused him. "Why are you laughing?"

"You say you don't want to be a queen. You don't like the title, and yet you will use it as a shield," he said. "It's funny."

"It's not funny. It's the truth."

"But you hate that it's the truth. You hate the fact that you are a queen. You don't want to be," he said.

"But it's what I am," she sighed.

"Not anymore. Not when you belong to me."

Erars's eyes darkened in a way she couldn't quite decipher, and she didn't want to ask more about it, fearing the answer. He could call her whatever he wanted, but she would not continue to play his games. Instead, she continued to try to manipulate him as well.

"You will just be the king, and I will be... your loyal knight?" she taunted. She poured herself some wine this time, taking a sip as she smiled.

"You could also be the queen at *my* side?" he suggested, making her choke on the wine she had just sipped.

Natava coughed, feeling the sting in her throat. Erars smiled, enjoying how he surprised her. He knew that would be her reaction, but he wanted it. The more time he spent with the intriguing and alluring Light, the more he seemed to crave her in ways he had never craved anything else before. He realised that it wasn't just his thirst for power that consumed him, but now Natava was becoming an obsession as well.

"You have lost your mind," she said.

"Because you don't want to be a queen?"

"I don't want to be *your* queen. Why would you ever suggest that?" she asked, shocked.

"But I intrigue you."

"What?"

"I see it, little Light. I see the way you watch me as well," he told her, not having missed the way she enjoyed asking more questions, especially about him, the way her eyes sparkled when he answered, and how she grew quiet whenever he spoke of her becoming his.

She could act like he didn't intrigue her, but he knew he did. It only fuelled the darkness within him that someone so pure could find him interesting as well.

Chapter 16

Natava was more than sure that Erars had lost his mind. How could he speak of her finding him intriguing? She knew it wasn't a lie, but she didn't want to admit that it was ever true. It shocked her that he would say it out loud. Would that not almost be a crime? A Light and a Shadow Lord finding each other intriguing instead of looking at each other only as enemies. It had to be unheard of. But there she sat, looking right at Erars, and she noticed he had not looked at her with disgust in his eyes once. He gazed at her almost as if he were intrigued by the form in front of him, and she was unsure how to handle that. No one had looked at her with such intensity before. She couldn't hold eye contact and glanced to the side, hearing a soft chuckle. He seemed to find her amusing quite often. Maybe she was just cheap entertainment.

"I do not watch you with anything but hatred in my eyes," she spat, finally looking at him again.

"That is not true, but I know I cannot convince you yet. The more time you spend with me, though, the harder it will be for you to deny the fact that you do look at me. You watch me and study me."

"I try to find a weakness."

"But we are going to work together now, aren't we?" he reminded her.

Natava bit the inside of her cheek, hating to hear him speak of how they were going to work together now. She would rather choke on the wine in her hand, but for now, she had to act to gain his trust. She gave him a small smile.

"We are."

"Great, then let's not look for any weaknesses in each other now," he said. "There is no need for that."

Yet the way he said it made both of them feel like there was every reason to. Neither had any trust in the other, but they were both playing a game, hoping to come out as the winner. Natava held his eyes, trying her hardest not to show any fear towards him. But she did feel afraid. She could sense his power, but Erars didn't seem like a hungry beast. As he had pointed out, he had patience, and that patience made him dangerous.

"Where is the veil?" she asked.

"In The Hallows."

"That place is said to be haunted and harbor all sorts of creatures. And we are going there, just the two of us?" she asked.

"We are."

"No, we will get killed or cursed," she snapped.

"I am already half-dead. I think we will be fine."

"I think you mean you," she retorted.

Erars shrugged. He had no fears about going to The Hallows. It was a dark place, and he thrived in that darkness.

"You want me to stay alive, don't you?" she asked, surprising Erars as he felt a strong pang in his black heart.

He did want her to stay alive. There was something that constantly drew him to her.

"I do."

"Then why would you take me to such a place?" she asked.

"Because I can't go alone."

"Of course you can."

"You're right, I could, but someone should watch you," he said.

"Yes, I love it when someone constantly watches me," she snapped, making him laugh again. "I am not that funny."

"But you are, Your Highness. Very funny."

She rolled her eyes, crossed her arms, and reclined back in her chair.

"I want weapons then."

"No."

"Then I will die," she said.

"With some food, water, and a little sun, you should be ready," he assured her.

"That isn't enough!"

"You're underestimating your powers now."

"I am not!" she retorted.

"You are, or you wouldn't be so scared to go. But maybe I should expect that from someone who was only trained to be a pretty queen."

"What did you call me?" she growled.

"A pretty queen. Is that all you are, Natava?"

He leaned forward, resting an arm on the table, and he knew he was provoking the hotheaded Light. It didn't take much to challenge her, and she began fuming, narrowing her eyes and leaning forward as well.

"You have no idea who you are speaking to."

"No?" Erars surprised her as he stood up, slowly stalking towards her. She kept her eyes on him the whole time as he positioned himself at her side. He put a hand on the back of the chair and one on the armrest, leaning closer to her, eliminating the distance. Her heart began beating faster, unsure where he was going with this. "You seem scared to me."

"I am not scared!"

She pushed closer, and so did he, until there was almost no distance between them. A strange energy seemed to swirl between them. What was happening? Natava wondered. She had not expected to feel such a shift from anger to... what was this feeling? It was strange and interesting, almost compelling her to move even closer. Erars noticed the change in her. Despite her words, she found him interesting too.

"Then if you're not scared, why are you trying to stay here?" he asked.

"You won't even give me a weapon."

"You don't need one. Trust in your abilities. A little faith can do remarkable things," he told her before finally stepping back and returning to his own seat. Natava kept watching him, unsure if he would turn back and challenge her again. So she continued watching him until he was back in his chair, smiling at her once more.

Chapter 17

Massana had ventured further west. Accompanied by a group of Halos and dressed in her old armor, it brought back memories. Not only bad ones, but also good ones of Hela. Memories of how they had helped each other dress and undress. It warmed her heart before sadness took over. It was quite unbelievable to Massana that she had ended up becoming queen. Hela's status had once divided them, making it impossible for them to be together. Later, Massana had been chosen as a good stand-in because of her closeness to Hela and her accomplishments.

Now she was back in the saddle, back in her uniform, riding towards the high tower located close to the shore on a cliff. Their journey had been easy and smooth, and she hoped to finally find answers among the priests of the Sun Tower about how things had unfolded the way they had. They slowed their horses as they neared the round and high tower. Massana swung her leg over the side and slid down from her horse's back. She instructed the Halos to stay ready and prepared, but that she would go inside alone. There was no need to show up with a whole group of Halos, appearing ready for battle in their white and golden armors. Massana approached the big sand-coloured doors and noticed that one of them was swinging back and forth, while the other had been completely pulled off its hinges. The Sun Tower was not marked on any maps and was located in the middle of nowhere. No roads led here, and there were no clues or hints on how to find it. It was a remote place known only to a few, and no priest ever left the place. High hills shielded it from sight, yet as Massana approached, she felt an eerie and thick silence. When she got close enough, she noticed a bloody handprint on the side of the tower.

"Shit!"

Massana hurried inside, only to find the chaos and bodies left behind. Long rows of bookshelves had been overturned, and scrolls and old books were scattered everywhere. The priests were strewn about the room, but their bodies had been arranged in a certain position. She couldn't quite make out what it was supposed to form, so she climbed the stairs that led up to a balcony overlooking the circular centre. A priest hung over the golden railing, dripping blood onto the marble floor, forming a large dried-up pool below. She looked at the bodies in front of her and saw that they formed a triangle—the symbol of the veil. It was a clear message, and she felt her anger rising. The Shadow Lords intended to break the veil. It was evident they did not expect to fail, and they would ruin all the hard work the Halos had put in. If they were able to break the veil, they were all doomed. Massana was uncertain if they could succeed in closing it again. Someone would have to sacrifice themselves for that to happen. She had been prepared to do it before, but was she prepared now?

Massana shook her head, horrified by the sight before her. She whispered a prayer to the Goddess of Light before descending the stairs. Once outside, the Halos watched her with intrigued looks, their questions evident in their eyes, but she shook her head again.

"All of them?" one of them asked.

"All of them," Massana confirmed.

"Who would do such a thing?"

"The same one bold enough to kidnap our queen, but I cannot say if it is one Shadow Lord or many."

"What if we are facing a whole group?" the Halo asked. "What if they have decided to work together now to destroy us?"

"Then we pray for strength."

"Pray for strength?"

"And prepare for war," Massana continued, before walking over to her horse.

She took the reins and mounted her horse, instructing the others to do the same. They all glanced at each other nervously. Many of them had fought in the previous war and did not want to repeat it. Massana turned her horse, and they all followed her, but their mission had been far from satisfying.

"What is this?" Natava questioned as she and Erars stood outside the large, dark house.

She observed the strange fog again, uncertain of what to make of it. She couldn't see an exit for them. It appeared as though they were the ones trapped. However, when she looked at Erars, she saw him smile. He snapped his fingers, and suddenly the fog started to move, creating a path in the middle.

"How did you do that?" she asked.

"Shadow Lords have many interesting tricks up their sleeves."

"Is that a threat?"

"Just information you can interpret as you wish," he told her before he started walking.

Natava had been provided with new clothes, similar to his. Dark blue with dark symbols on them. She had no weapons but carried supplies in a bag she had been provided. Erars navigated them through the fog, taking a turn. She was unsure how he knew where to go. Soon, they arrived at what looked like stables. A single dark horse stood inside.

"Am I to walk beside you?" she asked, annoyed.

"No, we ride together."

"Together?"

"Together," he repeated before going over to prepare the horse.

Natava watched, not liking it one bit.

"I want my own horse."

"I can do many things, Your Highness, but I cannot conjure a real horse out of thin air," he told her.

Erars mounted the horse and held out his hand to her. She hesitated, examining it.

"Well?" he asked. "Are we going to stay here all night?"

Natava sighed and grabbed the outstretched hand, allowing Erars to lift her up and help her settle in behind him. He initially placed her arm around him, but she quickly moved it back, opting to hold onto the sides of his jacket instead. He chuckled softly, enjoying teasing the Light.

"Now let's go."

He nudged the horse forward, and they left the large stable, passing through the fog once again. To Natava, it seemed endless. They rode for what felt like hours until finally reaching the edge of the fog, revealing a dark forest ahead.

"Where are we, exactly?" she asked.

"Somewhere hidden."

"Reassuring," she mumbled.

"Do not worry. In two days' ride, we will already be at The Hallows."

"So we are close? It must mean we are further south in Aneria."

"You're quick," he remarked, clearly impressed.

"I know our kingdom well."

"As a queen should."

They continued to ride in silence for a while, the quiet dark forest surrounding them. Natava couldn't see well and constantly felt as if something was breathing down her neck, while Erars seemed calmer than anyone she had ever met. He moved with the horse in a casual and relaxed manner.

"Why do you hate the other Shadow Lords?" she asked him.

"I do not hate them. I look down on them."

"Why?"

"There was a time when all that mattered to them was status. If you were born into the right family, you were the sort of person they wanted to be around. They ruled our world. But if you were an outcast or born into a lower class, you could never be perceived as anything else. You were beneath them, even if you had worked your way up through the ranks," he explained.

"And what sort of family were you born into?"

Erars glanced over his shoulder, smiling.

"The right sort," he told her.

"Yet you look down on the others?"

"I was born into the right family, but my father took one look at me and decided I was not good enough," Erars explained.

"Just like that? As a baby?"

"Shadow Lords have high expectations even for babies, and despite my mother being a princess, she had not provided him with what he hoped for," Erars explained.

"And your mother?"

"Our mothers die giving birth to us. One life for another."

"So, even as children, you drain the life out of them?" Natava asked.

"Was this not taught in your history books?"

"Not really. We don't know much about you, despite having defeated you."

"Do we look defeated?" he countered.

"I wouldn't say you are back to your glory days."

"They will come."

"Sure..."

"We are on the same side now. You want them to come, don't you?" he asked, glancing at her again. Natava forced a small smile.

"Yes, of course. As your trusted knight, what else would I want?"

"Queen," he corrected.

"What?"

"As my trusted queen," he reminded her.

"I did not agree to that," she retorted.

"You didn't have to. It will happen."

"I can't tell if you're trying to play me or if you're serious."

He smiled at her, then turned away and focused on the road ahead. His silence did not provide her with an answer, only making her more anxious. She truly hoped he wasn't serious because it made no sense for a Shadow Lord to want to pair up with a Light. They were born to be enemies, so why would an enemy want someone so close?

Chapter 18

Owin and his group of knights and Halos stood at the entrance of the dark forest. Even the trees had a black colour, and they observed the eerie silence of the place. A wide open space stretched between the forest they had just left and the one before them, as if the green forest refused to make contact with the darkness. Owin could almost understand why. The forest ahead exuded such a dark energy that it felt suffocating, and there was no sign of any animal movement. It was eerily quiet. They exchanged glances, none of them eager to take the first step. However, Owin had a greater purpose for being there. He was the first to step across the boundary and venture into the dark forest. The group followed him, moving at a cautious pace. They had left their horses behind since the trees stood close together, barely allowing them to walk side by side. Owin held his sword tightly, keeping it drawn as they made their way through the forest. Even the ground beneath them had a dark grey colour. How could grass and trees look like that? he wondered as he pressed on. It felt like they had been walking for a long time, but when Owin looked behind him, he could still see the path to freedom from this dark place. They were moving so slowly that it took them a considerable amount of time to progress further into the forest. Owin let the others catch up to him when he found a small clearing, but he could sense their tension.

"Do we know exactly where we're going?" Owin asked.

All he had been told was that the veil was hidden in this forest, but the exact location was uncertain.

"The forest will guide you," Sir Gawain explained.

"It will lead us to it?"

"It wants us to discover the secret we hid," added one of the Halos.

She was an older Halo, tall and broad, surveying the dark place as if she wished to set it ablaze.

"So we just keep walking?" Owin asked.

She nodded, and so they continued. They walked and walked, but they encountered no signs of living beings along the way. To Owin, it was almost a relief. They had brought supplies with them, so hunting was unnecessary. Moreover, it was a good thing they didn't come across any smaller animals because their presence would indicate the existence of larger predators such as giant spiders, snakes, or two-headed salamanders. Owin noticed the group growing tired quickly. Their slow pace hindered their progress, and the darkness of the forest made it impossible to determine whether it was night or day. They might have been walking the entire day, or only a short time had passed. However, witnessing the exhaustion of his companions, Owin knew it was time to make camp. Everyone gathered some food for a few small fires. Three members remained on guard while the rest settled in front of the fires or laid down to rest. Owin sat in front of the Halo who had spoken about the forest guiding them.

"Were you part of the team that sealed it?" he asked her.

The Halo looked up, her clear blue eyes reminding him of Natava, and his heart panged with concern. He hoped she was safe, still fighting, and had not lost herself.

"I participated in the battles," she said. "But I never entered the forest. A larger group did, but only four returned."

"Only four?" Owin asked. "How many were there to begin with?"

"Ten."

"Ten Halos, and only four returned? How?"

The Halo remained silent. She was toying with a stick in the fire, focused on it as if she were transported back in time, reliving the horrors.

"There are many things in this forest we should be aware of," she finally told him.

"But it seems like nothing lives here," he countered.

"They are here."

"Should we increase our guard?"

"It won't make a difference. They are already watching us, waiting to find a weakness and strike."

Owin looked at her, shocked.

"Are you saying we're walking straight into the jaws of the beast?"

"We are," she confirmed, before turning her attention back to Owin. "Do you want to turn back?"

"Of course not. We will find the veil and ensure it hasn't been broken, and then we will find our queen."

"If she hasn't already been drained."

"She hasn't. Natava is more powerful than that," he assured her.

"However, it's a valid question whether we will make it out alive."

"Why wouldn't we?"

"I told you, they are already watching us."

"Then why haven't they attacked yet?" Owin asked.

"They are patient."

"You said you've never been here," he retorted. "How can you possibly know that we're being watched?"

"Only four returned," she repeated.

Owin shook his head but didn't want to argue. He lay down on the ground, using his bag as a makeshift pillow, and closed his eyes. He fell asleep, but not long after a piercing scream jolted him awake, and he quickly scanned his surroundings. Everyone else was sitting up, on guard, but no one could identify the source of the sound.

"Where is Sir Jonah?" Sir Gawain asked, searching for the young knight Owin had spoken to a little while back.

Owin looked around and noticed an empty spot nearby. He surveyed the area, feeling as though something was breathing down his neck.

"Where are the guards?" Owin asked.

The group looked around, but no one could spot anyone on guard. Owin felt his heart freeze in his chest as a heavy silence descended upon them. They scanned their surroundings, trying to determine the source of the sound. Their fires had almost extinguished, indicating that a significant amount of time had passed. How long had they slept? Owin wondered. He turned to the Halo who had warned him about being stalked. He hadn't believed her then, but now he realised she had been right, and he scolded himself for not taking more precautions. But the Halo had seemed certain that there was nothing more they could do—either they would make it out or they wouldn't. Owin held his breath, listening intently, but it was deathly quiet.

Suddenly, they heard the sound of something moving swiftly, followed by another scream as a Halo disappeared into thin air. In the darkness, a light erupted, illuminating the forest, and a bestial scream reverberated through the trees. The wounded Halo returned, clutching her side.

"It's a giant snake!" she yelled.

"Shit!" Owin cursed, hating that the rumors of those snakes had turned out to be true.

Soon, he noticed a dark figure moving amidst the darkness, drawing closer and circling them. They huddled together, with the four Halos positioned on the outer side. It was clear that their light could inflict harm. They kept a close eye on the snake's movements when Owin saw something else stirring just after the snake had passed by him.

"There are more..." he whispered, just as the first one lunged, its enormous mouth wide open, ready to tear him apart. "Move!"

The knights and Halos quickly leaped aside as the snake charged towards them. Some managed to evade its grasp and landed safely on the ground, but another knight was snatched, and the snake swiftly slithered away, carrying him off while he screamed in terror. Owin turned as the second snake made its attack. He pushed himself up from the ground, swinging his sword and slashing it across the snake's massive face. It howled in pain and retreated, disappearing into the darkness.

"We need more light!" Owin yelled.

The Halos scrambled to their feet, forming a tight group with their backs against each other, and intensified their emanating light. The knights stayed close as the snakes continued to circle them, getting closer and closer. The Halos radiated even more light, causing the snakes to hiss and retreat farther away. They realised their prey wouldn't be easy to take down, and soon, the snakes disappeared completely. The Halos waited for a moment before allowing the light within them to fade, and they all collapsed to the ground, breathing a sigh of relief.

"Don't tell me the spiders are as big as those snakes," Owin said, turning to the Halo who had warned him to be on guard.

She was leaning forward, her hands on her knees, and she nodded. "They are."

"And do they also crave human flesh?"

"They love it," she panted.

"Wonderful."

Owin rose to his feet and surveyed the area. He heard the wounded Halo groan, prompting the other Halos to rush to her side. He approached them, observing the injured Halo on the ground, clutching her side as blood continued to flow. There was a large gaping hole in her side, and it was evident that she was bleeding heavily.

"Did the snake bite you?"

"No, I landed on something when it threw me to the ground," she gasped.

"Let's get her bandaged up."

The Halos swiftly began to bandage her up, but it was evident that this was not the ideal place for extensive medical treatment. She required proper care, but they were now far from the safety of the clear border, and splitting up would only make them more vulnerable. Owin glanced at Sir Gawain, who nodded slightly, indicating that he shared the same concerns. The wounded Halo's condition was critical.

"She needs proper medical attention," the older Halo stated.

"Her wounds won't heal quickly enough?" Owin asked.

"Not with a wound of this size," came the reply.

Owin was already aware of that, but frustration welled up within him. He scanned the surroundings, hoping to find more survivors, but it was only the one wounded Halo remaining, and her injuries were severe enough to make her survival unlikely.

"We should keep moving," he said.

The older Halo spun around, facing him. She stood up, towering over him in her impressive stature.

"What?" she demanded.

"We need to find the veil," he replied.

"But she needs help."

Owin said nothing, but his thoughts were evident to the older Halo.

"We need to get her help!" she insisted.

"You mentioned that this forest leads us to our destination. Won't it make it difficult for us to simply turn back? It will slow our progress," he explained, attempting to reason with the other Halo.

"Then we should split up."

"We need to stay together. We've already lost two men!"

"But they weren't Halos, and if we do nothing, she will die," the Halo argued.

"I'm... aware," Owin whispered.

The older Halo grabbed him by the collar of his jacket, pulling him closer and glaring at him with fury in her eyes.

"I will not let her die."

"We don't have a choice. This mission is too important, and our queen needs us," he snapped, pushing her hand away and glaring back at her. "We cannot risk everything for one person."

"It's easy for you to say when you aren't the one bleeding," the Halo snarled.

They drew closer, prepared to confront one another, but Sir Gawain intervened, stepping between them and pushing them apart as they glared at each other.

"Easy now, let's not become enemies," he urged.

"He's the one turning against us," the Halo snapped.

"Menora, that's not the case," Sir Gawain insisted.

Menora huffed and turned away, kneeling beside the wounded Halo. Sir Gawain moved closer to Owin, and they spoke in hushed tones.

"She won't make it," Owin whispered.

"No, but there's no need to say it out loud," the older knight reminded him.

"Are we supposed to act like it's not going to happen?"

"We'll make her as comfortable as possible," he replied, his tone sharp.

"I'm fine. I can walk," the wounded Halo interjected, her complexion already turning pale.

None of them agreed, but the Halo refused to give up and insisted they help her stand. Reluctantly, the others complied. She managed to get back on her feet, but as they resumed walking, it became clear that she would tire quickly. Owin knew he should display more compassion, but his concern for Natava made it exceedingly difficult.

Chapter 19

Natava gazed apprehensively at the imposing dark forest before her, uncertain of what to make of it. While the sun had replenished her, the foreboding presence of the forest filled her with unease. It felt as though an evil darkness loomed over the place, a silent warning of death to anyone who dared to venture in. She turned slowly, observing Erars as he tied the horse to a nearby tree. He wore a faint smile as he approached, his eyes fixed on the forest. It was clear that he relished the sight, which wasn't surprising considering his love for darkness.

"Shall we?" he asked.

"I would rather not," Natava replied.

"No? Are you already tired?"

"I don't like this," Natava said, taking a few steps back and shaking her head as she looked at the menacing forest.

"Scared? I thought you said you weren't scared," he taunted.

"This is different. Don't you feel it?"

"I do. It feels great," he countered.

"It's dark, and it's a death trap," she snapped.

"Nothing will touch you, Light. I will make sure of it," he assured her.

He regarded the forest as if it were a pleasant place for a leisurely stroll. Natava shook her head, but Erars crossed the border and entered the forest.

"Better hurry, Light. I'm not waiting," he said.

Natava cursed under her breath, telling him to go rot, but she hastened after him, aware that he wouldn't let her escape. He would catch up to her, and it was wiser to stay close to him as they entered the forest.

"It's... not good," she whispered.

"It's great," he countered.

"No, this feels wrong, and the stories about this place are not good."

"You can't believe everything you hear."

Natava turned to look at Erars, who appeared strangely calm. It confused her. While she understood that he thrived in darkness, she also knew that other creatures might find him to be a delightful meal.

"There are giant snakes here," she said.

"There are. And spiders too. They're quite repulsive," he chuckled.

"They devour people."

"They do."

"And there are other things as well. Evil spirits that haunt you," she said.

"Little Light, I didn't expect you to be such a believer. You seem too stubborn for that," he teased, glancing at her and smiling.

She glared at him, but then the sound of a snapping branch caused her to jump to the side, colliding with Erars, who stumbled backwards slightly before steadying them both. Natava pressed her back against him, peering towards the source of the sound. Erars noticed that she had begun to emit a soft glow, though he wasn't sure if she had noticed it herself.

"Did you hear that?" she asked.

"Yes, a branch snapped," he replied dryly.

"And what caused it?"

"Perhaps a spider coming to devour us," he leaned closer and whispered.

"You're not funny," she snarled, turning to him and realising how close they were standing.

He smiled at her, and she quickly moved back, creating some distance between them.

"We should be careful," she said.

"We are careful."

"No, we're wandering around as if we're strolling through a garden," she retorted.

"It's quite pleasant here."

"It's creepy."

Erars didn't find the forest creepy at all. The place fuelled him with power, while the Light beside him was unsettled. He glanced at her, watching her eyes dart in all directions, even tilting her head back to check for anything hanging from the tree crowns. He found it rather amusing, yet also intriguing that his powers were so drawn to her. They hungered for souls, but the hunger he felt wasn't of that nature. He reached out, brushing a finger down her cheek, startling her and causing her to recoil.

"Stop that. Why are you touching me?" she demanded.

"I simply find you interesting."

"I don't find you interesting. This is insane. This forest is dangerous!" she snapped.

"Aren't you trained to fight? You protected those small Lights from harm," he said.

"I am trained."

"Then why are you so scared?"

Natava narrowed her eyes, then turned away without speaking, continuing to walk.

Erars noticed her growing fatigue later in the day, and he stopped, causing her to nearly collide with his back as she had fallen slightly behind.

"W-What?" she stammered. "Is it a snake?"

"No, we're just taking a break."

"A break?"

"You look like you might faint soon."

"I'm fine," she insisted.

"We're taking a break," he stated firmly.

Natava now stood in front of him, arms crossed. "We should keep moving. The faster we go, the sooner we'll reach our destination."

"But you're getting tired, and we need you to conserve your energy. Who knows if other Shadow Lords have already captured a Light?" Erars argued.

"No one else is."

"What if the other Shadow Lords have already captured a Light?" Erars argued.

Natava didn't know if they had, but she believed that if something as significant as the veil that protected them from the Shadow World had been breached, she would have sensed it. They would all have sensed it, so she didn't believe it had happened.

"Ah, your mind is working hard," Erars said. "What are you thinking?"

"We would feel it if the veil had been broken."

"You're correct."

"We don't feel it. It has not been broken."

"That doesn't mean the other Shadow Lords aren't working on it or perhaps trying to summon more shadow creatures as well. If there is a tear, it could be possible," Erars countered.

"But if a tear can release the shadow creatures, why would they want to open it completely?" Natava asked.

"You have no idea what lurks beneath it." Erars replied.

"What hides there?"

"Very powerful creatures. Having them under our command will ensure that nothing can ever stop us again."

"Why didn't you use them the first time?" Natava asked.

"They were used, but when the opening was closed, it drained us. This time, the Shadow Lords will be prepared to prevent any Halo from closing it again."

"If another Halo or Light sacrifices themselves, it will be possible," Natava suggested.

"Then all the Halos and Lights must die."

"You're a monster," Natava accused.

"I am born from darkness," Erars stated matter-of-factly.

"How can you sleep?"

"I don't sleep, really."

"Never?"

"We don't need to. Nor do we need to eat. We just need to feed," Erars explained. He playfully reached for Natava, who instinctively moved away, causing him to laugh. He hadn't had this much fun in ages. The queen was bringing out another side of him.

"Do not touch me!" Natava warned.

"But it is so easy now that you have let me in," he teased.

"Let you in?"

Erars reached for her again, placing his hands on her neck and pulling her closer. Natava gasped as she found herself pressed against him.

"You do not burn me now," he whispered darkly, their breaths mingling.

"I-I am still weakened," Natava stammered.

"Someone as strong as you needs only a little fuel to unleash immense power. But now you do not burn me because you do not wish to."

"I definitely do!"

"Then why am I not screaming in pain?" he challenged.

Erars continued to smile, inching closer, yearning for more from the Light that stirred his blood and intensified his power. Natava wanted to prove that she wanted him gone, so she allowed her powers to come closer to her skin. Soon, Erars's expression changed as he felt the searing pain in his hands. He hissed and moved away.

"Shit," he cursed.

Natava smiled, clearly pleased with herself, and turned away from him, watching as he waved his hands in the air.

"I told you, I despise you."

"For now," he replied. "But we are still on the same side, aren't we?"

"We... are."

Natava realised that burning him had been a mistake. It wouldn't convince him that she was someone he could rely on. She understood that he kept emphasising their alliance to remind her of her place. She lowered her eyes, attempting to appear less defensive.

"You're a very interesting Light," Erars commented.

"I have been told that before," Natava mumbled.

They stood in silence for a while longer before Erars began walking again, and they continued their journey through the dark forest.

Chapter 20

Massana raced back to the capital, riding at full speed through the city streets, causing the citizens to jump aside. Her anger consumed her, and she paid no attention to her reckless riding. She needed to return and hope for good news from Owin. Perhaps the scouts had found clues about Natava's whereabouts or had located her. However, as soon as the gate to the square opened, Massana witnessed distraught Halos running out of the marble castle. Her blood ran cold. Without even waiting for her horse to fully stop, she slid down and stormed over to the other Halos.

"What is it?" she demanded.

"It happened last night. A Light has gone missing," a younger Halo explained.

"A Light?! I thought I ordered constant guards on them!"

"She seems to have slipped away while they were supposed to be sleeping," the Halo replied.

"Send out scouts! Find out!" Massana yelled.

"We already have," they responded.

Massana ran a frustrated hand through her hair, feeling overwhelmed. It seemed like everything was falling apart, and she was struggling to hold it together. No matter what she did, the world crumbled before her eyes.

"Has Owin and his group returned?" Massana asked.

"No..."

"Any news about Natava?"

"No..."

"So all we have is shit?!" she exclaimed.

Silence followed her outburst as no one dared to respond. Massana stormed inside, her loyal knight following closely behind. As they walked towards her study, she demanded an explanation.

"How did this happen?" she asked.

"A clever shadow," her knight replied, knowing that Massana understood what he meant.

Without a doubt, it was a Shadow Lord who had found a way to deceive the young Light and lure her outside. Massana knew what they wanted. They desired to break the veil, and a willing sacrifice was the key. What better sacrifice than a naïve young Light who hadn't yet learned about the horrors of the world?

"I don't understand how he could have tricked her," Massana said in frustration.

"The side of the wall hasn't been repaired. We believe he didn't try to enter but managed to communicate with the Light from the outside, convincing her to leave her room," her knight explained.

"I thought we had guards patrolling!" she snapped.

"We did, and they missed him."

"Incompetence!" Massana exclaimed, her thoughts clouded by anger. It was clear that the Shadow Lords had become bolder after their previous attack. Weakening their defences had invited their return. Perhaps the Light hadn't been lured out at all. Maybe she couldn't sleep, and it was her own decision to venture out. But that didn't calm Massana. They had the Light they needed, and it was uncertain whether they would be able to manipulate her.

"How old was she?" Massana asked.

"She was from the younger group," her knight, Calum, replied.

"How old exactly?"

"Eight," he answered.

"Eight..." Massana whispered, her heart heavy with concern, as they entered her study.

She angrily tore off her riding gloves, throwing them onto the desk, and began removing her armor. She should have done it in her chambers, where everything had its place, but anger clouded her judgment.

"Her mother?" Massana asked.

"Out searching," Calum replied.

"Her name?"

"Lora."

Massana knew who Lora was. She was a bright young Light with great potential. A clever and talented student, skilled in combat. Massana hoped that Lora could endure whatever was being done to her until they found her because they would find her; Massana swore to that. Just as she would find her own daughter, Natava.

"Is there any news about her?" Massana asked.

"About Lora?" Calum questioned.

"No, about Natava..."

"Unfortunately, no. No one has seen her since the party."

"But if Natava was their Light, then..." Massana trailed off, piecing things together in her mind. Something didn't add up, and a realisation began to dawn on her. "Natava wasn't their Light."

"What?" Calum was taken aback.

"Natava wasn't taken by the same ones who struck last night. Someone else has Natava."

"Are you suggesting Natava wasn't the target at all during the attack on us?"

"Natava is too old, less easily manipulated and stronger. They needed a child. But then who the hell took Natava?!" Massana shouted in frustration.

"Could it be that Natava is on her own mission?" Calum proposed.

"She wouldn't be that reckless."

Calum and Massana exchanged glances, the weight of their shared concern settling upon them. Massana slowly sank into her chair.

"No... she wouldn't be."

Natava had a small fire crackling in front of her while Erars sat opposite her, staring into the flames. She couldn't take her eyes off him, watching him intently. Sensing her gaze, Erars smiled and shifted his focus to her, but she glared back at him.

"You look good in black," he complimented.

Natava recoiled in shock, but her shock quickly turned to anger.

"Stop saying shit," she snapped.

"I am only being honest. Shouldn't we be honest with each other?" he replied calmly.

"Honest?" she mocked. "Why should we?"

"If we are going to work together, it would be best if we were honest," Erars explained.

Natava sighed, trying to calm herself. She couldn't let her anger control her, especially if she wanted to convince Erars to let his guard down.

"Fine. Why do you keep insisting that I have let you in or find you intriguing?" she asked.

"Because you have. For some reason, you and I are drawn to each other for different reasons."

"What reasons?"

"I don't know. I've never experienced this before. But I've learned that the world has mysterious ways of messing with us," he chuckled.

"You make it sound like a good thing."

"It can be, if you work it to your advantage. I didn't expect the Halos to become as powerful as they have, but at least they helped me get rid of those I needed gone."

"What?" Natava asked, confusion etching her face. "What do you mean?"

"I mean, the Halos never stood a chance until someone gave them a little nudge. A little information here, a little information there, and suddenly things started going their way."

"You're saying... Why would you... but you're a Shadow Lord," Natava insisted.

"I am."

"And you helped the Halos?"

"I did."

"Why?!" she exclaimed.

"Because I needed the other Shadow Lords gone. That's why."

"You're almost extinct. Don't you see how crazy that is? Your plan!" she argued.

"I see my plan working out. Well, almost. I still need to ensure that I'm the one who breaks the veil, not the other Shadow Lords."

"But you betrayed your own kind!" she cried out.

"I never betrayed anyone. I removed those who would always look down on me. I told you, my father didn't accept me. But I changed my life. I worked my way up through the ranks. I made something of myself, and still, it was never enough."

"It's all for power?" she whispered.

"Yes."

Natava shook her head, unable to comprehend the desire for power. She had never harbored such ambitions. To her, power was transient, like the wind. It shifted and was difficult to grasp. She couldn't fathom why someone would kill their own kind, send their enemies after them, just to gain more power. Erars could see the confusion and range of emotions on her face, her inability to understand. But how could a Light who grew up with care and was destined for a throne ever comprehend what it was like to be told you were nothing, and even after all your hard work, still be considered nothing? She never could.

"Why?" she whispered.

"You wouldn't understand. You were born for power. I created my own power," he explained.

"But you killed your own kind."

"You think they felt any affection for me?" he asked.

"I don't know about affection, but they didn't betray you to the Halos."

"You make it sound like such a bad thing. Didn't you benefit from it in the end?" he asked.

Natava shook her head. It wasn't that she didn't want the Halos to prevail in the end, but she couldn't grasp how Erars could do such things, claiming it was all for power.

"I did, but I don't get it. How could you do that to those who are like you?" she questioned.

Erars smiled a little. "Aren't you doing the same thing?"

"What do you mean?"

"You're on my side now. Aren't you betraying the other Halos?"

Natava fell silent, her heart pounding in her chest. Erars continued to smile. He already knew what the Light was attempting. He wasn't fooled, but he found the game amusing.

"Well?" he pressed. "Or are you lying to me?"

Erars derived great pleasure from playing with the young queen. Natava kept looking at him but remained silent. She narrowed her eyes slightly, then sighed, her expression almost sorrowful.

"You're right," she whispered, surprising Erars. "I am..."

He hadn't expected such a sudden shift or the powerful act she was now putting on. He leaned back slightly, his smile fading as he observed her.

"But we will lose, won't we?" she asked. "You will win... all of you will win."

Erars shrugged off his surprise and nodded. "We will."

"You will break the veil. You will make a Light sacrifice themselves. You will unleash those shadow creatures, and then we are all doomed. Shouldn't I choose the winning side? And if it's true that I will be your queen, why would I throw away such an opportunity?"

Erars had to admit, she was putting on a better act than he had expected. She wasn't a trained actress, but she was doing a decent job. She almost sounded sincere. However, he wasn't falling for it. He wouldn't call her bluff, but instead, he smiled a little.

"You're right. It's best to stick with the winning side," he agreed.

"Then I will stay there."

There was no longer a need for either of them to continue the charade, but Erars found it too entertaining. He was curious to see how far the Light would take it. Who would break first? he wondered. Who would let the mask fall?

Chapter 21

"Natava and Erars walked through the woods once again. Natava still felt a bit drained, but after resting and eating, she was regaining her strength. However, she didn't feel safe in the forest. It seemed like she was being watched. As she glanced at Erars, she noticed he remained calm, unaffected by the feeling. She wondered if he even sensed it.

"Erars?" she called.

He turned his head, looking at her. "Yes?"

"Don't you feel that?"

"Feel what?"

Natava looked around, her heart beating faster, and her powers reacting slightly to the perceived threat. "It's like we're being watched."

"Oh, I'm sure we are. This place has eyes and ears everywhere," he said.

"But why aren't you more concerned?"

"Concerned?" he repeated.

"Yes, concerned!" she insisted.

Erars looked around, appearing unaffected. Natava shook her head, feeling annoyed that he wasn't more cautious. It felt like he was leading them straight into the beast's cave without a second thought. She thought it would be reassuring if he acted more cautiously as well.

"Could you at least—" Natava was cut off as Erars grabbed her, swiftly turning her around and pulling her close. He wrapped an arm around her and pressed her against him. He placed a hand over her mouth, positioning his back against a tree. Then, leaning down to her ear, he whispered, "Shh."

His warm breath tickled her neck, sending pleasant shivers through her. She wasn't sure why she felt that way or why he had suddenly grabbed her, but moments later, something walked right past them. It was a giant black spider with red hairs covering its body. It moved slowly, and during that time, Natava stood with her back straight, her shoulders tense, and her heart pounding in her chest. Strangely, she found comfort in the warmth of Erars's body against hers, holding her in a protective embrace. He didn't press his hand hard against her mouth but kept it there softly. They waited for the spider to pass before he lowered his hand, but neither of them moved. A long moment passed, and then Natava looked over her shoulder, meeting his red eyes. He smiled, reaching out and brushing a small lock of hair behind her ear.

"Do you want to know why I'm not worried? Because I can easily cloak us," he explained.

"It would have been good to know sooner."

"But that would have ruined the surprise."

"I don't like surprises," she informed him, making him chuckle. He gently held her chin and brought their faces closer together.

"I'll remember that, my Queen," he teased before running his thumb over her bottom lip, sending a rush of warmth through her. Then Erars walked past her and continued on.

Natava stood there dumbfounded. She had no idea how to react or what to say. No one had ever done that to her, and the worst part was... she liked it. Her lower lip tingled from his touch, and her heart now raced for different reasons. What was happening to her? Why was she acting this way? She had to remember who the enemy was... because he was an enemy, right? Despite what he had done for the Halos in the past. Natava shook her head, breaking free from her trance, and turned on her heel to follow Erars. Neither of them spoke, and Natava barely looked at him, which amused him.

Owin sensed a shift in the air, as if it were growing thicker and thicker. He had a feeling they were close to the veil, and something was clearly wrong with it if he felt choked. They hadn't encountered any more monsters, but the injured Halo was slowing them down. Two other Halos were practically carrying her, which made them tired as well, burdened by the extra weight. They had taken a short break to gather their strength, but Owin was becoming anxious to keep moving. He knew they were close. He could feel it. However, they insisted on slowing down, and now he had to stand there and wait. Impatiently, Owin tapped a finger against the handle of his sword as he took on the duty of keeping watch while the others attended to the wounded Halo. He wanted to urge them to keep going, but he knew the other Halos would snap at him. They were wasting valuable energy, and he lacked the patience to wait when they were so close. Owin glanced at the Halos surrounding the injured one, talking to her and trying to keep her awake. He shook his head, considering it foolish to stop when they knew she wouldn't make it. Suddenly, someone slapped Owin's shoulder, causing him to jump slightly.

"You're practically shaking," Sir Gawain pointed out.

"I'm just anxious to keep moving," Owin replied.

"Give them a chance to say their goodbyes. The veil isn't going anywhere."

"How do we know that?" Owin asked. "Maybe it's tearing further open right now. Can't you feel it?"

"I feel it," Sir Gawain acknowledged.

"Then we should heed that warning."

"You want to rush in, hoping it will lead us to the queen."

"Don't you want to find her?"

"Of course," Sir Gawain said, "but your shaking and impatience are making everyone uneasy. Relax a little. Calm down."

"I can't, not when we're this close," Owin told him. "Maybe... Maybe I should go on my own."

"Owin!" Sir Gawain warned. "That's a terrible idea."

"But what if it isn't?"

"Don't take that chance."

"I can get there faster. I won't be far from you, and you can catch up."

"Going alone will only get you killed," Sir Gawain snapped. "You're staying with the group."

Sir Gawain returned to the others, but Owin's thinking was clouded. He looked ahead, feeling a pull towards the veil, and his foot took a small step forward. He glanced over his shoulder, seeing that the others were still tending to the injured Halo, offering her water and speaking to her. Owin took another step forward, then another, until his feet were moving on their own, leading him away from the group. He knew what he was doing was foolish, but for some reason, he couldn't stop himself.

Owin continued through the dark forest, soon losing sight of the others as they vanished. His heart raced in his chest, and the closer he got to the veil, the stranger he felt. He began to feel slightly sick, sweat breaking out on his skin, and indistinct voices whispered around him. Owin pressed on, with trees beginning to spread apart, no longer standing close together. He noticed that everything around him seemed to take on a grey colour instead of pure black. The ground beneath his feet seemed to undulate like waves. He didn't stop. Owin pressed forward until he reached the tree line. He walked past the last trees, finding himself in a clearing, and his eyes widened at the sight before him. A small crack in the ground lay a few feet away, emitting smoke. Fear filled his body as he stared at it, feeling his blood turn cold.

"*Come closer*!"

This time, he heard the whispers clearly. The crack wasn't large, but he could sense the evil lurking beneath. It was evident that the small crack in the ground wasn't a mere entrance to an underground cave or more earth. It was the crack between realms.

"*Come closer*!"

Owin felt compelled to listen. He took a small step towards the crack, and something began to form. Slowly, a shadowy hand rose from the crack, its fingers wriggling before waving him closer.

"*We're right here*," the echoing voice beckoned. "*Come see us. So few can see us.*"

Owin didn't know what came over him. The voice felt like a siren's call, making his feet move involuntarily, and the hand continued to beckon.

"*We can't all come out to play. Come to us instead. Play with us.*"

Owin was entranced, his feet inching closer to the hand. Soft laughter filled the air, like enchanting music.

"*Yes, come a little closer.*"

Owin continued towards the hand, but when a branch snapped further away, breaking the spell, he turned his head. He heard crunching sounds, someone approaching. Owin looked back at the crack, realising that the shadow hand had disappeared. He walked away, hurriedly finding a hiding spot behind a bush, and waited.

Chapter 22

Natava walked beside Erars, who continued to exude cheerfulness. They had encountered another monster, this time a salamander with two giant heads and sharp teeth, but once again, Erars had grabbed her, pulled her close, and cloaked them with his powers. It sent a surge of warmth through her, and she cursed herself for feeling even the slightest bit of comfort. She reminded herself that they were enemies, and yet she couldn't help but study the Shadow Lord. He didn't resemble the one she remembered from the past. Erars seemed different, and she hated that it intrigued her. He was inherently evil. All Shadow Lords were, and yet, despite capturing her, he hadn't tried to kill or torture her. Though she had been held in that room for two days, he had released her relatively quickly. He had to be cautious not to trust her too soon or give her too much opportunity to fight back. Erars wasn't stupid, and Natava had learned that quickly.

"Do you feel that?" Erars asked, his smile still playing on his lips as he came to a stop.

"What?" Natava had been too preoccupied with observing Erars to notice the shift in the air, but now she felt it. It was thicker, darker, and the hairs on the back of her neck stood on end, a clear warning of imminent danger.

"We're close," Erars said.

He felt nothing but power emanating from the cracked veil. The Shadow World provided him with strength, so he quickened his pace. Natava grabbed his hand, surprising him as he hadn't expected her to reach out.

"Maybe we shouldn't rush headfirst into the Shadow World," she suggested, her voice revealing her clear dislike of the situation.

"Haven't I already told you, Light? I can protect us," he said.

"You mean just you."

"If I wanted to feed you to the monsters, I would have done so."

"Maybe you're waiting for an opportunity to feed me to the shadow creatures," she retorted, causing Erars to roll his eyes.

"It has to be a willing sacrifice. Are you willing?"

"I am not."

"Then you're safe."

"That doesn't mean you don't take pleasure in feeding me to them," she snapped.

"With your powers, I don't think they can even touch you. Only I can," he boasted, running his finger down her cheek without getting burned.

"Stop that!" Natava pushed his hand away, and he chuckled before resuming pulling her along.

"Come now, Light. We're not far," he said.

"I don't want to be fed to those creatures."

"Then use your powers."

"So, you are planning to feed me to them?"

Erars continued to laugh, finding her fear amusing, but Natava didn't appreciate it one bit. Her heart raced, and she felt a slight wave of nausea as they approached the veil. Erars kept holding her hand, pulling her along, and while she no longer held his hand tightly, she still maintained a light grip. She knew she should let go, but strangely, the Shadow Lord gave her a sense of strength. She noticed the tree line, and Erars grew even more excited, tightening his grip on her hand and leading her closer. They soon left the dense trees behind and saw a small crack in the ground not far from them, with smoke rising from it.

"They actually succeeded," Erars said, impressed.

"They did," Natava mumbled.

"It must have taken quite an effort."

"How did they find this place?"

"Maybe in the same way I did."

"How did you find it?" she asked.

"I tortured a Priest of Light for it."

"You did what?!" she shouted.

"I tortured—"

"No, I heard you. Have you lost your mind?" she asked, pulling her hand away and finally being reminded of why Erars was just as cruel as the others. "That is evil!"

"I needed answers, and he wouldn't give them to me."

"So, that's your solution?" Natava asked.

"Trust me, Your Highness, if you were desperate enough, you would do the same thing."

"I would not!"

Erars turned to her, moving a little closer, revealing a darker side of himself for the first time. It caused her to draw back until her back met a tree. He closed in, narrowing the space between them, and looked at her angrily, trapping her.

"Yes, you would," he said darkly. "Anyone would. If you want something badly enough, you won't let anything stand in your way."

"It's barbaric," she whispered.

"It's survival, and it's not pretty."

Erars turned away from her, looking back at the crack. He approached it while Natava remained pressed against the tree, curious to see what would happen next. Erars circled the small crack, observing it, when something started emerging from it.

"Well, well," he said with a slight smile.

"*We have so many visitors today. A handsome Shadow Lord,*" an echoing voice spoke.

"Visitors? Multiple visitors?" Erars asked, looking around.

Suddenly, a powerful roar erupted as Owin emerged from his hiding spot and charged towards Erars. Owin had been concealed in the bushes, watching Erars and Natava appear from the other side of the crack. He had been overjoyed to see her, but also fearful. Had Erars already corrupted her? Had he turned her into a willing sacrifice? All Owin could think about was freeing her, so he leaped out of hiding, ready to strike down the Shadow Lord. He let out a warrior's roar and swung his sword through the air, cutting Erars on his arm, eliciting a hiss and causing him to step back.

"*Yes*!" the voice laughed, finding the fight to be an amusing spectacle.

Erars quickly retreated from Owin, who continued swinging his sword. Erars utilised his own shadow powers to cloak himself, confusing Owin, who looked around. However, Erars had no intention of staying for long. He knew that if this knight was in the forest, others were as well, and they would be after the Light he possessed.

"Owin!" Natava called out.

Owin spun towards Natava, who smiled and seemed delighted to see him. It filled him with hope, but then he noticed Erars appearing beside her.

"Natava!" he shouted and pointed.

Natava turned her head, noticing Erars wearing that dark and angry expression once more.

"You're not going with him," Erars stated as Owin raced towards them.

Erars pushed his hand through the air, creating a giant shadow wall. With the veil cracked open, it was easy for him to draw power from it, and the wall became thick and impenetrable. Owin continued to strike, curse, and pound his hand against it.

"Natava!" he shouted.

His voice sounded muffled from the other side as Natava pressed herself against the shadow wall, pounding her fist against it as well.

"Owin!" she yelled.

Erars watched her for a moment, observing her desperation to break through. It didn't take much for him to put two and two together. He noticed as Natava kept calling the knight's name, and he felt a deep, dark anger rise within him, his powers swirling inside, demanding that he kill the knight who seemed so desperate for his Light.

"Take down the wall!" Natava demanded, turning to Erars.

"No, we came to see if it was true that the veil had been cracked open. Now we know. Now our true mission begins," he said darkly.

"Our true mission?"

"We're going to find those Shadow Lords and stop them from completing the final part. If anyone is removing the veil that separates us from the Shadow World, it's me," he declared.

Fear gripped Natava. The way Erars spoke almost froze her blood, and she didn't like the look in his eyes. Erars began to move away, but when he noticed Natava wasn't following, he turned to look at her, sending a clear message through his eyes. Natava sighed, longing to stay. She had been accustomed to seeing Owin every day, and now she had been separated from him for many days. She missed her friend. However, she couldn't stay, so she reluctantly followed Erars. He smiled darkly as he saw her walking past him. His Light could not escape his claim on her now. He wouldn't let her go, and no lovesick knight would take her away from him.

Chapter 23

Owin continued hammering his hand against the shadow wall, desperately trying to break through, but his efforts were in vain. He kept calling out for Natava, but there was no response. He knew she had disappeared, and when the wall eventually came down, he realised they were nowhere to be found.

"Natava!" he shouted. "Nat!"

But there was no answer. Owin grew desperate, running a hand through his hair and feeling his heart pounding in his chest. He had been so close to getting Natava back, but she had vanished once again, still held captive by the Shadow Lord. How could he free her? He didn't know this particular Shadow Lord, but perhaps someone else did. Owin remembered that Massana had fought against the Shadow Lords for a long time and might recognise him. Owin hurried away. The shadows were calling out to him, but he was determined not to turn back or listen to their enticement. He found the group, still moving at the same slow pace, and was surprised to see the wounded Halo still alive. However, Sir Gawain was far from pleased with Owin and immediately began shouting upon seeing him.

"What do you think you're doing?" Sir Gawain shouted. "I told you not to leave the group!"

"I know, but I found it," Owin responded.

"What?"

"I found the veil, and it has been cracked open. Some shadow creatures are managing to break through, but there's more," Owin said, breathing heavily as he was still worked up from everything that had happened.

"More?" Sir Gawain asked.

"I found Natava."

Everyone looked at him in shock, struggling to believe what they were hearing.

"Was she the sacrifice?" one of the Halos asked.

"I think so, but I scared them away. He didn't have a chance to do anything to her."

"Who?" Sir Gawain questioned.

"I don't know. A Shadow Lord."

"Only one?"

"Yes. I attacked him, but he separated us with a massive shadow wall that I couldn't break through. When it came down, they were both gone. Him and Natava."

"They will be back," Sir Gawain sighed.

"I believe so too, but we can't stay in the forest. It's too dangerous," Owin said, feeling awful that he had to go back when he was so close to reaching Natava.

"It is. We need to return and gather a larger group. At least now we know the queen is alive. But we must rescue her and find a way to mend the damage that has been done to the veil. I don't understand how one Shadow Lord could open even a part of it," Sir Gawain muttered.

"Perhaps the Shadow Lords are truly working together, and he only brought Natava with him because he didn't need an army for the sacrifice. Maybe he didn't anticipate that we would come here," Owin suggested.

"Some strange things are indeed occurring," another knight chimed in.

They all agreed, nodding in unison, before deciding to retrace their steps. However, the journey away from the veil proved to be more challenging than their approach.

Natava walked alongside Erars again, who had grown very quiet after their run-in with Owin. He didn't tease her or look as cheery. Somehow, she found his silence more disturbing than his taunting words. She had almost begged for him to turn quiet, but now that he was, she would rather have the cheerful Erars back. While that side also made her feel a little disturbed, she was more used to it than this silent and almost murderous-looking Erars.

"So where are we going next?" she asked, but the moment she broke the silence, Erars stopped.

She stopped too and turned, as he had ended up a little behind her.

"What?" she asked.

"What does that knight mean to you?" he asked.

"What?" Natava was taken aback by his sudden question about Owin, but she did not want to tell him anything. Owin was her best friend, and the last thing she wanted was to risk him getting killed. "Nothing. He is a knight."

"Is that why you call him by his first name without any title being added?" Erars questioned.

"He is just another knight."

"I know a lovesick fool when I see one."

"Because a Shadow Lord knows what love means," she mocked.

Erars's eyes turned darker, and he moved closer to her. Natava was unsure what to expect from him, but suddenly he placed his hands on her neck, pulling her closer and kissing her. There was a giant spark exploding in both of them as their opposite powers clashed in a whole new way. It shocked them both, making them gasp, but it wasn't an unpleasant feeling. Soon, it felt like a battle took place inside of them, as their powers met through the heated kiss, but it only made them warmer, more desperate for each other. Erars deepened the kiss, slipping his tongue inside her mouth, and Natava grabbed onto him, pressing herself against him. She had never felt anything like it. It felt dark and sweet, and she was unsure if she truly hated it or truly enjoyed it. She couldn't find the will to stop. She leaned into the kiss, feeling how it overtook her, and Erars's hands moved underneath her shirt, touching her bare skin. Another giant spark erupted within them both, making them moan softly, while she tugged at his clothes, feeling so desperate for him. She wanted more. It felt like an addiction to something bad, but the longer the kiss continued, the more she craved him.

He began kissing his way lower, down her jaw and neck, his hands moving higher, and she leaned her head back, feeling warm. Natava pushed off his jacket, causing him to momentarily move away from her. She took off her own jacket and threw it to the ground before Erars was on her again. He ripped her shirt from her body and began working on the string of her pants. Natava felt like she was in a trance. Something happened as their powers clashed together. Somehow, the dark and light were drawn to each other, longing to touch and taste.

Erars pushed her to the ground, leaning over her and undressing her completely. He moved back to admire the sight of her, the Light, in front of him—her golden skin and smooth body. He leaned down to kiss her again, his hands exploring her body, one of them finding her breasts, kneading and squeezing. She gasped as his powers seeped through his skin, causing black veins to spread on her body, but somehow it didn't progress further. It was only a slight effect, feeding off her energy, and where her hands touched him, he felt a slight sting as her powers tried to touch him too. Erars leaned down and sucked on one of her nipples, making her pant and whimper before he removed his own shirt, eager for her to touch more of him. He had never before felt drawn to a Light like he was to Natava. He had never felt any sort of attraction or tenderness towards them. That was not like him, but touching this Light, *his* Light, made him slightly lose control.

He moved further down her body to taste her. Natava gasped at the powerful and wonderful feeling spreading through her as his tongue licked her, bringing her pleasure. She reached down, gripping his short hair, pressing him closer as he found that sweet spot of hers to tease and suck on, making her climax in pure warmth. She called out his name, arching her back as she came for him. Erars thought he had witnessed beautiful things in this world. He thought he had seen all there was to see, but nothing compared to seeing his Light explode for him. He made her come again before moving away, watching her pant and look at him with hazy eyes. When he stopped touching her, he observed reality slowly settling in, but he wouldn't let his Light leave him just yet. He leaned over her, kissing her and removing his pants as the spark erupted within them again. Their powers fought one another, clashed together, but didn't harm them. It felt good and wrong. They both knew this shouldn't happen. It had never happened before, but before either of them knew it, Erars had lowered his pants, positioned himself, and entered her. He stretched her, making her gasp at the intense invasion. She was too far gone to notice the slight discomfort, continuing to kiss him as he moved inside her. Both of them felt the pleasure building.

Natava pushed him back a little, and they turned, with her ending up on top of him. His hands grabbed her hips as she bounced on top of him, and he noticed the black veins once again spreading where he touched her, but not extending far. He could just see the end of them moving past his fingers. He urged her to move faster, both of them desperate to climax again. The passion intensified as they let out pleasurable sounds, expressing the delight they both felt. Natava reached her peak, panting loudly, her moans filling the forest, and Erars was not far behind, climaxing inside her and finally finding release.

They both slumped down, the energy shimmering as they had both reached climax. Natava, with her hands on his chest, pushed up, reality flooding back to her as she realised what had just happened. Erars was smiling, looking satisfied, while she began to panic. What had come over her? Not only had she engaged in an intimate encounter with a Shadow Lord, but it had occurred in this dark forest filled with horrific monsters, and she had never before been with anyone. She was the protected princess, destined to rule and bear an heir. Instead, she had condemned herself, surrendering to the enemy she was supposed to despise. What should she do now?

Chapter 24

Owin and the rest began their journey back home. The wounded Halo didn't make it out of the dark forest, but the other Halos refused to leave her behind. They brought her out of the forest and buried her closer to the green lands. They couldn't perform a larger ceremony as they were busy returning to the capital and informing the others about what had happened. They rode their horses hard, taking minimal breaks for rest. The knowledge that their queen was still alive but likely to be used as a sacrifice heightened everyone's anxiety. They needed to act quickly if they were going to save Natava from that evil fate. However, upon Owin and his group's return, they received troubling and confusing news.

Entering the meeting room, Owin found Massana, his father, and a few other advisors engaged in a conversation. The atmosphere was heavy, and he immediately sensed that something was amiss.

"What is going on here?" Owin asked.

Massana looked at him with sadness in her eyes and began explaining the disappearance of a young Light. Owin was deeply confused. He believed Natava was the intended sacrifice, so he couldn't comprehend why another Light had been taken. They took their seats around the long table and began recounting their journey, the losses they had suffered, the discovery of the crack, and Natava's appearance with another Shadow Lord.

Massana's expression grew strange when Owin mentioned that Natava had been accompanied by a single Shadow Lord. Owin provided a more detailed description of the Shadow Lord, but Massana seemed unfamiliar with him. This only fuelled her anger and increased Owin's confusion. He wondered what the problem was with Massana and why she reacted so strongly when he shared his story. Massana abruptly ended the meeting, making the advisors, some of the Halos, and the knights leave. Everyone could sense that something was troubling her, but Owin chose to remain with his father, hoping to obtain some answers.

"Massana?" he called out as she stood up and began pacing around the room, her white-golden dress flowing with each sharp turn.

Owin turned to his father, but his father's expression remained inscrutable, and Massana's behavior only added to the confusion.

"What is happening?" Owin asked. "Didn't you hear that Natava is still alive?"

"Yes, I heard," she responded, her anger apparent in her tone.

"That's good news, but we need to act quickly before she becomes the sacrifice."

"That's the thing, Owin. We don't believe she is a sacrifice!" Massana snapped, finally turning to face him with anger burning in her eyes.

"What? That doesn't make sense. How can she not be?"

"Being with a Shadow Lord for almost two weeks doesn't automatically make her a willing sacrifice!" Massana declared.

"Perhaps he was manipulating and taunting her," Owin suggested. "The Shadow World is alluring. I felt it. It can make you come closer."

"Did she seem compelled to get closer?" Massana countered.

"I intervened, trying to fight off the Shadow Lord and free her," Owin explained. "I don't understand your anger. Why aren't you more concerned?"

"Why would they take another Light if they already have one?"

Owin was perplexed by this, so he shrugged in response.

"Maybe she isn't the sacrifice. Maybe she's on some misguided mission to prove herself once again. She doesn't want to be queen. She wants to handle this on her own," Massana accused.

"Wait... what?" Owin asked, his confusion deepening.

It felt as though Massana was speaking a language he couldn't comprehend. Massana sighed heavily, walking over to her chair at the end of the table and resting a hand on it. She appeared exhausted, as if she had aged a hundred years, and Owin couldn't fathom why. What had occurred while he was away? Why was Massana suddenly seeming opposed to Natava, the Light she had raised and cared for? Massana had expressed complete trust in Natava before, and now it seemed she believed Natava had betrayed them.

"Think about it, Owin. Natava disappeared after the attack, but she's an adult, trained to understand the horrors inflicted by the Shadow Lords on this world. She wouldn't be easily manipulated. At the age of five, she killed a Shadow Lord with her powers. However, a young Light is more susceptible to manipulation. They could make her believe she's doing the right thing or use the allure of the Shadow World to deceive her. It would be easier to target a young Light who is unable to protect themselves against their tricks. Natava is smarter than that," Massana explained, her voice filled with exhaustion. "But she's also reckless, wild, and stubborn."

"Do you really think she would use the party to her advantage? Just to get her own way? To escape being queen and prove herself as a Halo?" Owin questioned, finding it difficult to believe. He couldn't imagine Natava acting so recklessly. Owin understood her desire to prove herself, but she would never do anything so foolish. They had been together almost their entire lives. He knew his friend, and she wasn't stupid.

"Why not?" Massana responded wearily.

"Because that's ridiculous!"

"Natava has done other ridiculous things."

"But then why would she be with a Shadow Lord?"

"Perhaps she encountered troubles. Maybe she's playing him," Massana suggested. "But I don't believe she's the one who needs our help. Natava got herself into the situation she's in. She can get herself out."

"She'll be killed! Drained!" Owin argued.

"She'll be fine," Massana said, taking a seat. "We need to focus on the Light who actually needs our help."

"Natava needs our help! She's our queen, doesn't that matter?" Owin questioned.

Massana remained silent. The other Halos who had stayed behind seemed to share Massana's perspective, and his father stayed quiet too. Owin knew that many saw Natava as wild and unfit to rule. Even among the Halos, she didn't have the best reputation, but Natava had deliberately made them believe her to be unfit. She had wanted to become a Halo. Natava had wanted to fight for the good in life. She had a pure heart, and Owin had no doubt about that. However, everyone around him was doubting their queen. Owin shook his head, finding it unbelievable that they would turn against her so easily. They believed Natava could handle her own troubles, but he didn't have a good feeling about it. The way Natava had called his name, the way she looked at him as if he were there to save her, it indicated that she was in trouble. Something had happened during the attack that no one knew about.

"No, I don't believe it," Owin stated firmly, standing up. "I don't believe Natava would just abandon us."

"Sit down, Owin," his father commanded.

"No! She's our queen. She deserves our loyalty and help. Why doesn't anyone care?!" he shouted, but everyone remained silent. "It's unbelievable. I know you have doubts about her, but she's not bad. She may seem wild to many of you, but there's more to Natava. She's fit to be our queen, and she needs our help now. We owe it to her."

Everyone continued to stay quiet, and Owin shook his head, unable to believe that they were so quick to turn on Natava. He refused to accept that Natava had simply left to play the hero and prove herself. As he was about to walk away, his father grabbed his wrist.

"Don't go out there," his father warned.

"I'm going to find our queen and bring her home," Owin stated firmly.

Calum shook his head, not wanting his son to leave once again. There was no guarantee he would return. No one would accompany him on a mission to bring back the queen, as rumors had already spread that she had abandoned everyone to pursue her own mission and prove herself instead of being the pillar they all needed during these uncertain times. Owin couldn't believe how many were willing to give up on her so quickly. Massana was already a strong leader, and this was the perfect opportunity to test their new queen, but they believed she had failed.

"I'm going," Owin said resolutely.

"No one will go with you."

"That's fine. I wanted to go alone anyway."

"You're needed here, Owin!" his father shouted.

"No, my queen needs me."

"Owin!"

His father tried to hold him back, but Owin broke free from his grip and left the meeting room to prepare for his journey. He wouldn't let anyone stop him. Even if he had to go alone, he didn't mind. He simply wanted his friend back, and he was determined to ensure she returned home safely.

Chapter 25

Massana sank back in her chair, feeling a deep sense of exhaustion that words couldn't adequately describe. She had dealt with a great deal in recent days, and the scouting teams had yielded no results. No one could determine the whereabouts of the young Light or where the Shadow Lord or Lords had taken her. The veil had been cracked opened, making the Halo's sacrifice almost meaningless. It made Massana think even more about Hela and the loss of her mother. Hela had wanted to enter the Shadow World, but her mother had done it instead. Now that sacrifice might have been in vain. If the Shadow Lords were to tear open the veil once again, it would be the end of their world. Massana was uncertain if they could close it.

Last time, no one had expected the Halos to attempt to trap the shadow creatures in their former realm, and the opening had been so massive, stretching for miles, that the location for reopening the world had become a secret. Where it had been sealed was where it was supposed to be opened. The information had never been written down. Only a few knew where Hela's mother had entered. But now that secret was out. The Priests of Light, who held the knowledge, had all been killed and tortured for their information. The Shadow Lords seeking this knowledge had not pursued the Halos who knew, including Massana herself. They would only meet their own demise.

However, Massana wished they had come for her. She could have prevented this escalation, but now it felt as though she couldn't stop the chaos from spreading. Though things were currently quiet, with no news of any powerful shadow creatures, she knew it was only a matter of time. This was the calm before the storm, and they had no queen to rally around. Natava was on her own mission, acting as though she wasn't needed there. It greatly annoyed Massana. How could Natava venture off on her own like this? Yet, in a way, Massana wasn't entirely surprised. She knew Natava's nature, but she had never expected her to take it this far.

"I'm going after him," Calum declared, rising from his chair.

"Leave him be. You couldn't stop him last time, and you won't stop him now. Let both our children go on their dangerous missions. Let them learn from it," Massana replied.

"He might die in the process! He doesn't possess Natava's powers."

"But she doesn't have his skills as a knight. I've witnessed knights vanquishing many formidable creatures. Don't underestimate your son."

"I'm not underestimating him, but I know he can be as stubborn as our queen, especially when it comes to her," Calum remarked. "I won't let him die for her."

"Dying for her is part of his duty," Massana reminded Calum.

The knights had pledged their loyalty, vowing to die for their Halos if necessary. In a way, it was Owin's duty to lay down his life for Natava. Calum had never thought such a scenario would come to pass, as Natava was meant to stay safe within the walls that were being rebuilt now, a process that was taking longer than expected to restore them to their former glory.

"No, I won't allow this," Calum insisted.

"He's leaving," Massana informed him. "You can't stop him."

"But I will try."

Calum left the meeting room to go after his son. He refused to let him die for something that seemed almost futile in his mind. Massana sighed, feeling even more drained as Calum departed. He was an important person and advisor to her, and she wished she could do more to help and perhaps even prevent Owin from going. However, she had seen the way Owin looked at Natava. She understood his feelings for her, and she knew better than most what being in love could drive someone to do.

She had acted recklessly at times in battle when it concerned Hela, willingly risking her own life to try to save her. Hela had often scolded her for such actions, but would later come to her, kissing her and confessing that she had grown angry because the thought of losing Massana was too difficult to bear. That was precisely how Massana had felt. She couldn't bear to lose Hela either, and in the end, she had. After Hela's mother sacrificed herself, everything changed. Hela became queen, creating an irreparable rift between them. Naturally, Massana didn't want Natava to be harmed, but she couldn't keep attempting to save her from the edge she danced on. Perhaps this was what Natava needed to learn. Hopefully, she would emerge from it unscathed.

Owin finished packing his belongings when his father burst into his room, slamming the door shut in a dramatic fashion. Owin sighed, rolling his eyes. He had no time for theatrics. He wanted to leave now so he could track down Natava. Owin hoped she wasn't too far away, but he wouldn't stop searching until he found her.

"You're not going!" his father yelled.

"But I am," Owin replied.

"Owin, it's too dangerous! You'll get yourself killed."

"It's a risk I'm willing to take," Owin told him, swinging his bag over his shoulder, now filled with provisions. He tried to walk past his father, but once again, his father tried to stop him, blocking his way. "Stop this!"

"No!" his father said. "You need time to calm down and think."

"I don't believe Natava left us just to prove she's more than a pretty queen," Owin snapped.

"What?"

His father hadn't heard everything that Natava's betrothed had said, but Owin had. It still made his blood boil. But despite hearing the hurtful words spoken to her, he didn't believe she had run off. She cared for everyone here, regardless of what they thought of her. Natava would willingly sacrifice everything for them. She already had. She didn't want to be queen, but she had taken on the responsibility anyway and had tried her best. Natava had even attempted to talk to the prince, her betrothed. Though it ended poorly, she had given it a chance. She could have left. She could have thrown a tantrum. She could have ruined her own coronation or the ball, but she didn't. Natava did her best. How could it be that Owin was the only one who saw that?

"I don't think Natava left us. I think she's in trouble," Owin explained.

"It doesn't make sense, Owin. Why take her?" his father asked.

"I don't know. I understand that it doesn't add up. How a younger Light would be a better sacrifice than her. But I'm going to find out. I'll find Natava and get the whole story," Owin said firmly.

"I don't want you to die for a queen who was ready to abandon us in our time of need."

"But that's not what I believe."

"But what if it's true?" his father asked.

"Then I'll have learned a lesson."

"You might not get that far, Owin. Please stay. We need more people here."

"You're doing fine on your own, and I believe I'll do fine on my own as well."

"Owin, the Priests of Light are dead. Slaughtered just to obtain the knowledge of where to crack the veil. Shadow creatures are still entering our world. A Shadow Lord, or perhaps many, have taken a terrified young Light who is now alone. She's just a child, and she might even die before they force her to sacrifice herself. That means they'll come back for more. You're a skilled fighter, and we need you here," Calum pleaded.

"And what about our queen?"

"What about her?"

"What if you're all wrong?" Owin asked, seeing the surprised expression on his father's face. "What if she truly needs our help, and here we are, doing nothing? What if she's the one in danger, scared and alone?"

"Owin..."

"What if she's the one who truly needs us?"

"The young Light needs us!"

"Maybe they both do. And if our queen returns and realises none of us searched for her, what then?" Owin questioned. "We've let her down. We've betrayed her. Why would she ever show us any respect after that?"

"Massana and I agree that Natava—"

"But you don't know Nat! I do! I know what she's like, and the façade she puts up in front of all of you is fake. She does it hoping you'll choose someone else to be queen. She does it to give herself more freedom. But I know what lies beneath it all, and I won't let my friend be crushed by the shadows. She doesn't deserve our disloyalty now. She needs us to prove that we stand by her, that we believe in her."

His father fell silent, staring at him, and Owin held his eyes as the silence stretched between them. Eventually, unable to bear it any longer, Owin took a step back and grasped the handle of his sword.

"Now, you can let me pass, or we can settle this with a fight," Owin pressed.

His father's eyes widened in shock at the challenge in his son's voice. Owin was prepared to do whatever it took to bring their queen back. He would fight for her, even against his own father. And once he found her, he would prove to everyone that they were wrong about her.

"Well?" Owin demanded.

"Please, reconsider."

"I have, and I'm going."

"What if you find out that Natava chose this?" his father asked. "What if she left willingly?"

"I've already told you. If that's the case, then I'll have learned my lesson. But I don't believe it's true. I found her, Father. I heard the way she called out to me. She's not on some mission to prove she can be more than the queen everyone wants her to be. She's trapped."

"Do you truly believe that?" Calum asked.

"I do."

Calum sighed, not wanting to let his son go, but he also knew there was no stopping him. His desperation was even enough to draw his sword and challenge him for the right to leave and find their queen. Calum despised it with every fiber of his being, but he stepped aside, showing his son that he was free to go.

"She will disappoint you," his father warned as Owin walked past him.

"You're the ones who disappoint me," Owin stated before leaving.

He made his way back to the courtyard where his horse was waiting. It hadn't been taken to the stables yet and was already prepared for their journey. Owin glanced back at the marble castle one last time before mounting his horse and riding away. He would find Natava, and he would prove to everyone that they were mistaken about her.

Chapter 26

Natava sat in front of a small fire, the silence between her and Erars stretching for almost three days. She knew what was going on in his mind by the way he looked at her. He constantly brought back the memory of their intense union in the dark forest. It was a mixture of their opposing powers that made it so addictive and passionate. They collided without overpowering each other, and Erars had only felt more energised as he fed off her pure soul. Natava hadn't felt drained from it. Instead, his actions had filled her with a sense of need and power. It was overwhelming, and she couldn't comprehend how it had happened. One kiss, and the world had faded away. The timing of their encounter couldn't have been worse, and no matter how she tried to deny or rationalise it, nothing worked. And now, she understood the look in Erars' eyes even better. It was hunger, and it had grown more intense.

Erars wanted her again. Their previous encounter had been unlike anything he had experienced before. Despite living for many years, he had never found pleasure to be particularly interesting. His ambitions were greater, his needs different. But Natava brought something else out in him. He hadn't expected their kiss to lead to such a loss of control, ending with them fucking in the forest. However, he had no regrets. His powers yearned for her even more, pushing him towards her. Yet, for now, he allowed the queen some space. He knew she wouldn't be able to escape him forever. She would come back to him because, as they both realised, nothing else mattered when they were together. Their powers drew them closer, evoking intense emotions and an insatiable craving. So, he knew it was only a matter of time. She would want him again, perhaps even beg for him when she couldn't bear it any longer, and he would be there.

"Where are we going?" Natava finally broke the days of silence, her eyes fixed on the flickering flames.

"To where I believe the other Shadow Lords are hiding," Erars replied, but Natava's eyes were not on him. She seemed lost in her thoughts.

"How much farther?"

"A few more days. We will soon reach a town where we can gather supplies, and you can rest in a proper bed. But stay close. That town is filled with the worst kinds of people."

"I'm already stuck with you. I think I'll be fine."

Erars laughed, finding his Light's comment amusing, as he always did.

"Don't underestimate the darkness, Light. Sweet things like yourself attract it."

"I've learned that," she snapped, her words sparking a fire in her eyes as she met his gaze.

"Yes, I'm sure you have," he chuckled.

"I can keep them at bay."

"Can you?" Erars questioned, aware that he had gotten a strong taste of her. He had touched, licked, and fucked her until they both reached their peak in that very forest she had been concerned about. With him, she had let go completely and surrendered to the intensity of their passion. He wanted to experience that again. He couldn't wait to taste her once more.

"I can!" she declared, though both of them knew it was a feeble attempt to assert her power.

"There's no need to feel guilty for wanting me," Erars assured her.

"We are enemies!"

"Do we have to be?"

"Yes, we do! You want to take over the world!"

"I thought we were on the same side," he taunted.

"Let's drop the act already. You saw through me long ago!"

"You're right. I knew you were never on my side, but now I'm a little unsure," he admitted.

"Unsure?"

"Why else would you have come for me?" he asked.

"You're terrible. Erase that memory. Pretend it never happened," she told him.

"No, I'll let it warm me as you grow accustomed to the thought of my hands on your body again. Or did you not enjoy my touch?"

"I hated it."

He chuckled, shaking his head, fully aware that she didn't hate any part of their moment together. Her coldness towards him now was merely a result of the guilt she felt. But he knew it would change. No one else would touch his Light but him. There would only be Erars.

"You loved it. But I'll give you some more time to get used to the idea," he said.

"I won't let you destroy this world, Erars!" she snapped.

"Not destroy. I will rule it."

"Rule it, destroy it. Isn't it all the same to you Shadow Lords? You have no remorse. You're willing to feed off any innocent soul, any child you find on the street!"

"Children, despite having the purest souls, do not sustain us for long."

"What?" Natava asked, her voice filled with confusion.

"They do not sustain us. We need grown people. But the longer people live, the more tainted their souls become. It's a hard balance to find," Erars explained.

Natava looked puzzled, not fully understanding. The Shadow Lord she had encountered had tried to touch her, but had she misjudged his intentions? No, the way he looked at her was very different from Erars. It was hunger, but hunger for her purer soul.

"That can't be," she said.

"It's true."

"No, I killed one of you when I was five."

"What?" Erars drew back, shocked.

"I was alone in the streets. A Shadow Lord found me and tried to feed off me."

"He must have been desperate if that's true. Did he seem desperate?" Erars asked.

"He seemed hungry."

"Hmm, well, cities were the best places to find souls to feed off, but often they were tainted. Maybe he intended to take you and protect you from the bad things in the world before feeding off your soul."

"That doesn't make it any better!" she snarled.

"What were you doing in the streets alone?" he asked.

Natava shrugged. "Who knows? I don't remember."

"How can you not remember?"

"My mother was attacked, and she ended up fleeing with me. She died, and I was lost. One night, I was found by that Shadow Lord, and I ended up killing him. The light I emitted was so powerful that other Halos saw it and found me."

Erars became even more intrigued by his Light, studying her closely. He had heard stories of the lost princess being found, but he hadn't known about the powerful light she had emitted when she was only five. No ordinary Light should have been capable of such a display, but it showed just how powerful she was.

"Do you want to find out?" he asked.

"What?"

"What happened during the time you can't remember."

Natava felt confused. She couldn't understand why he was asking about something she couldn't recall. The memories had never resurfaced, so what would change now?

"I can't remember."

"But you can. It's just locked away," he said. "I can unlock it."

"How?"

"It would require me to use my powers on you, but it seems you enjoyed it," he teased.

Natava narrowed her eyes, disliking the reminder of how his powers had somehow intensified their time together. However, her curiosity was piqued. She could finally get answers about what had happened during her time away from everyone, how she had ended up on the streets, and everything in between. She looked at Erars for a long moment, and he continued to smile.

"Nervous?" he asked.

"I shouldn't accept anything from you," she explained.

"But you already have, and I have tasted your sweet body. What difference would it make if I learned what happened to you all those years ago? It wouldn't erase anything else."

Natava could see the logic in his words, and it would provide her with answers. However, she was determined not to let another passionate encounter occur. Their first one would be forgotten, and no one else would even know it had happened.

"Very well, you may use your powers on me," she said, noticing Erars' growing excitement.

He moved from his spot and approached her. As he did, her heart began to race, and warmth spread through her body as memories of them fucking flooded her mind. The echoes of their moans still resonated in her ears. She swallowed hard and tried to maintain an indifferent façade, not wanting to reveal how deeply he affected her. Erars positioned himself on his knees in front of her, reaching out. Natava instinctively pulled back as his hands drew closer.

"I have to touch you," he said.

"Only search for what I can't remember," she warned.

"Very well."

He smiled a little smugly, understanding why she was prolonging the process. She was afraid that the moment he touched her again, they would end up naked and fucking on the ground. He would remain focused, though. Even he was curious to see this other Shadow Lord she had encountered and killed. Natava inched closer to him, and he placed his hands on her cheeks, eliciting a small gasp from her. They both felt the powerful spark once again, but neither of them moved. Erars allowed his powers to flow to his fingertips, feeling a tingling sensation. He then began to feed off her a bit, causing her to close her eyes tightly as it hurt more this time with him taking more energy.

Flashes of her past began to appear in his mind. He saw a woman finding Natava and taking her to an orphanage. He witnessed the abuse she endured there and how she eventually ran away from it. No wonder his Light couldn't remember. Her young mind had buried all the darkness of the orphanage, where children were punished severely for even the slightest mistake or accident. It was a wonder her purity remained so strong, but Natava stayed resilient through it all. More images flashed before his eyes, and he saw the Shadow Lord she had encountered. Erars understood his intentions. The Shadow Lord had planned to take Natava and hide her from the world, but the young Light recognised the danger. The light in her memories erupted with such intensity that it was no surprise the Halos had found her. She had killed the Shadow Lord, one that Erars recognised. He had once been a powerful figure but had ended up in the shadows of the dirty streets as well. This brought Erars a sense of satisfaction, and he took even more energy from Natava. He heard her whimper and quickly snapped out of it, releasing her and noticing her slight exhaustion. Erars leaned back, his expression growing more serious, and Natava took notice.

"So?" she asked.

"It seems like you ended up in a difficult situation," he explained. "An orphanage, and not a good one. You escaped from it, and that's how you encountered the Shadow Lord. Sometimes our minds choose not to remember the bad things, and it seems like yours has blocked out all of that."

"So, I was found."

"Yes, you were."

"At least I didn't spend all this time on the streets," she sighed, turning away. However, the answers Erars provided did not bring her the relief she had expected. It hadn't truly given her anything. While she still couldn't remember it, she now knew that her time in the orphanage hadn't been pleasant, and that brought her no happiness.

"You didn't really want to know, did you?" he asked.

"I thought I did, but I don't feel any lighter."

"Sometimes we don't remember for a reason. But I was right. You're very powerful."

Erars sat down beside her, and though Natava noticed, she didn't say anything.

"Killing him is the first real memory I have. That's what I'm meant to do. Even to you," she admitted.

"But you haven't."

"You weakened me."

"And now?" he asked. "We've stopped pretending. Do you want to kill me now?"

"I do," she said harshly, redirecting her gaze towards him. However, he raised an eyebrow, challenging her statement.

"But there are other Shadow Lords that need to be dealt with," she clarified.

"Ah, of course," he chuckled. "The other lords."

"After they are taken care of, I will deal with you."

"Please, my Light, do tell me how you will take care of me," he teased.

Natava shook her head, rolled her eyes, and returned her focus to the fire. Erars continued to let out a soft chuckle that evoked a strange feeling within her. Gradually, the atmosphere grew quiet, and they both sat there, gazing into the flames.

Chapter 27

Natava looked at the sign that seemed to be on the verge of falling off. Mud Hill, that was the name of the town. Not a very creative name, she thought as she observed the muddy road that everyone was walking through. The sky was dark, and it seemed like rain was either approaching or had just passed. Erars and Natava were still riding on the same horse, but as they reached the outskirts of the town, they both dismounted. She glanced around, noticing the dirtiness of the people and realising that it was a poor town. Having studied the maps of Aneria all her life, she knew they had moved further north. Mud Hill was not far from the glorious city of Ruby, named after the beautiful gem as the walls shared the same colour. Ruby was a wealthy city with a royal family residing there. While they held authority within the city, Natava was the queen of all of Aneria, although there were smaller kingdoms scattered throughout the land. Some of them resisted being under her rule, and she knew Massana had faced challenges as well. However, they now faced a greater problem: repairing the veil. They could not afford to let it tear, or they would all be doomed. The previous attack had already taken its toll on them, and they were ill-prepared for another.

"Shall we?" Erars asked as they entered the muddy town, passing through the small wall that encircled it.

Natava could sense the negative energy that hung over the place, leaving her with an unpleasant feeling. Erars, on the other hand, seemed relaxed once again. He appeared to fit in effortlessly in any shady location they visited. Erars led them to several shops, restocking their food supplies, before taking them to a small inn where he booked a room. When Natava realised he had only reserved one room, she was about to protest, but a fight broke out right in the middle of the inn. A table snapped as two burly men clashed on the ground. Erars swiftly grabbed Natava, pulling her closer and holding her there while the innkeeper, a giant of a man, intervened and separated the fighters, tossing them both out amidst laughter.

"What kind of place is this?" Natava whispered in annoyance.

"A lively one," he whispered back in her ear.

She sighed and shook her head before finally getting some food to eat. They found a place to sit down.

"We are not sharing a room. Order another one," she demanded.

"No," he replied.

"Erars, order a separate room."

"No," he responded once again, his smile unwavering.

He settled for sipping some wine while she ate her meal. Erars had noticed that due to Natava's immense power, he didn't need to take much of her pure power to feel energised. His Light could easily sustain him, and they could have fun while doing so.

"I'm serious," she asserted.

"Really? I thought I heard a joke," he teased.

"You're unbelievable!"

"Thank you."

"That wasn't a compliment," she hissed.

He chuckled, well aware that it wasn't, but finding it too amusing to resist teasing his Light. It was so easy to elicit a reaction from her.

"We are not sharing a room."

"Why not?" he asked. "We have been sleeping near each other throughout this entire journey."

"Yes, but that was out in the open. We are no longer in the open," she reminded him.

"I'm aware."

"So let's not get trapped in a small room together."

"Maybe I want us to be trapped together," Erars remarked, smiling at her.

"Then maybe I should get us another room," she retorted.

"Natava, it's safer this way. This place is not good."

"I am trained to fight."

"But have you ever been in a real fight where your opponent wants you dead?" he asked.

"I fought during the attack at my coronation ball."

"Before that?"

Natava fell silent, and he nodded slightly, understanding that the queen had been well-protected her entire life. Despite her wishes to become a brave Halo, she was ill-prepared for the harsh realities of being a protector. Erars believed this journey was the longest one she had undertaken, and it had taken her far from home. Naturally, the future queen had been shielded from harm. He would have done the same thing. And now, he would do whatever it took to protect her. If anyone dared to lay a finger on his Light, they would meet a gruesome end. That was a promise he made to himself.

"I am still trained for it," she asserted.

"No, you are trained to be a queen," he reminded her, speaking softly so that no one else could hear the important title she held. In a town like this, no one could be trusted.

"I have received training! My knight trained me."

"Ah, yes. Your knight," Erars spat.

Natava noticed the venom in his voice and examined him closely.

"Are you jealous of Owin?" she asked.

"Jealous?" The word was foreign to Erars. He had never experienced jealousy before. Why would he? He harbored a great deal of resentment towards the other Shadow Lords, but jealousy had never been a part of it.

"Yes, because he desires me, and because he is the one I should be with," Natava said, smirking smugly now.

Erars leaned in closer. There would be no one else who would possess his Light. She was now his.

"Listen, Light, you are mine now, and whatever your knight desires from you is not going to happen. He can pursue you all he wants, but it won't grant him your affections. Besides, you said 'should'."

"What?" Natava questioned.

"You said you 'should' be with him. That doesn't sound like you want to be with him, and I don't believe a queen should have an affair with her knight," Erars reminded her.

Natava was unsure of how to respond. While she cared deeply for Owin and had enjoyed their intimate moment together, she was uncertain about her true feelings for him. When he kissed her, she thought there might be something more, but it was nothing compared to when Erars had kissed her and done so much more. With Owin, she had maintained control, never losing herself in the kiss. But with Erars, it felt as though the entire world had vanished, and indeed it had, as she had ended up naked on the ground.

"Well?" he pressed. "Did you sleep with your knight?"

Natava remained silent, and Erars smiled, seeing right through her.

"You do not love him."

"What do you know about love?" she asked.

"Not much, but I can see it in your eyes. Besides, if you truly loved him, you would not have hesitated."

"I do love him."

"But are you in love with him?" he questioned.

"Why does it matter to you?"

"Because, Light, you are attempting to provoke my anger, and I would be extremely careful with that. People get hurt when I am angry, and while I will never touch you in a way you do not enjoy, I can't say the same for your knight. Don't make me hunt him down and hang him from a tree," Erars warned.

"You're sick!"

"I am defending what is now mine, as Shadow Lords do."

"No, you are treating me as if I am a part of your shadows. As if you are my master!"

"Then get up and leave," he told her.

"What?"

"Go, little Light."

"I can just leave? You would let me?" she asked.

"You could stop me with your powers, after all. You are strong enough."

He was right about that, Natava thought, but she remained seated, looking at him. Erars looked right back at her, appearing calm, and Natava continued to observe him for a little while longer. She had no intentions of leaving. She needed to stop the other Shadow Lords from opening the veil, but there was something more to her reluctance. Something she vehemently denied because it would mean admitting that she wanted to be around Erars and enjoyed what he did to her. Natava wanted to test him, though, so she stood up. Erars continued to watch her with a calm expression. She walked away from her seat, but she didn't hear him following her.

When she turned and saw that he wasn't even looking in her direction, she felt a peculiar pang in her heart. Natava sighed and walked back, taking her seat again. Erars smiled.

"Did you forget something?" he asked.

"I still need to kill those Shadow Lords," she informed him.

"Ah, yes, of course. Don't make me think it has anything to do with me."

"It doesn't."

"Of course, Light."

Natava sighed deeply once again and shook her head, but she couldn't deny how good she felt sitting there again. She knew she shouldn't feel this way, but Erars was doing something to her that she couldn't quite explain. They continued to enjoy their food and drinks in silence. Natava listened to people singing and playing music, observed another fight breaking out, and watched some people getting angry over a game of cards. As she sat there, a strange feeling blossomed in her heart. Suddenly, she found joy in the fact that she wasn't confined to some castle. Suddenly, she was free to explore and experience. She would never have been allowed to visit a town like this. It was dangerous and filled with criminals, yet there she sat among them, looking nothing like the queen she was, and she relished in the freedom of it. She relished the fact that she could simply exist without being criticised or burdened by her duties. In that moment, she was just another person among them.

Erars noticed the calm that washed over his Light and smiled. She had found her place there, and he found it captivating. It transformed her, revealing a new side to her. The night wore on, and neither of them spoke much. Erars made sure that Natava ate a substantial meal, preparing her for the upcoming battle. Her powers would be far more effective against the other Shadow Lords than his own. That was why he preferred to have others fight on his behalf. Shadow Lords' powers weren't as powerful when used against each other. While they could harm each other, their shared nature made it easy to anticipate their moves. It resulted in an endless cycle of battle that Erars didn't have time for. However, his Light could easily overcome them. He eagerly anticipated the shocked expressions on their faces when they appeared together. Erars knew they made an odd pair, but he was growing accustomed to it and even enjoying it. He hadn't expected to be so drawn to her when he took her. Initially, he believed he could treat her like any other person he had encountered, but that turned out not to be the case. The more time he spent with her, the more he craved her.

As the night progressed, people began leaving the inn until only a few intoxicated individuals remained, nursing their drinks without causing any trouble. Natava started to grow tired, and she and Erars made their way to the shared room. The sound of the door closing seemed particularly loud to Natava. She nearly jumped in response, and then she felt Erars right behind her, drawing closer and causing a slight shiver to run down her spine. But it was a delightful sensation. She closed her eyes slightly as he inched even closer, his lips grazing her neck before planting a soft kiss near her ear.

"You shouldn't..." she whispered, but did not sound as if she hated it. Natava was unsure where her resolve had vanished.

After experiencing a taste of freedom, realising there was no one to scold her or remind her of her duties, she momentarily forgot she was a queen. When Erars grasped her hips and pulled her towards him, revealing how hard he had grown, she lost all reason. She turned in his arms and reached for him, kissing him passionately, relinquishing any restraint she had. Merely looking at him stirred something within her, and she couldn't resist herself. *Just one more time,* she told herself. Just one more passionate night, and then she would put an end to it. They began undressing each other, growing desperate to feel the touch of naked skin and taste each other.

This time, Natava took greater control, pushing him onto the small bed, dropping to her knees before him, and leaning in to take his erection into her mouth, moving her head with fervor. Erars grabbed hold of her hair, hissing with pleasure, relishing the sweet suction of her mouth. He dictated the rhythm slightly, urging her to move faster before pulling her away. He lifted her from the floor, turning them around and placing her on the bed. Reaching between them, he found her sweet spot and began rubbing her clit, igniting her desire for him. He then positioned her with her hips raised, settling himself behind her and thrusting deeply into her, both of them moaning with pleasure. Their powers once again intertwined, creating a fiery fusion that intensified their connection. Erars took her hard and passionately, gripping her hips with increasing force, causing black veins to spread where he touched her.

"Goddess!" she cried out when he hit the right spot inside her, making her body tense with pleasure, yet not quite pushing her over the edge. He reached around her, stimulating her sensitive nub, and she came hard, calling out his name.

He pulled her close to him, continuing to thrust vigorously, pursuing his own release as he held her tightly, adoring her neck with his lips.

"*You are all mine, Natava. It isn't your knight who pleasures you. It is the person you are supposed to hate and never allow this close. But you are. You are stepping into the darkness with me, and you will remain there. I will never let you go,*" he promised.

Natava knew she shouldn't feel the warmth spreading inside her upon hearing his words, but she couldn't stop it. Why couldn't she stop? Tremors ran through her body as she clung to him, and she reached lower, touching herself until they both reached climax simultaneously.

Erars thrust deeply inside her, releasing himself, experiencing indescribable pleasure. Nothing could compare to his Light.

Chapter 28

Natava woke up with a heavy arm wrapped around her waist. This time, she hadn't bothered to get dressed and found herself nestled against Erars's warm body. She could sense his hunger for her once again and cursed herself internally. There was no excuse for the pleasure she had found this time. She had more than willingly participated, reaching for him and deriving immense satisfaction. Their first round had quickly led to a second before they both rested, and now it seemed his body craved more. The warmth she felt only intensified her desire for another round, but she couldn't let it continue. She needed to deal with the other Shadow Lords before confronting Erars himself. Perhaps killing him would free her from the magical hold he seemed to have over her. Frustrated, she pushed away his arm, causing him to groan as he was abruptly awakened from his slumber. Erars opened his eyes, observing the captivating sight of the beautiful naked form leaving the bed. However, his view of Natava was quickly obstructed as she began dressing. She turned around while putting on her boots and noticed him watching her intently. He remained comfortably sprawled in bed, propped up on one arm, his eyes filled with desire.

"We should get going," she said.

"We still have some time," he replied.

"Not if we want to stop the other Shadow Lords. They are hard at work while we are sleeping!" she argued.

Erars couldn't deny that the other Shadow Lords were indeed attempting to tear the veil apart. He usually wasn't so easily distracted, but when it came to his Light, it seemed he could effortlessly forget about his mission.

"Very well," he conceded. "Let's go."

They both got out of bed and dressed. Unbeknownst to Erars, Natava watched him as he dressed, admiring his powerful physique that sent shivers down her entire body. After getting dressed, they gathered their belongings and headed downstairs. The inn was still relatively quiet. They had arrived late the previous night, so they were also waking up late, with the sun on its way down. However, Erars preferred the night. He retrieved his horse from the stable, making sure it hadn't been stolen, and they set off from the muddy town.

"How far north are we going?" Natava asked.

"There is an old underground city beneath Ruby," he explained.

"I've never heard of such a city."

Erars glanced at her, a faint smile on his lips.

"No wonder. It used to be ruled by some of the more powerful Shadow Lords. Many important meetings took place there. It was almost a festive place."

"A festive place?" she repeated.

"Some places are known for throwing more parties," he reminded her.

After leaving the town, Erars mounted his horse and reached down to help Natava up behind him. They continued their journey together.

"How long will it take to reach our destination?" Natava asked.

"Just a few days," he replied.

"Will we be making more stops in other towns?"

"I don't think it will be necessary. We have enough supplies to sustain us, and we'll reach Ruby soon. We can always buy more provisions there," Erars explained.

"Perhaps I should get a horse of my own," Natava suggested, prompting a smile and a shake of the head from Erars.

"But I enjoy our rides together," he said.

"I do not," she replied.

Erars found amusement in her response, knowing that Natava was fighting against falling deeper into his trap. She displayed admirable stubbornness, but it was difficult to ignore what had transpired between them the previous night—twice. If she would only surrender herself, it would have happened again this morning. However, she wasn't ready yet. Nonetheless, Erars knew that moment would come soon when his Light would shine only for him.

"How many Shadow Lords do you think we will be facing?" Natava asked.

"There must be a larger group if they were able to weaken the veil, but I can't say for certain if they're all hiding in the same place," he replied.

"What if they are? It would be the two of us against... many!"

"Well, your powers are more effective against them than mine, so..." Erars trailed off.

"So, I'll be fighting alone?" she retorted.

"With your powers, you shouldn't have much trouble. Remember, you've already killed one Shadow Lord," he reminded her.

"Yes, by accident!"

"You stopped the shadow wave."

"And I passed out from it. How much energy will it take for me to take down a whole group of Shadow Lords?" she countered.

"You will be fine. Have faith in your abilities," Erars assured her.

"I see why Shadow Lords are called 'slippery' as well. You're letting me do all the hard work!"

He chuckled, acknowledging that he was indeed doing so. It made things much easier for him.

"Don't worry. I will protect your back."

"I thought men were the ones always wanting to show off," she mocked.

"Only idiots," he replied.

"What?"

"Idiots like to show off, but smart ones know how to use others to their advantage."

"Sure, let me die at the hands of the other Shadow Lords," she snarled.

"That won't happen," he assured her.

"No? Are you going to be my hero now?"

"I am no hero. Let's not forget who the 'bad one' is."

"I have not forgotten," she said.

"Why do you have so little faith? Has no one given you reason to believe in yourself?" Erars asked. "I would think that someone with your powers would have been constantly told how magnificent she is."

"I wasn't meant to become a Halo," she explained. "I was meant to be a queen."

"And shouldn't a queen know how to protect herself and her people as well?"

"Yes, through politics," she replied.

Erars turned slightly in the saddle, looking at Natava with confusion. She sighed and nodded in agreement.

"How boring," he stated, eliciting a slight smile from her.

"And marriage to a complete ass."

"Awful," he said, shaking his head and refocusing on the road.

"He was. He thought I was nothing more than a pretty queen unfit to rule on my own. He wanted all the control and heirs. I'm glad I spilled wine on him."

"Ah, so that's what happened," Erars laughed.

"What?"

"I was at the ball."

"You were there?"

"I was going to steal a Light, remember?" he asked.

"Yes, I remember. I thought you stayed in the shadows."

"You could say that. I disguised myself and used an invitation to a lord to gain entry. I found some small Lights that I was going to take, but then I heard a commotion and saw someone storming off. I now realise that it was you. You spilled wine on your betrothed?"

"I did, and I was scolded for it. But he was driving me insane," she argued.

"I don't blame you for spilling it on him. He deserved it," Erars said, glancing over his shoulder and noticing a small smile on Natava's lips.

"Some thought I went too far."

"I see others haven't given you any confidence in your powers. Do you have any idea what you're capable of?" he asked.

"I think so."

"You think so?" Erars asked, finding it hard to believe that she had such little confidence.

"Yes, I think so. Listen, I haven't used the same level of power I had as a child. I haven't had a reason to," she explained.

"Then it's time to start preparing. You'll need it for the upcoming fight."

"And how am I supposed to prepare?" she asked.

"I suppose it's time I helped another Halo," Erars said, leaving Natava confused.

Chapter 29

"Is that really all you've got?" Erars asked, sitting on a large rock while his horse grazed nearby. Natava stood a little further away from him, conjuring a faint shimmering light from her body, but it wasn't as impressive as what he had seen at the party.

"What?" she asked.

"It was pathetic," he stated.

"Excuse me?!" she exclaimed.

"You heard me. Pathetic. You can do better than that," he insisted.

"It's not that simple!"

"But it is. Your light is a part of you. It is that easy. You did it when you were a child, so go ahead and do it again," he ordered.

"You want me to hurt you?" she asked.

He smiled, and Natava shook her head.

"You could try, but that small shimmer won't harm any Shadow Lord," he taunted.

Natava could feel herself growing increasingly annoyed, and she clenched her fists. Erars noticed and believed that anger might be the catalyst she needed to unleash her powers. He knew she had the potential to do more than just produce a small shimmer.

"You're going to get yourself killed, and here I thought you wanted to act like a big Halo and show me some power," he continued.

"I am trying."

"And failing," he mocked.

Natava felt her anger rise, and soon her body began glowing more brightly, but as soon as she noticed it, her anger subsided, and the glow diminished.

"Has no one trained you to use your powers?" he asked.

"Not much. I don't think they wanted me to know too much," she replied.

"Perhaps they feared you would become dangerous."

"But I am a Light," she countered.

"People fear what they can't understand. You've been controlled your whole life, and now you need to learn to embrace the chaos inside you," he explained.

"That goes against everything I've been taught," she said.

Erars nodded. "I know."

"How can I just forget everything I've been taught?"

"Because your life and everyone else's depends on it," he reminded her.

"But even after I kill the Shadow Lords, you'll still try to break the veil," she said. "Teaching me this won't serve your purposes, will it?"

Erars laughed a little and nodded. "I know what will happen."

"Then why are you doing this?"

He shrugged, appearing unfazed, and that puzzled Natava. She studied him for a moment, then realised the reason for his lack of fear: confidence. He possessed a level of confidence that she didn't. Despite teaching her how to use her powers, he believed she wouldn't be able to defeat him. He thought she wouldn't be strong enough to challenge him, or perhaps he believed he could outmaneuver her, never having to face her directly. Or maybe, because they had been intimate, he now thought she could never harm him. But she would. She wouldn't allow whatever was happening between them to stop her from taking him down. Aneria depended on it. Everyone across the Long Sea depended on it. If Erars became the only Shadow Lord drawing power from the Shadow World and tore it open, he would plunge the world into darkness once more, instilling fear in all. What had she been thinking, coming to him again? What was wrong with her? Natava didn't have the answers, and she was afraid to delve deeper into those questions due to what she might discover. So, she focused on attempting to unleash her powers once more, but all that emerged was a feeble glow.

"Pathetic again," Erars taunted.

"Maybe I truly am," she snapped.

Erars shook his head and then stood up from the rock, walking over to her. He reached out and placed his hand on her stomach, causing her to gasp. He moved around her, running his hand over her body before grabbing her hip and pulling her back against him. Leaning closer, he buried his face in her neck, eliciting a small whimper from her.

"You're not pathetic," he whispered. "You just don't understand the depths of what you can do."

"W-What can I do?" she asked.

"Ruin this world."

She spun around, looking at him in shock. "I am not like you."

"Doesn't mean your powers don't carry destruction as well," he replied.

"They don't," she stated firmly. "Your powers bring destruction. You're the one ruining everything!"

"No powers are inherently good or bad," he explained. "It's only how we choose to use them."

"Then be better," she countered, eliciting a slight smile from him.

"You truly don't see how controlled you have been, do you?"

"I know I've been locked up like some precious little thing. I was lost for years, after all."

"Yes, but you don't believe me when I say people fear you."

"Why would they fear me?" she asked. "I am supposed to be their queen."

"Yes, you were born to be their queen, but that doesn't mean they don't also worry about you being their ruler."

"That has nothing to do with my powers. I acted like a reckless child for a long time, hoping they wouldn't make me queen," she retorted.

"Or maybe they have been fearful of you ever since you emanated so much power as a child," he suggested.

"No, Massana always said I was meant for greatness. That's why I am queen."

"Or maybe she had doubts too. Perhaps she tried to impress upon you that being great was your only option while also limiting your abilities. Have you ever thought about that?" he asked, causing Natava to fall silent as she pondered his words. "Maybe being a pretty queen was what she wanted you to be, or at least one who wasn't too in control of her powers."

"She was scared I would meet the same fate as my mother."

"Ah, yes, the incredible Hela. The most powerful and ruthless Halo, and a righteous queen," Erars mocked, provoking anger in Natava.

"She was an amazing queen!"

"Perhaps, but she didn't possess your powers," he said. "And for the sake of the crown, she had to change as well."

"What do you mean? Change how?" Natava asked.

"By giving up true love."

"You don't know what love is," Natava retorted.

"No, but I know that your mother and our former queen, Massana, were lovers," Erars revealed, leaving Natava taken aback. She shook her head in disbelief.

"No..."

"Yes! They were a formidable force on the battlefield, but when they weren't fighting, they sought solace in each other's arms. However, they did not rule together. Hela had your father as her king."

"That's... No... Massana would have told me!"

"Not many knew," he responded.

"How did you know then?"

"I know many things," he replied.

"Right, hiding in the darkness, waiting for the carnage to be over. Isn't that the behavior of a coward?" she questioned.

"Oh, perhaps it's the behavior of someone biding their time, waiting for the perfect moment to strike. Acting brutally and destroying everyone in your path is not how you win the game. Sometimes it requires patience, sacrificing a little, and then striking when your opponent is unprepared and vulnerable," he explained.

"My mother and father were in love."

"Were they?"

"I was told..."

"You were told," he countered. "You never witnessed it. Do you know how fabricated history can be?"

"What?"

"Yes, because only the survivors get to tell the tale. Not the dead ones. While your mother may have been a queen who cared for her people, she was also ruthless."

"A ruthless queen?" Natava questioned, disbelief in her voice.

"Hey, I don't blame her. It's better to take them down before they can grow too powerful," Erars explained. "But again, your mother actually chose her king. No one chose for her. That is the sign of people fearing her, not daring to even try to control her. She held power, and she made sure to maintain it. Where is your power, Light? Who has taken it?"

While Natava felt like everything Erars was saying was like a punch to the gut, it also clarified many things for her. He was right that she had been controlled, but now she saw how deeply that control had affected her. It had almost paralysed her. At the age of five, she had taken down a Shadow Lord without any training, and she had created a light so powerful that other Halos from far away had discovered it and followed its sight, finding her. During that attack on the marble castle, when she had used her powers again, it had drained her quickly, and she had passed out as a result. Had she really been so controlled that her powers had been taken from her? Did her mother know that others were trying to control her too? Was that why she became such a brutal force? Natava had many questions now, but she also saw things much more clearly.

"Were they really scared of me?" Natava whispered.

"Do you have any idea how many people your mother killed?" Erars asked.

"People?" she questioned.

"Enemies. Yes, they were enemies, but she didn't only go after Shadow Lords. There were other people as well who got in her way. Again, I don't blame her. I would have done the same. But it seems like you haven't been given the harsher view of her," Erars explained. "Although I believe your grandmother was not that different."

"Then what happened to me?" she asked, desperate for answers.

"Maybe they tried to break that cycle. Maybe they felt like they had to because of the powers inside you. It was better to keep them in check so you wouldn't get any ideas. With power comes a hunger for more," he explained.

"I can't believe this... Massana and my mother... And then she raised me, and she... she wanted me to marry, yet she never married... Now I know why, and she... Ah!" Natava exclaimed loudly, feeling her anger reach new heights.

She had never felt like this before. It was almost frightening, but she couldn't calm down. She was furious at the realisation of how she had been manipulated. She had thought Erars was the manipulator, but all along she had been confined by those around her. People had gossiped about her, thinking she was unfit to rule, and she had always attributed it to her childish behavior. But what if it was more than that? What if they saw the brutality within her? The fear they held for her mother projected onto her? Natava began to glow brighter and brighter, illuminating the dark forest where they were resting. Erars felt the intensity of her power and instinctively moved further away, ensuring he wouldn't be harmed. Natava realised she couldn't lose control now. If she unleashed a powerful light again, it might draw attention to their location. Taking a deep breath, she regained her composure and suppressed her powers. When she looked at Erars again, a formidable energy surrounded her.

"What else?" she asked.

"What else?" he questioned.

"What else can you tell me? How blind have I truly been?"

"You're the queen, Natava," he said. "You don't have to marry anyone. No one can force you. Having an heir or not having one is up to you."

"But it's for alliances."

"You don't need that. You're strong enough on your own," he explained.

"They would come for me."

"That's when you show them why it's a bad idea, just like your mother did," he told her.

Natava nodded, savoring his words. She crossed her arms and smiled briefly, but then her expression turned serious, and she pointed at him.

"I am certainly not having an heir with you. When we get to Ruby, I will make sure it cannot happen," she reminded him.

"I'm unsure if it's even possible," he said. "We are opposites. What would that child become?"

Natava remained silent, but she knew she had to ensure that there would never be a child. Fortunately, she knew how to prevent it.

Chapter 30

Natava felt a bit confused as they entered the giant city. It had big red walls, almost as tall as the ones surrounding the marble castle, and the people were all dressed in expensive, well-covered clothes suitable for the colder climate of these parts. Natava's own attire wasn't quite fit for the colder weather, but it would do. They weren't planning to stay for long, or at least she didn't think so. She went to a shop selling herbs and mixtures where she found what she needed. After consuming the mixture, she rejoined Erars, who was waiting for her, and they continued walking down the busy, stony roads.

"I thought we were going beneath Ruby," she said.

"We are," he replied.

"But then why are we in Ruby?"

"We're just looking for the entrance," he explained.

"Here?"

"Yes. The perfect hiding spot is in plain sight."

"Aren't you afraid someone would find out and ruin this hiding spot?" she asked.

"Not really. It has been here for many years, and so far no one has discovered it," he assured her.

They walked for a while, and then Erars suddenly stopped and looked around. Natava was confused, studying him until she realised something.

"You don't know where the entrance is, do you?" she asked.

"I do. It's... um, been a while," he admitted.

"So you don't know?"

"Just give me a moment to think. A lot has changed since I was last here."

Natava sighed and leaned against the wall of a nearby house, observing Erars as he struggled to find the entrance. He continued to scan the surroundings and then suddenly perked up, tying his horse nearby. Without needing to be told, Natava followed him as they approached what appeared to be an empty and rundown building.

"What is this?" she asked.

"Our way inside," he replied.

"But it says 'beware'." She pointed out to a sign that was barely hanging on the door.

The rundown building was partially hidden behind others, and they had to walk down a small alley before it came into view.

"Yes, it's always a good way to scare others away. Just write 'beware'," Erars chuckled.

"Beware of what exactly?"

He shrugged and stepped onto the first step of the little porch.

"Who knows? That's what makes it scary," he said, entering the building.

Natava followed him, unable to think of any other course of action. They walked into the dark building, and he closed the door behind her. Natava struggled to see where they were going, but then Erars reached out and grabbed her hand, leading her to another door at the opposite end. They entered a pitch-black room, and she couldn't see anything, but then she heard a cracking sound. Erars grabbed her hand again, and they continued walking. Natava expected to collide with a wall, but they didn't.

Instead, she felt a slight downward slope, as if they were descending further and further. It was a bit disorienting, but she understood that they were heading towards the underground city hidden away from the world.

"Does any Halo know about this?" she asked.

"If they did, do you think it would still be standing?" he whispered in her ear.

She hadn't expected him to be so close, and she let out a soft gasp, but continued to let him guide her through the narrow tunnel. Erars could see perfectly in the darkness, and he knew when they left the tunnel. In a few places, streams of light penetrated the darkness, and Natava's vision improved as they reached a small path with an edge that led straight down into darkness. She gasped, shocked, and moved closer to Erars, who chuckled softly.

"Welcome to our hidden world," he said.

"Not funny," she muttered.

"It was to me."

"What is this?" she whispered as she stared at the city in the distance, seemingly carved out of the stony walls. She had never seen anything like it, and it was almost breathtaking.

"It used to be a glorious place of ours. Now it's quiet and almost deserted," he explained. "Now let's go."

Erars seemed more urgent now that they had arrived, and he walked ahead of Natava along the narrow path. They stayed close to each other, making sure not to get too far apart. They crossed a long, wide, stony bridge before reaching what looked like a street, but they were the only ones walking on it.

"Should we really be out in the open like this?" she asked.

"If they are here, they already know we are too. I bet they have shadows that warn them," he replied.

Natava felt a certain darkness in the air, an indescribable heaviness, and she wondered if more powerful shadow creatures were lurking down here. She wouldn't be surprised if they were. Erars continued walking, and she followed closely behind. The street gradually inclined, leading to a grand stony palace. Erars stopped not far from the large staircase leading to the palace's entrance. Natava looked at him, confused, but Erars began scanning the surroundings, his confusion deepening.

"Something isn't right," he said.

"What?" she asked.

"It's... quiet," he replied.

"Does that mean they're not here?" she questioned.

Erars was about to respond when something growled behind them. They both turned and saw a group of large shadow creatures in the shape of tigers approaching. Their bodies appeared translucent, but they knew they would solidify upon impact.

"Shit," Natava cursed.

"Time to use your glowing powers," Erars urged.

"I've only had a few days of training!" she retorted.

"Use them!"

Natava delved deep within herself, tapping into her powers, and just as the first creature lunged, she emitted a brilliant light from her body, causing the shadow creature to scream and disintegrate. The remaining creatures advanced once the light dimmed slightly, but she quickly drew from her powers again, and they vanished into thin air. Afterwards, silence descended once more, but neither of them moved, listening for any other creatures that might be approaching.

"Now what?" she asked, but Erars didn't answer.

He began walking up the staircase, and she followed closely behind. He pushed open the door, storming inside, and Natava entered right behind him. She was confused about why he was in such a hurry, but soon they found themselves in a large courtroom. However, there was no one there except for the two of them.

"Fuck!" Erars exclaimed.

"Were we wrong? Are they not here?" Natava asked.

"No, they were here, but they've moved," he replied.

"Moved? Where?" she asked.

"My guess is that they got what they wanted," he explained.

"Wanted..." Natava repeated, her voice trailing off as she realised what he meant.

Driven by a surge of determination, she stormed off, searching the big stony castle for any clues. She wasn't sure if she would find anything, but she had to know for sure. Had other Lights been taken? She burst into a room that still felt slightly warm, sensing a sweeter energy in the air that indicated a Light had recently occupied it. Natava immediately knew that one of her kind had been there. She scanned the room, searching for any signs, until she spotted a soft white ribbon lying on the ground. She picked it up just as Erars found her, entering the room and sensing the lingering presence of the Light as well.

"They've taken one," she whispered.

"It seems that way."

"For how long have they had her?" Natava murmured, not expecting an answer, and Erars didn't attempt to provide one.

He started to leave the room, and she quickly followed suit. They arrived at a large room where a map lay on a table, and they both circled it, searching for any clues. A knife was embedded in the table near the location of the marble castle, and Natava gently ran her fingers over the map just beside the knife.

"It seems like they have everything they need," Natava whispered.

"Unfortunately."

"But it has to be a willing sacrifice."

"Perhaps the Light was easier to manipulate than we thought. Maybe they have already convinced her," he speculated.

"Can they frighten her into doing it?" Natava asked.

"No, it must be of her own free will, but they can exert some degree of coercion."

"Making her believe she is acting of her own accord," Natava added.

"Yes, and that would be deemed acceptable."

"How much of a head start do you think they have?" Natava asked, her fear growing as she clutched the ribbon tightly in her hand.

"Too much," he said. "By the time we reach The Hallow, that Light will have already slit her own throat, spilling blood on the ground and unleashing the shadow creatures. And guess who they will be indebted to."

Natava heard the clear anger and resentment in his voice, and he let out a frustrated groan that echoed through the room.

"For centuries, I have waited, and now they are the ones breaching the veil?!" he snapped.

Natava rolled her eyes. It was clear that all he cared about was his own power, while a young Light was on the verge of being sacrificed to open the veil. It disgusted her, and she glared at him.

"She's just a child!" she shouted.

"And? We were all children once. Did life treat us kindly?" he retorted.

Natava recoiled slightly, realising she had no argument against his words. It didn't mean she wanted to let the young Light come to harm. She walked over to Erars, grabbing him and holding up the ribbon.

"We need to save her."

"We won't make it in time," he snapped. "What good will it do?"

"We can stop this!"

"I'm not here to prevent the release of the shadow creatures."

"Isn't that why you came here?" she argued.

"I came here to prevent *them* from releasing the shadows. I still intended to be the one to break the veil, but now I can't. Those shadow creatures will be loyal to the ones who set them free."

"If we ride fast enough..."

"No, I'm going back," Erars declared, pulling away from her and walking out of the room.

Natava quickly followed, hurrying after him and feeling a surge of anger at his sudden retreat.

"So, you're going into hiding again?!" she shouted.

"I am doing what I need to do to survive. As I always have," he said, continuing to walk.

Natava looked around and noticed a small stone on the ground. She picked it up and threw it at Erars, hitting him on his back. He was taken aback by the unexpected attack, stopping in his tracks and turning around.

"Did you just throw a stone at me?" he asked.

"Yes!" she yelled.

He approached her, coming closer until he was standing right in front of her. His energy was dark and angry, a side of him she hadn't seen often. It shocked her, but she stood her ground, meeting his intensity head-on.

"They will be unstoppable now. You know who else holds grudges besides the Shadow Lords?" he asked.

Natava shook her head, not knowing where he was going with his statement.

"The Shadow World. Every creature down there has been locked away for centuries. Do you think they don't know who imprisoned them? Do you think they don't hold a deep grudge against the Halos? And once they are free, who do you think they will come for first?" he explained.

"I know who they will come for," she said. "But that doesn't mean we should give up now!"

"That is exactly what it means," he argued. "We should go into hiding. Do you think the other Shadow Lords don't know the part I played in the first war? Do you think they are unaware of the traitor among them? They may not come for me right away, but they will come. Go into hiding, Light. It's all you can do now."

"No!" she yelled.

"No?" he questioned.

"I am not hiding!"

"Well, I am not going to let you die," he said.

"Oh, so now you're my hero," she taunted. "I thought you said you weren't one."

"That doesn't mean I won't keep you safe. Now let's go."

"No!"

"Don't be difficult. They will slaughter all of you. They will restore their reign of terror, and it will be a harsh and brutal world once again, especially for women," he stated.

"And would it have been any different in the dark world you would have ruled?"

Erars shrugged. "Probably not, but in that world, I would have been the hunter, and they would have been begging me for mercy while you sat at my side."

"I am not your queen!"

Erars smiled slightly, clearly disagreeing, but Natava didn't want to argue about it. She crossed her arms and glared at him.

"There is still time," she said.

"You're imagining the impossible. There is no time!" Erars snapped. "We need to return to my house and keep our heads down."

"We don't know if they have truly succeeded! Maybe they have just chosen to stay hidden in the forest!"

"Do you really think they would leave the safety of this city to venture into the forest?"

"Yes," she responded.

Erars raised an eyebrow.

"Why not?" she challenged. "They would be closer to the veil, and when they finally have the Light on their side, they can go straight to the veil and spill her blood to achieve their goal."

Erars shook his head, disagreeing with her perspective.

"No, they have what they wanted, and now we should be smart and go into hiding before they send their creatures after us. I'm not even sure my fog can keep them at bay, but it's the safest option," he explained.

"Erars, we need to fight!"

"No, I don't need to do anything."

"Are you really going to be a coward?" she asked.

"Tell me, who survives? The coward or the hero? Because I know that a hero charging headfirst into battle has a higher chance of dying," he responded.

"But what about the glory—"

"Fuck glory," he interrupted. "It's useless if you're dead in the ground, isn't it?"

"But there might be a chance that you could save everyone else."

"So, you want to be a sacrifice?" he questioned.

"What?"

"You just described a sacrifice. Someone willing to give themselves up to save everyone else. Is that who you want to be?"

Natava hadn't realised that her words described a sacrifice, but now she understood their true meaning.

"Because if that's what you want, you should have said so earlier when we were at the veil. Then we wouldn't have gone on this long journey, and we could have removed the veil already."

Natava felt the urge to punch him or use her powers on him, but she remained calm and shook her head.

"You know what I meant."

"If you're looking for a hero, you're looking at the wrong person," he said darkly, before spinning on his heel and walking away.

Natava knew she couldn't accomplish this task alone, and she didn't have time to seek help from others. She needed Erars. As she watched him walk away, feeling desperate and unsure of what to do, an idea suddenly struck her. She realised there might be one thing that could change his mind. Uncertain if it would work, but feeling a calling inside her, she had to try.

"I will be your queen!" she shouted after him.

Erars froze in his spot, his entire body tensing as her words echoed through the vast underground world. He had never realised how much he longed to hear those words. Despite his claim earlier, hearing her say it made his whole being vibrate with need. Not completely sure if he had heard correctly, he turned slowly to face Natava, who stood some distance away, watching him intently.

"What did you say?"

Chapter 31

It was as if time had stopped between Natava and Erars as they locked eyes. Her words still echoed in the air, but now there was silence, and neither of them spoke. Natava could feel her heart racing in her chest as she observed Erars standing at a distance, his eyes slightly narrowed. But Erars was longing to hear those words again. She took a deep breath, knowing that ultimately she was becoming a sacrifice. However, she wasn't being sacrificed to an evil Shadow World, but rather to a Shadow Lord. Surprisingly, Natava had to admit that it felt easier than she had anticipated.

"I will be your queen," she repeated.

Even upon hearing it a second time, Erars couldn't fully comprehend the fact that she would surrender herself completely to him. There was nothing in her mind resisting it in the slightest. He started walking back towards her with quick steps, stopping in front of her and looking intently at her.

"One more time," he said, raising a finger.

"I will be your queen if you go with me to The Hallows," she told him.

Erars watched her for a long time, and she felt uncertain about what was going on in his mind. Fear gripped her—fear that he would turn on his heel and walk away, which she didn't want to happen. She needed his help if she was going to accomplish this. Surprisingly, he was the only one who had truly taught her the meaning of her powers, the only one who encouraged her not to give up easily and not to let others decide her fate. She knew she was sacrificing herself to Erars for the sake of everyone else, but she couldn't deny the selfish part of her that desired it. This time, no one had instructed her to sacrifice herself. She made the choice to offer herself to Erars in exchange for his assistance.

"So you would be mine? Do you understand what that entails?" he asked, a dark smile playing on his lips.

"I would be yours."

"But what does it mean?" he asked, wanting her to fully comprehend the commitment she was making.

"I would stand by your side. I would fully devote myself to you, without fighting against anything that transpires between us. I would demonstrate my loyalty to you," she promised.

He moved even closer, causing her to take a step back. He reached out and gently held her chin, ensuring she couldn't escape from him.

"And would you allow me to touch you? Whenever I desire to?" he asked.

Saying yes was not difficult, as she enjoyed his touch, but she wanted to give the appearance of resistance, so she prolonged her response.

"Whenever you want, but you cannot open the Shadow world."

His grip tightened, and she winced, before he released her and looked at her with frustration.

"Then why the fuck am I even doing this?" he demanded.

"Because by marrying me, you will gain everything anyway," she pointed out, surprising him with the proposal of an actual marriage.

"What?" he asked, wanting to hear more.

"We would marry. You would be my king. Aneria would be yours, not shrouded in darkness, but still under your rule. Imagine all the Halos bowing to you instead of lying dead in the ground."

"I enjoy seeing them dead in the ground," he declared.

Natava sighed, briefly closing her eyes, and then refocused on the conversation.

"But you enjoy it even more when people crumble before you, when they realise how powerful you are," she reminded him. "Having them bow to you would make an unprecedented statement. You would reign over everyone."

Erars began to understand where she was leading with this, and he was quite surprised by how much he warmed up to the idea. He had expected to rule in a dark world, with her as the small Light shining by his side. He would ensure that no shadows could extinguish it, and she would continue to radiate. However, now she spoke of him stepping into the light with her, ruling alongside her there, and he relished the thought of seeing the Halos bowing before him. He would crush them in an entirely different manner. They would despise seeing a Shadow Lord on the throne, but it would demonstrate the true extent of his powers. He didn't have to crush the world to conquer it. He could ascend through the ranks as he had done for centuries—through patience and cunning. Erars nodded slightly, finding himself increasingly fond of the idea.

"It's very tempting," he agreed.

"Then let's go to The Hallows."

"But how can I be certain that you won't attempt to kill me once we've defeated the other Shadow Lords? Where is my assurance?" he asked.

"What do you want from me? To kneel before you and bow right now?"

He chuckled, relishing the idea, and Natava thought he was serious. She began to kneel, but he swiftly grabbed her arm, pulling her back up and enveloping her in his arms, drawing her closer. She gasped, taken aback, but soon warmth spread through her.

"Swear it to me," he said.

Natava was surprised that he only wanted words, but she would gladly give them to him if it meant he would accompany her and put an end to the other lords.

"I swear—"

He pressed a finger to her lips, shaking his head.

"Kiss me. Say it without words."

She stared at him, stunned, blinking rapidly, but then nodded slightly. He lowered his hand, looking at her expectantly. Slowly, she moved closer to him, the tension between them building, the energy becoming so thick that it was difficult to breathe. Finally, she pressed her lips to his, starting gently and then deepening the kiss. She thought it would once again take control of them, but it didn't. Erars moved his lips against hers, and she felt the heat rising, but he pulled back before it could escalate further. When he did, he looked at her in a way that was indescribable. His eyes appeared... tender, although that word couldn't capture the intensity of warmth and passion she saw. She was completely taken aback, unable to speak, and simply gazed up into his eyes, relishing being looked at with such power.

"Accepted," he whispered before placing another soft kiss on her lips.

"What?"

"I believe in your promise," he said, stepping back.

"Because I kissed you?"

"Are you going back on your word now?"

Natava shook her head, but she felt utterly bewildered. She couldn't comprehend how a kiss changed anything. She hadn't even made him a true promise. How could he trust her word or a kiss as proof? It made no sense to her, and she continued to look at Erars. He smiled slightly, but what his Light didn't know was that he had used a touch of his power, as he often did when they touched or were together, and in that moment, he glimpsed into the pure depths of her heart. She believed she was deceiving him, but the only person she was fooling was herself. Buried within her light was a small piece of him, one she had unwittingly taken and held onto, and he knew that fragment would forever bind her to him. She wouldn't be capable of ending him when the time came. She thought she could, but Erars knew the truth. He knew that she had already grown so deeply attached that there was no turning back. It was a good question as to when his Light would realise it.

"Shall we?" he asked when she remained silent.

Natava nodded, and they began to leave the dead city. They walked back down the narrow path and through the dark tunnel. He took her hand once again to guide her out of the rundown house.

"I will need a horse of my own," she said as they stepped outside.

"Agreed."

They walked back to the bustling street, still holding onto each other as they searched for a seller. It didn't take them long to find long stalls filled with horses, poking their heads out and receiving pats from passersby. Some even offered them treats, and the horses had become accustomed to the pleasant attention, expecting it from anyone who approached. Natava smiled as a deep red horse emerged from its stall, nuzzling her and demanding a treat as well. Natava ran her hand along its forehead and instantly knew she wanted this horse. The seller was easy to negotiate with, and soon the red horse belonged to her. Natava and Erars walked back towards the city's entrance, where people were still streaming in and out. They mounted their horses and glanced at each other. The sun was setting, and they both knew time was running out.

"How far are you willing to go?" he asked her.

"Didn't I just promise to marry you and make you the King of Aneria?" she countered, making him smile.

"Yes, you did, but a hero is willing to do whatever it takes to protect everyone."

"And I am marrying you."

"But we might be too late," he reminded her.

"What?"

"If they open the veil, Natava, how far are you willing to go? Hmm? Will you be the one to close it, or will you make someone else do it?" he asked.

"What?!" she exclaimed. "Make someone else do it?"

"Why not? You're the queen. There's a reason why your grandmother sacrificed herself and not your mother. Your mother was the future. You are the future. So tell me, who will it be?" he asked, his question only filling Natava with pure fear. She hadn't considered what would happen if they didn't make it in time. What if they removed the veil and unleashed countless shadow creatures? Would she be the one to venture into the dark depths of the evil world and offer herself? Or would she assign someone else? Natava wanted to tell Erars that it would be her, but the words eluded her.

Erars witnessed her internal struggle, but it only made him smile, as he didn't pay heed to his Light's talk of sacrificing herself for everyone. How long had she forsaken everything for the sake of others' desires? She didn't seek a crown, nor did she want it, but she wore it.

"Let's go," he finally said, breaking her trance, before they set off.

Chapter 32

Natava was impatiently pacing around, unable to find any rest. She felt nervous and scared. They had been riding through the night, but their horses needed rest as well. She feared that at any moment she would sense the powerful shift in the air, signaling the release of the Shadow World from its prison. Shadow creatures would pour out, reclaiming their world and plunging it into darkness. There might be nothing they could do to prevent it, unless someone was willing to sacrifice themselves. Was it her? Was Natava the one who would venture into that evil realm and allow herself to be consumed by it? She didn't know what to do, but she knew she needed to make a decision quickly. Soon she might not even have the luxury of choice and would have to act purely on instinct and see where it led. She preferred to make a deliberate decision now rather than being forced to decide in the heat of the moment.

"Could you stop that?" Erars asked, growing tired of watching Natava pace back and forth incessantly.

She stopped and turned to him, looking angry. "No."

She resumed her pacing, and Erars rolled his eyes, becoming frustrated with her anxious and restless energy. Pushing away from the tree he had been leaning against, he walked over to her and caught her arm as she walked in his direction. He wrapped his arms around her, holding her close.

"Enough," he told her, his voice tender. "We can't get there any faster."

"I know, I'm just thinking."

"About what?"

"The sacrifice. It will be me, won't it?" she asked.

"That's up to you, but it's a bit challenging to keep your promise to me if you're trapped in the Shadow World," he reminded her.

"But who else?"

"Anyone else. You're not the only Light out there."

"But I am the queen. I am supposed to be willing to—"

"Sacrifice yourself?" he mocked.

"Yes!"

"Why?"

"I'm... the queen."

"You didn't want to be," he reminded her. "So why are you now the one who has to be trapped in the Shadow World like your grandmother?"

"Do you think she's still there?"

"I think they devoured her alive."

"Erars!" she scolded, but he smiled and pressed her closer to him.

"I don't know, but I don't want to see you walked down there. If you do, I might just have to come and rescue you," he told her, causing her heart to beat faster.

"What?"

"Yes, I would tear open the veil again, and I would get you out."

"Then my sacrifice would have been in vain," she said.

"It doesn't matter to me. I would have both: a world full of shadows and my queen," he declared proudly. "I won't let you sacrifice yourself. You promised to be mine, and I'm going to hold you to that promise."

"Somebody has to do it. Besides, what would you choose? The other Shadow Lords ruling or me sacrificing myself?" she asked him.

Erars pondered over it. He didn't want the other Shadow Lords to be in power. He had worked so long and been so patient. It was all meant to be his, but now the others were vying for the same thing, ruining his plans. It might even cost him Natava, and he wasn't willing to let go of his Light that easily. What would he choose? Power or the queen standing before him? Natava raised an eyebrow when he remained silent, then pushed away from him and resumed pacing. Back and forth she went, when suddenly a snap echoed through the dark woods. The sun was slowly rising, but they couldn't see very far despite the nearby fire burning.

"What was that?" she whispered.

Erars said nothing, but both of them looked in the direction of the sound. They waited, expecting something to happen, but when everything remained quiet, they turned back to each other.

"Probably just a rabbit," he said.

"Erars!"

A shadow moved swiftly behind Erars, catching Natava's attention. The Shadow Lord managed to react in time, disappearing into thin air right before a sword sliced through the air. Erars reappeared behind Owin, who had attempted to sneak up on him and attack. He kicked him forward, and Owin stumbled a few steps before turning around and running the sword through the air once again. Erars vanished once more, but this time Owin was prepared and faster. He swung the sword, cutting Erars's cheek, before Erars vanished completely, not reappearing.

"Come out, you coward!" Owin shouted, gripping the sword tightly.

"Owin?!" Natava exclaimed, shocked.

Owin remained on guard, but he moved closer to Natava, gently taking her arm and positioning her behind him. She was stunned to see him there.

Natava was certain he had returned to the marble castle or would have arrived with a group of knights, but it was only Owin. She looked around, thinking she must be mistaken and that others would appear momentarily, but it was only Owin who stood there. He scanned their surroundings, causing them to inch backwards, guiding her towards safer ground.

"What are you doing?" she asked.

"It's all right, Nat. I'm here now," he assured her.

Natava was about to speak when she felt someone grab her from behind, pulling her away. Owin sensed it too and whirled around, seeing Erars holding onto Natava and giving him a fierce glare.

"Let her go, you monster!" he shouted.

"Come and get her."

"Stop it!" Natava yelled, causing the two men to turn their attention to her. "Just wait, Owin."

She turned to her best friend, who stood there looking confused. He had been riding for a long time, slowly tracking them down. He had moved swiftly on his own and asked numerous locals if they had seen Natava. It took a while before anyone mentioned spotting her, but soon he was on their trail. He had lost them in the Ruby City, but a local had informed him that they had been seen leaving again. Owin wasn't sure why they had travelled all the way to the north of Aneria, but he reserved those questions until he had Natava back. He had pushed his horse hard, almost causing it to break down, but he had managed to catch up to them and found them resting in a small clearing, away from the main road. Owin had observed Erars holding Natava strangely, with his arms around her, and watched them talking, but he hadn't thought much of it. Not until now. Not until he saw the protective arm Erars had wrapped around her waist and how Natava didn't even resist his touch. It made Owin stand up straighter, his posture changing, and he lowered his sword slightly as he scrutinised them both.

Natava noticed the change in him. It was subtle. Owin didn't wear his emotions on the outside. As a knight, he couldn't. But she knew her best friend. She knew how he reacted to things, and of course, seeing her in Erars's arms would be shocking. How would she even explain it?

"Owin..."

"What is going on? Tell me he has manipulated your mind. Tortured you even," he snapped.

"It's more complicated than that."

"What?"

Owin looked betrayed. To him, there was nothing complicated about the Shadow Lords. They were inherently evil, but now Natava insisted there was more to it. How could there be? he wondered.

"Listen, we are on the same side."

"What?!" he exclaimed. "I don't work with Shadow Lords. Natava!"

"He is helping me."

"Helping you? Is that why he's holding you in such a tender embrace?"

"I..."

"Are you letting a Shadow Lord touch you?" he asked, sounding even more betrayed.

"Owin..."

"Did you... fuck him?"

Owin had never spoken to her in such an accusatory manner, but his mind conjured up the worst possible scenarios, and he grew so angry that he trembled. Natava moved away from Erars, approaching Owin, but he raised his hand, signaling her not to touch him. She halted, keeping a small distance between them, and offered him a faint smile, hoping to find some peace between them.

"Did you go on a mission?" he asked.

"A mission?"

"Massana and the others believe you abandoned us in a time of need," he explained. "Did you?"

"No! I was taken! Erars took me!"

"Then why doesn't it look like you want to get away from him?" Owin demanded.

"I do! I did..."

"Did?"

"We're working together now," she explained.

"A Light... and a Shadow Lord?" Owin questioned, and she could hear how absurd it sounded. She had struggled to accept it herself, but it was true. She was collaborating with Erars, and she knew she needed his assistance to accomplish their goal. But it would also be helpful if she could have her best friend by her side.

"I know how it sounds, but we went to The Hallows seeking the same thing. To see if the veil had been breached," she explained.

"You weren't meant to be his sacrifice?" Owin asked.

"No, or... at least I wasn't intended to be sacrificed then."

"How reassuring."

"It changed. I'm not a sacrifice, not unless... I choose to be."

"What?" Owin asked, looking at her in shock.

"The Shadow Lords who captured the young Light may already be at the veil, about to breach it, and someone will have to close it," Natava explained.

"And that someone is you?" he asked, not believing his own ears.

"Aren't I the queen?"

Owin shook his head. "If you go down there, you'll truly let down your people. They need a leader, not a dead one."

"I agree," Erars interjected, smiling, but Owin glared at him, refusing to find any common ground with the Shadow Lord.

"Someone has to do something," Natava snapped.

Owin continued to glare at Erars before finally turning his attention back to Natava.

"Do you truly believe he's helping you?" Owin asked.

"He is."

Owin shook his head. "I thought you were smarter than this, Nat."

Natava recoiled, unable to believe her best friend would say such a thing.

"I am not a fool!"

"You're trusting a Shadow Lord! He wants you to sacrifice yourself, but not to close the veil. He wants you to spill your blood. You're going with him straight to the altar, offering yourself up for his desires!" Owin snapped.

"If he wanted me dead, he would have made me harm myself already!"

"He needed more time to manipulate you," Owin accused, pointing his sword at Erars. "And you allowed him to. Now step away."

Natava found herself caught between the two men, and she quickly shook her head, raising her hands.

"No! Owin, listen, we're working together!"

"You can't trust a Shadow Lord. He's getting exactly what he wants by removing that veil!"

"No, he isn't. He doesn't want them to be the ones to do it."

"Exactly! He wants to be the one to do it and become our master, Natava. He's no different. Now step away!"

Natava continued to shake her head, but when she glanced at Erars, she saw him readying himself for another confrontation with Owin, taking a step forward as his powers began to emanate from him, causing shadows to dance over his skin. But she wouldn't let them fight, because she knew it would only end in death.

Chapter 33

Erars wasn't going to lose Natava. If that veil was breached before they could stop the other Shadow Lords, he would take Natava with him, go into hiding, and never let anything harm her again. No Shadow Lord or love-struck knight would stand in his way. Natava belonged to him, and he would never let her go. Owin was ready to strike him down, but Erars saw that it was no longer just about protecting Natava and bringing her back. His eyes had transformed, filled with pure anger and anguish. He wanted to utterly destroy Erars because Natava had surrendered herself to him. He had tasted her sweetness and reveled in it. Now, the knight wanted to erase the fact that a Shadow Lord had come so close to the beauty between them. Owin didn't want someone like Erars near her, but that only made Erars smile even wider. He had come very close, and he would gladly do it again.

"I'm not moving, Owin. I need his help!" Natava declared.

"His help?" Owin accused. "He's going to betray you. He wants to open the Shadow World. He desires the power that comes with it. Can't you see how you're being deceived by him?"

"It's not true."

"No? How so?" Owin asked.

Natava fell silent, and that was all Owin needed to hear. He had already pieced it all together. It was crystal clear in his eyes as he observed the two of them. He had witnessed the tender way Erars held her, and how Natava leaned towards him instead of away. Owin wasn't blind to the signs of their mutual attraction. He could see what was happening, and it made his blood boil. But what was even worse was how his perception of Natava changed completely. He no longer saw his friend. He saw a traitor. Someone he felt disgusted by, and it caused him to take a step back.

"Are you telling me you have feelings for him?" Owin asked.

"We made a deal," Natava replied, trying not to reveal too much of the truth because she wasn't ready to admit it yet.

"What kind of deal?"

"If he helps me, I will marry him. That's why I trust him, because he will ultimately gain control of Aneria anyway!" she explained, sounding almost happy. However, Owin thought it was the most ludicrous thing he had ever heard, and he shook his head.

"You would marry him?" Owin asked, the sense of betrayal evident in his voice.

"It's the only way."

"No, it's not! How about not marrying him?"

"I need his help!"

"You have mine!" he shouted, pointing to himself. "I will always stand by you, Natava."

"Owin, I need him."

"You need... *him*?" he questioned, the words sounding foreign to him.

"He can help us navigate through the dark forest faster. He can cloak us."

"I would gladly help you, Natava, but I fail to see why you need him. Actually, I fail to understand how you can even defend him! He's a monster. He's one of them!" Owin shouted. "He's not a good person and never will be, and you're willing to make him your king?"

"He needed something too," Natava explained.

"Exactly! He only agreed to help you if he also got something in return. He didn't suddenly do it out of the goodness of his heart. Can't you see that you can't trust him?!" Owin yelled.

"Why do you think we made a deal?"

"And what happens when he becomes our king?!" Owin asked.

"What then?"

"Exactly! He will destroy us. He will revert the world back to how it was, and how will you fight against him then?" Owin asked. "You've made him our ruler. Will you be able to overthrow him as well?"

Natava remained silent. She hadn't discussed with Erars what their rule together would look like. What would Erars want from the people? How would he treat them? Natava glanced back at Erars, but he had become unreadable. She slowly turned to Owin, who shrugged slightly, giving her a meaningful expression.

"I don't know," she answered honestly.

"But you're willing to risk all of us to find out?"

"What would you have me do?" she asked. "The other Shadow Lords might be breaking the veil as we speak, and we still have several days' ride ahead of us. What do you expect me to do?"

"Let me help," Owin said.

"We would be two people!"

"You're already two people now!"

"But he is a Shadow Lord!" Natava defended.

Owin looked at her with hurt in his eyes as she spoke those words, but it wasn't a lie. Owin was skilled with a sword, but where they were going, they needed more.

"And what am I?" Owin asked. "Just dead weight?"

"I never said that. I want you to come with us."

"You want what?" Erars asked, causing Natava to sigh as yet another person was displeased with her now.

She didn't turn around to look at him or try to explain anything. She remained focused on her friend, who she felt slipping away bit by bit. He was slipping from her grasp, and she didn't know how to keep him.

"I want you to come," she emphasised. "You're my friend, and I need you."

"It seems you already have plenty of help," he accused.

"Owin..."

"Do you even need rescuing, or was I wasting my time?"

"I did... in the beginning," she said. "But I have chosen a different path now."

"To work with a Shadow Lord," he accused.

"Owin, there's no use arguing about this!" she snapped.

"No, because you have already turned against us. Against me. You know what those monsters do. You've fought against them before. But now you stand by him like he's your friend. Like the rest of us mean nothing to you now."

"It's not true!" Natava yelled. "You're my best friend. I would never trade you for anything. Owin, I do need you!"

"No, I don't think you do. You have all the help you need, but I won't be there to save you when he stabs you in the back."

"Owin, please..."

Owin began backing away, so Natava lunged forward and grabbed his arm. He roughly pulled away, looking at her as if she were a stranger. She had never seen such a look in his eyes. He turned away again, and she called out to him.

"This isn't about us!" she shouted.

Owin froze with his back to her.

"This is about all of Aneria! They need us!" she pleaded.

Owin stood there for a moment, then slowly turned towards her. "You're right, and you're letting them all down."

"Please, Owin, I'm trying to fix everything. I'm trying to save us before it's too late."

"You're only going to make it worse. Trusting a Shadow Lord will be your doom. Do you think anyone would trust you or follow you when they know you lie with the likes of him?" Owin asked, making her feel dirty, as if being touched by Erars had somehow tainted her. Perhaps it had. Natava couldn't say she was surprised by Owin's reaction. She had felt dirty. She had felt guilty. But every time Erars touched her, something changed. It was as if he was always meant to be close to her.

"I need his help," she whispered. "But I need you too."

"No, you don't," he said. "You've chosen a side, and I was foolish enough to choose you."

"Owin..."

"I never believed anyone when they said you were unfit to rule us or when they said you were too wild or reckless. I never believed a word they said because I thought I knew you."

Natava felt the sting of tears in her eyes, her heart breaking.

"But I didn't. I don't know you. I don't know what the hell happened to my friend, but apparently she never existed."

"She did! I'm still your friend, Owin!" she shouted as he began to walk away. "Please! Please come back!"

But Owin wasn't listening. He kept walking until he disappeared into the dark forest, and Natava felt a piece of her heart walk away with him.

Chapter 34

Erars watched the entire show unfold in front of him, observing his Light clutch her hair in panic and then fall to her knees. He saw her shake as if she were crying and walked closer. He wanted to comfort her, although he didn't know how. Comfort was something he had never been shown or taught. Nonetheless, he reached for her, but before he could touch her, Natava had collected herself, forcing away the tears in her eyes and getting back on her feet. When she turned to Erars, he saw nothing but coldness in her eyes, as she refused to let her friend's betrayal break her. Her knight was a fool, he thought. Natava still extended her hand to him, but all he did was walk away. Erars didn't expect the knight to trust him, but he believed the knight's love was strong enough that he would trust his queen. He hadn't wanted Owin to come with them, but he couldn't deny that more help was needed, and it would have been good to have more people on their side. Natava took a deep breath before straightening her back.

"Should we get going?" she asked.

Erars didn't like how she shut off, as if she were no longer present in this world, but he understood it was what she needed to do right now because they had to save Aneria, and there was no time to cry.

"Yes, let's get going," he agreed.

They retrieved their horses, which had rested for a while, but neither of them had slept. They mounted them and began riding away. They rode in silence all day, even into the night, before giving their horses another break. Erars didn't like the energy surrounding his Light now, especially because it tainted her sweetness a little, as she felt left behind by her friend. Erars walked over to her as she filled a waterskin from a fresh stream. She didn't drink it but just looked at the bottle in a crouched position. Erars stopped by her side, arms crossed, but she did not look at him.

"He is the fool," Erars finally spoke.

Natava glanced up at him, but she didn't really want to talk about Owin. It hurt to even remember the look on his face as he turned away from her. It had stung like crazy, and she just wanted to forget and focus on their mission.

"He is right..." she whispered. "We make no sense. Making a deal with you makes no sense. Your kind is not known for your honesty."

"We actually are," Erars corrected her.

Natava stood up and looked at him, confused. "What?"

"We are known for honesty. We don't lie because we know how powerful the truth is. But to you, we are slippery bastards because we can hide in the darkness and reappear beside you in a second, killing you in an instant. The things we have done make us look like monsters and the most evil beings in this world. We may not seem like the most honest people, but we don't really lie. We have no use for it. We enjoy the truth because it can destroy you."

"A lie can too."

"But once a lie is discovered, everything truly crumbles," Erars explained to her.

Natava wasn't sure she agreed. A lie could make everything crumble too, but she didn't want to argue about what was most powerful. It didn't matter really. Whether or not Erars was known to be truthful, it wouldn't change the fact that Owin had still turned away from her, and she couldn't blame him. No one could trust a Shadow Lord, not when she had grown up learning about all the horrific things they did. No one wanted to trust them. They believed their lives would be in danger if they did, and Natava wouldn't just trust any Shadow Lord now. Erars was different. He might want the same from the Shadow World: power, but he would gladly accept the crown in a different way. She didn't think she could have offered the other Shadow Lords the same, or that they would even take the time to listen. They wanted the Shadow World opened again, so they could all rule in the same way they did before. They wanted the old ways, while Erars was ready to change. But how much would he change?

"Once we marry, what then?" she asked him, shocking him with the change of subject.

"What?"

"Owin did ask something interesting. How would we rule together? I am assuming it is together, or do you want to do it all on your own?" she taunted.

Erars smiled a little, stepping closer. "I am not used to sharing power."

"I won't let you hurt people."

Erars had envisioned a different way of ruling. He had never imagined having a queen by his side or Aneria free from darkness. Now, Natava had made him an offer he couldn't refuse, but it also meant altering his vision for the future. Could he do it? Could he change the way he desired to rule? He wasn't known for his kind heart or compassion. He lacked both, and yet the image of his queen feeling betrayed by his actions, turning away from him because of the goodness within her heart, made him feel... hurt? The feeling surprised him, but then he realised that she had awakened something inside him as well. She made him feel more than he had in his many years in this world. It was both irritating and refreshing.

"No, I don't think you would allow me," he agreed.

"So how would it work then?"

"I would lock you up, and we would go from there," he joked, but she raised an eyebrow, not finding his joke amusing.

He chuckled a little, then lowered his arms, placing his hands on her hips and pulling her closer to him.

"No, I truly don't know," he admitted.

"What do you mean?"

"I had envisioned the way I would be king. I had seen the old ways, the way the Shadow Lords once ruled."

"I won't allow us to return to that," she declared.

"No, I didn't think you would, and I am surprising myself by saying that I am okay with it."

"Are you?"

"Aneria will still bow to me, but don't think that I won't remain true to what I am—a Shadow Lord. If anyone gives me a reason to be cruel, I will be."

"Perhaps it can be a topic of discussion."

"Discussion?" he questioned, sounding unfamiliar with the concept.

"How we handle things."

"No, they will be handled in my own way," he stated, causing Natava to sigh and shake her head.

"I don't want cruelty to define us."

"Then it's fortunate that I will be the one known for it."

She continued shaking her head, disagreeing with him, and Erars smiled, pressing her even closer to him and reveling in the feeling of her warm and soft body.

"It will be a different kind of reign, but we won't know how we'll do it until we actually sit on the throne," he said.

Natava nodded slightly. She knew he was right. It would be challenging to determine the specifics of their rule without having the opportunity to experience it firsthand. It had never been done before—having a Shadow Lord and a Light ruling side by side. She was meant to rule on her own. She knew her father didn't truly rule. It was her mother who took charge. Now she understood better how her mother wielded power. She was more ruthless than Natava had realised, but she had never really known her mother. Natava had been raised by Massana, who now questioned her like everyone else. She heard what Owin had said. She heard how everyone doubted her loyalty and questioned whether she stood with them. Would Owin go back and tell everyone that she had aligned herself with a Shadow Lord? Would they demand that she abdicate or choose someone else to rule? Natava had never desired the crown, but she also didn't want to be hunted out of her own community and family. Where else could she go? To Erars's dark world? Maybe it wouldn't be so bad, she wondered, but she couldn't say at the moment what would happen.

She had no idea where Owin was or what he might do next, but his look of betrayal was still etched into her mind. He appeared so betrayed, as if she had deceived him their entire lives. She had never done that. She was his friend, and he was hers. However, she wasn't sure if the rift between them could be mended now. After all, he had turned away from her. But would he ever want to know her again? Natava had to admit that she had changed, but she didn't believe it was for the worse. She saw things more clearly now, and while no one understood why she was with Erars, she didn't believe it had to be a negative thing. Not if Erars continued to change as well. If the darkness within him could be contained, there was hope.

"You're right," she agreed. "We won't know until then. But what if we never get the chance?"

"You mean if they open the Shadow World?"

"No, I mean what if Owin tells everyone about us? What if they're waiting with torches and pitchforks to chase us away?"

Erars burst into laughter, but Natava was serious and gently shoved him.

"I am serious!" she exclaimed.

"I know, that's why it's so amusing," he chuckled.

"You don't think they would?"

"Oh, they definitely would, but once again, you're underestimating yourself. Remember who holds the power, and you'll be fine. A queen doesn't bow, so why are you allowing them to rule you?" he asked, stepping away and returning to their belongings.

Natava didn't know what to say. She hadn't considered that possibility and watched curiously as Erars stopped by the fire. She walked over and joined him, standing by his side and giving him a small smile.

"For some reason, you're the only one not trying to rule me," she remarked.

"You wouldn't truly be my queen if I ruled over you," he said. "You would be my slave."

She shook her head slightly, but the smile remained on her lips. "Am I everyone's slave?"

"You have allowed them to decide many things for you. Are you really going to let them dictate how you will rule?" he asked.

"I thought I didn't, but now I see the reality of it. I am the puppet they manipulate, and I let them do it."

"Then stop," he said. "Don't let your knight make you doubt. Don't let him decide for you either. Choose what you want to do and make the others follow. That's what a leader does."

“You make it sound so brutal, though.”

“It’s not pretty because some people need to be whipped into line.”

“But I’m not like that,” she told him. “I don’t whip people.”

“No, instead you allow them to control you.”

“I don’t want that either.”

“Then find a way to reclaim your power because it belongs to you and no one else. Stop letting them have it.”

His words were harsh, but necessary. She knew she couldn’t let this continue. She was meant to be the one making decisions for everyone. That’s what a queen did. She wanted to act in the best interest of all, but she couldn’t allow others to rule over her. So why was she letting them? Even if they couldn’t accept Erars, she made the choice for the greater good. With his help, she had a better chance of stopping the other Shadow Lords, and they had to accept the decision she had made.

Chapter 35

An urgent message had reached Massana, who hastily made her way to her chambers and donned her armor. She gathered a group of knights and Halos, intending to personally go to The Hallows and prevent the Shadow Lords from breaching the veil. The message, brief and unmistakably penned by Owin, informed her that the veil was on the verge of being shattered, and she had to act swiftly. Owin had not provided any further details or appeared as the messenger, but she would investigate his whereabouts later. Perhaps he was already waiting by the forest that led to the Shadow World. Time was of the essence, and they all prepared themselves, mounted their horses, and set off at a rapid pace. The journey would take some time, but she hoped to reach their destination before it was too late. She was resolute in her determination not to allow the Shadow World to be unleashed once again, wreaking havoc across the world.

They rode relentlessly for days, only pausing briefly for rest, which enabled them to arrive at the dark forest relatively quickly. Their horses grew restless in front of the dark forest, its powerful energy emanated from it, putting them all on edge. Disembarking, they secured their horses a short distance away, as riding through the forest would be impractical.

"How long has it been since you were last here?" Calum asked, his eyes fixed upon the black forest.

“A very long time...” Massana replied, memories flooding her mind. She had once contemplated sacrificing herself to the Shadow World in place of Hela, but it was Hela’s mother who intervened during their dispute over who would be the chosen one. Massana recalled the expression on her beloved’s face as she realised her mother had gone instead. She caught a fleeting glimpse of the woman stepping into the dark realm before a bestial scream resounded throughout Aneria, followed by the gradual closure of the crack. Massana had held her friend back as her mother vanished from sight. The pain of that moment lingered, and if the Shadow World were unleashed, someone else would have to descend into its depths, surrendering themselves to its consuming darkness.

“Let’s not stand here,” Massana said, taking the first step forward.

No one was eager to be the first to proceed, and Massana understood the dangers concealed within the forest. Beasts of various shapes and sizes lurked, all possessing poisonous or lethal qualities. It was essential to remain vigilant and prepared for anything. They quickened their pace, forming a tight formation with a smaller group encircled by a larger one. They were taking turns shifting to the outside position and continued to move as a group as best they could. The densely packed trees hindered their advancement, forcing them to go slow.

“I can already sense it,” Calum remarked, trailing behind Massana.

“Yes, they are watching us. They’ve been doing so since we entered. They stalk us, waiting for the perfect moment to strike and devour us,” she explained.

“It’s no wonder so few have ventured out of the forest.”

“But there’s something else in the air. Can you feel it?” Massana asked.

“I do sense something.”

“The Shadow World knows it’s on the brink of liberation. It’s pushing against the crack.”

As they traversed the forest, Massana noticed an even denser and more sinister energy. It didn't resemble the full opening of the Shadow World, but she could discern the dark vibrations and the mounting impatience of the shadow creatures yearning to be unleashed upon their realm.

"Do you think Owin is already here?" Calum wondered.

"I don't know. I didn't see his horse anywhere, but this forest stretches for miles. Perhaps he's staying close to the veil. The monsters tend to avoid that part of the forest. Even they find the creatures unsettling."

"In that case, we should be even more wary," Calum stated.

"We should. It took us years to figure out how to close the veil, and even longer to get close enough. We lost many good Halos. We used to have a much larger group. Even after all these years, our numbers haven't remained the same," Massana explained.

"You don't require the same numbers," Calum reassured her. "You don't need an army."

"Now we may need them," she replied.

"We will rescue the Light before they can do anything to her. They won't unleash those evil creatures."

"Goddess, I hope you're right."

Suddenly, a colossal snap echoed through the forest, reminiscent of a falling tree. Massana scanned her surroundings, uncertain of its origin. The sound repeated, and soon a tree hurtled towards them.

"Jump!" she shouted.

The group split in two, and as they landed vulnerable on the ground, a horde of beasts descended upon them. Not just snakes and spiders, but massive rats, salamanders, and other grotesque creatures assailed them, screeching and attacking with savage fervor. Just as one of the creatures lunged towards Massana, poised to swallow her whole, she unleashed a brilliant burst of light. The beast recoiled, allowing her to swiftly rise to her feet. They were being picked off one by one, torn apart and savagely slaughtered.

"Shit..." Massana muttered.

Natava did not feel any joy upon seeing the forest again. She had disliked it the last time, and her sentiments had not changed. However, there was no turning back now. They had to keep moving forward. As Natava and Erars stepped into the forest, an unsettling sensation coursed through her, causing her to feel on edge and tremble.

"Do you feel that?" she asked.

"Yeah, the Shadow World senses something is happening," Erars replied. "They know they are on the verge of being freed."

Erars and Natava exchanged apprehensive glances. Erars wasn't certain if he could hide fast enough if the veil were opened now. This might be his final day in Aneria, and the thought did not sit well with him. He had fought fiercely to survive. Abandoned as a baby, he had endured and climbed the ranks to become the formidable Shadow Lord he was today. Would it all come to an end today? Would he die alongside his Light? He glanced at Natava, experiencing a peculiar sensation. Surprisingly, the thought of dying with her did not displease him. However, he would prefer if neither of them had to perish.

They continued walking for a while until Natava suddenly stopped, noticing something on the ground. Erars followed suit, turning slightly as she ended up behind him.

"What is it?" he asked.

Natava crouched down and picked up a piece of white and blue fabric. She held it up and showed it to Erars.

"It's fabric," she stated.

"And?" he pressed.

"It bears the seal and colours of the knights who serve the Halos," Natava explained. "Look."

She extended the fabric towards him, and he took it, examining it closely. He observed the swirling symbols with a sword crossing over them. She was right, he thought. The fabric undoubtedly belonged to one of the knights in service of the Halos.

"Well, they could have been devoured when your knight was here," he suggested.

"But it's not dirty, and it has been a while since we were last here," Natava pointed out.

Erars studied the fabric once again. He noticed a small amount of blood on one corner and reached out to touch it, only to realise that the blood was not dry. A drop suddenly fell onto his hand. He looked at it intently before tilting his head back, feeling his black heart freeze in his chest.

"Natava," he whispered.

"Yeah?" she replied.

"Do not move."

Confused, Natava looked at Erars. She had been examining the fabric in his hand but noticed that his gaze was directed upward. She followed suit and gasped softly when she saw the lifeless bodies suspended in the tree crowns, cocooned in spider webs, while massive spiders continued to tightly wrap the corpses.

"Oh... Goddess," she whispered.

"Walk slowly towards me," Erars commanded. "I need to touch you to cloak both of us."

Natava swallowed hard and took a step towards Erars, causing a small leaf to crunch beneath her boot. She froze momentarily but saw that the spiders were preoccupied with their fresh meal. She continued taking cautious steps, getting closer to Erars. However, her progress was interrupted when she accidentally snapped a dry branch beneath her foot. Both of them froze, but the sound of strange hissing filled the air. Natava looked up to see the spiders, now alerted to their presence.

"Natava, here!" Erars called out.

Reacting quickly, Natava lunged forward just as the spiders descended from the trees. Erars caught her, immediately cloaking them and pulling her close. The spiders looked around, confused, as their prey seemed to have vanished. They emitted clicking and hissing sounds as they communicated with one another. Trembling in Erars's arms, Natava waited anxiously to see what would happen. They couldn't afford to make any noise, or the spiders would discover them. The huge, hairy bodies of the spiders surrounded them, with some having a completely black colour while others appeared red and dark blue. The hairs on their bodies almost brushed against Natava and Erars, who did their best to avoid contact. Erars held Natava even tighter, his heart pounding in his throat as he contemplated the dire consequences if the spiders realised they were standing right beside them. Could Natava muster enough power to repel them all? Could he? They waited patiently, their hearts racing, but then the spiders began crawling back up the trees, returning to their previous task. Natava and Erars waited a while longer before slowly and silently retreating. Once they had put enough distance between themselves and the spiders, they broke into a run, gradually slowing down once they felt they were at a safe distance. They turned to each other, panting and reflecting on the perilous encounter.

"Those were my knights!" Natava exclaimed.

"I know," Erars acknowledged.

"They are here!"

"They are dead now," he confirmed.

"Are we certain? Are they truly gone?"

Erars explained, "They inject their victims with a paralysing venom that also affects the lungs, causing them to suffocate. They are gone."

"But there were so many!" Natava exclaimed.

"Perhaps your knight informed the others. He might have sent a message with a raven, which could have arrived quickly."

"But do you think there are more?" Natava panicked. She had not expected others to be here, at least not yet. The sight of the knights being devoured by the spiders weighed heavily on her mind. Who were these knights? How many of them were there? Were they all dead? The pain in her heart intensified as she imagined them becoming meals for those monstrous creatures.

"I don't know, Natava," Erars said, stepping closer and placing his hands on her neck to redirect her attention. "They are no longer our concern. They are gone, and we need to find our way back to the veil."

Natava took a deep breath, still feeling the ache within her, but she knew he was right. Their goal was getting to the veil. They couldn't go back to save the deceased. No matter how much she longed to give them a proper burial and spare them from becoming food.

"You're right," she whispered.

"Let's proceed with greater caution. I believe the Shadow World is stirring up trouble, unsettling the beasts as well."

"Okay," she agreed.

They moved forward more carefully, maintaining a swift pace. Erars continued using his power to conceal them as he held Natava's hand. He knew the beasts weren't easily deceived, and if they heard any sound, they would pursue it.

Chapter 36

Natava and Erars found a small clearing where they could rest and maintain better visibility of any potential threats. Despite their fatigue, they remained vigilant, their eyes scanning the tree crowns to ensure they wouldn't be taken by surprise. Natava was still shaken by the sight of the knights being consumed by spiders, but she knew that the horrors of the Shadow World would be far worse if it was unleashed. She focused her mind on that thought, attempting to calm herself during their brief break. Neither of them spoke, both consumed by their own thoughts and keeping a watchful eye on their surroundings.

"Do you think Owin was among them?" Natava finally broke the silence.

"Maybe," Erars replied, seeing the fear on Natava's face. What else could he say? He didn't have the answers, and they couldn't go back to verify. "But if the Shadow World is opened, there will be no doubt about your knight's fate."

"Do you think they would kill all of us?"

"They would certainly eliminate most of you, making an example of some while allowing the weaker ones to live, as a warning to those who dare to resist," Erars explained.

"Was that your plan?" Natava asked, her tone tinged with accusation.

"Something along those lines," he admitted.

She shook her head, disapproving of his answer.

"But I am going to rule differently now, right?" Erars asked, observing Natava's surprised expression. She nodded in agreement, a small smile appearing on her face.

"Yes."

"I know what it means to be a Shadow Lord, and I'm not that different from most—"

"That's not true," she interjected. "You could have tortured me, changed me completely, but you didn't. Why?"

Erars shrugged slightly. "The moment I saw you, I felt something. My powers were drawn to you."

"You wanted to feed off me and kill me?"

"I do draw a little energy from you when we're together. It gives me strength," he said with pride, causing her to sigh and roll her eyes. "And you seem to enjoy it. It excites you."

"Erars!"

"I had no intention of killing you. I never even planned on taking you away. I made a spur-of-the-moment decision, and it turned out to be a good one."

"A good one?" she questioned.

"I have you now, don't I?"

"You do," she conceded with a small smile.

"I gain a crown, and I have the Light."

"You seem to be the winner in all of this."

"I always intended to come out on top," he boasted.

She rolled her eyes and shook her head, but the smile remained. It didn't matter to her if he saw himself as the victor, as long as the Shadow World remained sealed. That was Natava's ultimate goal, and she would do everything in her power to ensure it didn't happen.

"Of course, you had a lifelong plan."

"I did, and it almost worked," he remarked. "If it hadn't been for those other Shadow Lords. I should have anticipated that they would make a move as well, but I thought I had dealt with them effectively."

"Perhaps you waited too long," she suggested.

"Discovering the exact location where the veil was sealed was no easy task," Erars explained. "It took me many years."

Natava nodded slightly, choosing not to delve further into the matter since she already knew how he had acquired the information.

"I just hope we can stop them before someone has to sacrifice their life," she whispered.

"It won't be you."

"But someone has to."

"You made a promise to me," he reminded her.

"And how can I keep that promise if the Shadow Lords destroy the world?" she countered.

"How can you keep your promise if you're trapped in the Shadow World?"

They locked eyes, neither knowing what to say. It was evident they didn't agree on what should come next. Natava wanted to make a decision at that moment. Was she prepared to sacrifice herself or not? However, it was equally clear that Erars was ready to prevent her from doing so. What could she do? She felt trapped, uncertain if there was anyone else willing to take the necessary steps. If they waited, the Shadow Lords would undoubtedly eliminate them all to ensure the veil could never be sealed again. They wouldn't risk the possibility of anyone entering and disrupting their "perfect" world. The situation became incredibly complicated, for they couldn't allow the Shadow Lords to reign once more. Chaos would engulf the world, with death reigning supreme.

"I don't know what to say," she whispered.

"Say that you're done sacrificing yourself," he urged.

"But if the veil is cracked open, we may have no choice."

"There is always a choice."

"I'm not so sure."

Erars disagreed, sighing deeply and looking away. He wouldn't allow his Light to sacrifice herself. He would protect her from the powerful clutches of the Shadow World, even if it meant sacrificing all of Aneria.

Natava had decided to take a short nap, but she was abruptly awakened by a spreading sense of foreboding. She looked over at Erars, who was on guard duty. He wasn't facing her but instead was staring into the forest.

"Do you feel that?" she whispered.

"It has begun," Erars replied.

Erars suddenly started moving in the opposite direction. Natava hastily got up, shocked, and hurried after him, grabbing his arm.

"What are you doing?"

"It's too late, Natava. Can't you feel it? The process has already started. The ground is opening up!"

Just then, the ground beneath their feet began to tremble, and a deafening roar reverberated through the forest, causing their ears to ring.

"We have to stop it!" she exclaimed.

"No, we don't have to do anything! The veil has been opened. It's too late now! We need to run!"

"Run?!" she exclaimed in disbelief.

"Yes, run. We will be among the first they come for. I am a traitor, and you are a Light. We need to go!"

Erars broke free from her grip, assuming that Natava would follow him. But when he glanced back, he saw Natava running in the opposite direction.

"Natava!" he shouted after her before quickly making a wall of shadows in her path.

Natava collided with the barrier, stumbling backwards, and then turned to face Erars. "What are you doing?"

"I won't let you go back there!" he shouted. "I won't let you become their sacrifice!"

"It's not your decision! We have to do something!"

"Not this. We will find another way."

"Don't make me fight against you, Erars."

"Now you want to use your powers? Show me what you've got, Light," he challenged.

Natava and Erars locked eyes, neither of them moving. But then the ground began to shake beneath their feet, and Natava watched as the darkness in the forest intensified. It became nearly impossible to see. Erars struggled to maintain his balance, leaning against a tree for support. Natava started to emit a radiant glow, using her powers to enhance her vision. However, she noticed Erars getting distracted, and she saw the shadow wall he had created fading away. Without hesitation, she jumped through the dissipating wall and broke free, ignoring Erars's cries.

"Natava!" he shouted, but she kept running.

Chapter 37

There was no time for hesitation, Natava realised. She couldn't allow the world to descend into chaos. She didn't want to be a sacrifice, nor did she want to be trapped in the Shadow World. However, what other choice did she have? She couldn't let everyone die when she had the power to prevent it. Natava knew there was no turning back. She would be consumed by the darkness, but she was the only hope they had. Natava continued running towards the crack between realms, feeling its pull growing stronger with each step. It wanted her there, yearning to devour her.

Suddenly, she almost got crushed by a massive snake fleeing from the darkness of the Shadow World. She jumped aside, landing on the ground, and watched in awe as more beasts followed suit. She moved back to avoid being trampled, unable to fathom that these monstrous creatures were running away in fear when she herself had been terrified of them. And if they were afraid, she knew she had a good reason to be terrified. Getting up from the ground, she resumed her sprint.

However, the ground started shaking again. She grabbed onto a nearby tree, witnessing the ground giving way. Natava maintained her radiant glow, which provided some visibility, but the energy was thick and suffocating. The closer she got to the Shadow World, the harder it became to breathe. When the tremors subsided, she followed the crack towards a large, open clearing where a gaping hole had formed, and shadows spilled out like a torrent. They flowed upward, reaching for the sky and spreading across the ground. Hiding behind a tree, Natava felt a force pushing against her as chaos unleashed itself. She couldn't locate the little Light, but she knew that she was dead if the Shadow World had indeed been unleashed. In the distance, a group of Shadow Lords reveled in the mayhem that engulfed Aneria. There was a significant number of them, and it seemed unfathomable that so many had united, but their alliance had paid off, shrouding Aneria in their sinister shadows.

Natava knew she couldn't remain hidden. She had to summon every ounce of strength she had and protect the world from the encroaching darkness. She had to close the crack before an overwhelming number of creatures emerged from it. Taking a deep breath, she steeled herself for the imminent battle. The Shadow Lords would undoubtedly fight fiercely to safeguard the opening. As she prepared to move around the tree, someone grabbed her. She gasped, pulling her fist back, ready to strike, but she froze when she saw who it was.

"Massana?!" she yelled over the sounds of bestial screams and evil being unleashed.

Massana stood before her, her long brown hair disheveled, her body covered in sweat and blood. Her armor was in ruins, but she tightly gripped her sword. She gave Natava a faint smile, and Natava immediately embraced her, relieved to no longer be alone.

"How are you here?" Natava asked.

"It took some time, but I fought my way here," Massana explained.

Natava pulled back slightly, then glanced over her shoulder at the still-standing Shadow Lords, reveling in the chaos.

"We have to stop them."

"I know," Massana replied.

"I have to go down there."

"Natava..."

"It's my duty, isn't it? You said I was destined for greatness. Maybe this is it."

Massana looked crestfallen, but she firmly grasped Natava's arm and smiled.

"We face this together," Massana said.

"Together."

Natava summoned an even more powerful glow, and Massana did what she could with her own abilities. Despite feeling weakened and the spreading shadows in Aneria hindering them, they emerged from hiding and ran towards the Shadow Lords. The Shadow Lords noticed their approach and quickly commanded the shadows to attack. Natava halted, seeking deep within herself to find her formidable light. It surged forth until she radiated with the intensity of the sun. The shadow creatures and the Shadow Lords recoiled, unable to withstand her light. She continued to unleash her power, determined to create a path leading to the entrance of the Shadow World. She only had to maintain it for a little while. Natava pushed herself even further, allowing her light to blaze brighter, illuminating Aneria. She sensed the shadows and the Shadow Lords screaming in agony, begging her to stop. Trembling, she noticed a protective barrier forming where the shadows couldn't touch. The Shadow Lords cursed and yelled but vanished from sight, unable to withstand her light any longer. She smiled, allowing her radiance to dim slightly, but before she could make her move towards the entrance, she saw Massana rushing past her.

"Massana!" she shouted.

Natava ran after her, hoping to intervene, but Massana was already far ahead of her. She wouldn't let Natava die. She wouldn't let the woman she considered her own daughter get trapped in the horrific Shadow World.

It was her duty to shield her from the evil below. Natava was destined for greatness, but that didn't mean to sacrifice. It meant protecting the world.

"Massana, no!" Natava cried out as Massana reached the edge of the entrance, looking down at the immense wave of shadows advancing towards her.

They had been pushed back by both the light emanating from Natava and Massana's power. Massana looked back, catching sight of Natava charging towards her, and she smiled before allowing herself to be consumed by the seemingly infinite darkness. As soon as Massana disappeared, the beastly screams grew louder, and a roar echoed through the air. Natava lost her balance as the ground shook beneath her, falling to her knees, unable to proceed as everything trembled violently. She had never witnessed or heard anything like it before, but she continued to call out for Massana, hoping in vain that she would return.

"Natava!"

Out of the darkness, she saw Erars emerge in the distance, searching for her but unable to reach her as the ground continued to quake. They watched as the crack began to close, gradually shrinking until it sealed shut entirely. Natava watched helplessly as the gateway to the only mother figure she had known vanished before her eyes.

"No..." she whispered.

The trembling ceased, and the darkness disappeared. Erars cautiously approached, kneeling beside Natava and placing his hand on her back.

"What happened?" he whispered.

"Massana... she... went down there," Natava told him, tears streaming down her face. "Why did she do that?! I was going to go!"

She turned to Erars, who reached out and gently wiped away her tears, his expression filled with sadness.

"Perhaps she knew that it wasn't your sacrifice to make," he said.

"But it was! I am meant for this!"

"Are you?" he asked.

Natava stared at him in disbelief.

"Where does it say that? You possess great power, but does that mean you have to die because of it?"

Natava was at a loss for words. She looked at him with a vacant expression. Erars helped her stand, and as soon as she was on her feet, she clung to him.

"She's gone..." she sobbed. "No..."

Erars held her tightly, his hand soothingly moving along her back. Although the pure darkness had dissipated, an evil energy still lingered in the air. The Shadow World had once again been sealed, but countless creatures had escaped, and Erars knew that this was far from the end. Aneria would now be consumed by its darkness, and the Shadow Lords, having lost their connection to the Shadow World once more, would not be deterred. Especially now that they had gained an army of powerful shadow soldiers. They were all in grave danger.

"She closed it..." Natava whispered.

"Yes, she did."

Natava pulled back slightly but knew that darkness now loomed over the world.

"It's not over, is it?" she whispered.

"No, it's not."

"What do we do? So many shadow creatures escaped, Erars," she said.

"I can't convince you to go into hiding, can I?" he asked.

She smiled through her tears.

"No."

"Maybe this is what you're meant for then," he suggested.

"Maybe..."

"They will need a leader to rally behind."

"Can I be that leader?" she questioned.

"Either that or come into hiding with me," he said.

"I can't hide, and you shouldn't either."

"Natava, I'm a traitor."

"But maybe your powers are exactly what we need. Maybe you can turn the creatures against their masters. You're not a weak Shadow Lord. We both know," she said. "You're needed."

Erars didn't know how to respond. He had never been regarded in the way Natava looked at him, as though he were a true hero destined to save them all. He was unsure of how to feel about it. Erars never thought he would be considered someone's hero or even desired to be one, but he didn't correct her. They simply looked at each other before Natava straightened her posture, realising it was time to rally support.

"We need to go. Find other survivors. Protect the other Lights," she said. "We need to warn everyone."

"They already know," Erars replied, knowing everyone would have felt the shift in the air.

"Then we need to fight back," she declared. "We can't stay here."

Natava was about to turn away when they both heard a peculiar sound. It resembled the ground giving way once again. They turned and observed the ground slowly beginning to open.

"I-I don't understand," Natava said. "Massana sacrificed herself!"

Erars extended his arm in front of Natava, ensuring she didn't approach too closely in her desperation to understand what was happening. They watched as the crack expanded further and further, and then... stopped? Erars and Natava looked at it with curiosity, unable to comprehend why there was a small hole in the ground again. But then smoke began rising, slowly taking on a dark colour, followed by an eerie cold sensation enveloping them both. Near the hole, the smoke transformed into a shadowy figure, gradually assuming a human form. Its red eyes began to glow, only to change to a blue hue. The shadow solidified, shaping a woman. Her hair turned blond, and she was adorned in armor resembling that of a Halo, similar to Massana, but it was not Massana who stood before them. The woman in front of them smiled evilly, her appearance bearing a striking resemblance to the portraits of Natava's mother. She resembled... Natava herself. Natava struggled to believe it was true, but she couldn't find any other explanation for the resemblance.

"Grandmother?" she asked.

The shadow's smile twisted into a more sinister expression before reverting to its shadowy form and rising into the air with a powerful, high-pitched scream. Erars and Natava both looked up but could discern little in the darkened sky, as the shadow blended with the darkness and vanished. They heard that peculiar sound again and witnessed the crack closing. After it sealed shut completely, they observed it for a while, but nothing else emerged. Silence fell, and no one dared utter a word. Natava slowly turned to Erars, who appeared even paler than usual. For a moment, he couldn't meet her eyes, but then he slowly faced her. Natava could see the answer in his eyes, and she knew he saw the question in hers, but they remained silent for a while longer.

"Don't tell me..."

Erars seemed at a loss for words, unsure of how to respond. However, Natava needed to hear it, regardless of her fears. She dreaded the answer but had to know if it was indeed possible.

"Erars!" she exclaimed, gripping his arm tightly. "Don't tell me it's true!"

Erars swallowed, having never encountered such a situation before. He never believed such a thing could be possible, but they had witnessed it firsthand. Erars had seen the former queen, the one who had sacrificed herself. He knew what she looked like, and there was no doubt in his mind as to who emerged from that crack.

"Erars!"

"It appears we know what happened to your grandmother," he whispered, observing Natava take a step back. "She has returned."

To Be Continued...

About the Author

Anne T. Thyssen, a Danish/English writer, discovered her love for writing at the age of six. Even as a young child, she dreamt of becoming a writer and sharing her stories with the world. However, it wasn't until 2019, when she felt burned out and was under lockdown because of the overwhelming presence of the COVID-19 pandemic, that she truly dedicated herself to her craft.

Anne made her debut in 2021 in her country, Denmark, with the short story collection "Hvem Fxck Er Jeg?" and later published a novel called "Flugten Fra København".

It wasn't long then Anne discovered the wonders of publishing online and really got her career started by publishing on the online platform Dreame, captivating her readers with her series "Wolves' Fated Mates". After reconnecting with her passion for writing, she continued to spread across many platforms and, already at the age of 22, had published over 50 books.

Anne does not keep herself limited by certain genres, but embraces the opportunity to explore various writing styles, captivating readers from diverse backgrounds and interests.

She continues to use each day to write and sharpen her talent while exploring more ways to reach people from all over the world.

ISBN: 978-87-94501-04-0

Printed in Great Britain
by Amazon

26067799R00152